FOREST OF THORNS AND CLAWS

J.T. HALL

RIPTIDE
PUBLISHING

Riptide Publishing
PO Box 1537
Burnsville, NC 28714
www.riptidepublishing.com

Forest of Thorns and Claws
Copyright © 2017 by J.T. Hall

Cover art: L.C. Chase, lcchase.com/design.htm
Editor: Carole-ann Galloway
Layout: L.C. Chase, lcchase.com/design.htm

ISBN: 978-1-62649-587-6

First edition
May, 2017

Also available in ebook:
ISBN: 978-1-62649-586-9

FOREST OF THORNS AND CLAWS

J.T. HALL

RIPTIDE
PUBLISHING

This book is dedicated to the individuals who work and sacrifice to protect our planet's natural wildlife.

TABLE OF CONTENTS

CHAPTER ONE

Donovan McGinnis paused to wipe the sweat from his brow with his camouflage T-shirt, then peered through a dense curtain of strangler fig. Ahead of him, sunlight highlighted a small clearing in the rainforest. Behind him, three men, all members of the Tiger Conservation and Protection Rangers, held still and listened. They were kilometers into the rainforest—about two and a half hours away from their base camp near the village of Ketambe. It was important to keep quiet and tread carefully. Here in the jungle, wild animals weren't the worst threat.

Worst were the poachers and their cleverly hidden snares.

This was the front line of an epic battle, but not one that most of the world was aware of. Every day, Donovan and his men fought to preserve what little rainforest was left on the Indonesian island of Sumatra, home to some of the rarest creatures on Earth. A lot of people didn't even know that there was such a thing as a Sumatran elephant or rhinoceros. The orangutans tended to draw the tourists, and their population was in better shape. But the most endangered of all was the creature he loved best.

The Sumatran tiger.

"Stay there," Donovan whispered. Amin, his best tracker, nodded and signaled to the other men. Amin was in his early twenties, beardless as many of the locals near the jungle tended to be, with short black hair and brown skin. He wore cargo shorts and a dark-brown T-shirt, the better to blend in with the dark undergrowth of the rainforest. He was Donovan's lead assistant at the research center.

Slowly, Donovan parted the vines and stepped into the clearing. Moving cautiously, he searched through a cluster of orchids on the forest floor, alert for signs of disturbance. High over their heads, leaves rustled, perhaps with the wind.

The jungle was quiet today. That wasn't a good thing.

Using a long collapsible walking stick, he poked the underbrush, noting broken stems and vines which appeared to have been arranged. It didn't take long for him to find something—a thin, braided rope beneath a cluster of vines. A taut line and a loop was a classic tiger snare. *The poachers were here, all right.* At least this one was empty. With deft fingers, Donovan felt for the trigger and deactivated it, breathing easier once it was done.

"Found a snare." He waved for the others to come forward. They gathered up the pieces to throw into the evidence bag, as Amin logged the location.

"That's eight you've uncovered so far today." Amin sounded impressed. He took the bag once Donovan was done with it, handing it back to one of the porters.

Donovan sighed. Not yet sundown, and already so many traps. The poachers were getting more desperate—only about a hundred tigers were left in this particular forest, and the forest itself was being gnawed away by coffee and palm oil planters. The big corporations funneled money to the nearby farmers in the hopes they'd do the dirty work of clearing the forest and planting the illegal crops. Most of the time, the provincial government turned a blind eye. Sometimes trying to combat it all felt like a hopeless task. In fact, tomorrow he'd be over in Blangkejeren to testify against a paper company trying to take even more of the supposedly protected national park.

But despite the conflicts between the local government and conservationists like himself, Donovan loved Sumatra and this area in particular. The jungle was magical to him. The locals believed there was actual magic in the area and called this forest *"Hutan Duri dan Cakar,"* which translated into "Forest of Thorns and Claws." The thorns referred to actual thorns in the plant life. Enduring the prick of such thorns was said to bring health and long life.

He kept hoping for a glimpse of the claws today. Claws of the tigers, that was.

Using the walking stick for support, Donovan stood. "Eight, right. I think we've cleared this area. We'll keep moving toward the west. Stay quiet. We could still run into whoever's setting these things."

The fact that the jungle was so quiet worried him. Even the birds and monkeys were keeping clear of this area, which meant there was probably a large predator somewhere nearby. It might be a man. As they began walking, Donovan kept a hand near his rifle, strapped to his shoulder. Vines and ferns brushed his bare legs; it was too humid to wear trousers out here, so he did as the locals did and wore long shorts instead. Also plenty of mosquito repellent.

They'd been walking for maybe fifteen minutes when he heard something thrashing in the dense undercover ahead. Donovan signaled his team to be silent and brought out a pair of binoculars. With a sinking feeling, he tried to spot the source through young teakwood trees and bird of paradise plants.

A frantic yowl confirmed his fears. That sound could only come from a large cat.

"Get the tranq gun ready! I'm moving in closer to see how badly it's been trapped." Donovan was no longer concerned about noise. If it was a young tiger, its mother would have already been on them; therefore it had to be a solitary animal.

He kept watch for more snares as he crept closer. Branches swayed maybe twenty meters off, but he still couldn't see the animal. This wasn't good; it meant the tiger was probably rolling on the ground, perhaps injured. "Radio the home station," he told Evan, one of the junior rangers and a conservationist from Germany. "We may be bringing this one back with us."

Evan quietly began to report the incident to the rehabilitation center as Amin handed Donovan the tranquilizer gun. Donovan checked his watch. They were going to need reinforcements for an extraction. *There goes the rest of the day.*

"Hang back for now. Once it goes down, I'll need everyone to help me free the animal." Donovan gripped the gun in one hand and tucked his collapsible walking stick into his backpack's side pocket. As he drew closer, he focused on where the snarls and growls pierced the jungle. It was a positive sign that the tiger was making so much noise. A noisy tiger was a live one.

Crouching low, he climbed over a dead branch, then rounded a large rubber tree and finally spotted the animal in a clump of tall reeds. The tiger's orange and black coat showed clearly through the foliage as the creature flailed, its left front paw trapped by the cruel rope of the snare. The tiger snarled in anguish.

It was a small specimen, most likely a female. There was blood where the snare had cut into the animal's paw, probably also cutting off circulation. Yeah, they'd want to keep this one overnight, in case she had broken bones or damaged ligaments. Females were particularly important to the breeding pool; this one appeared to have just reached maturity, making her vital to their conservation efforts.

The tiger yowled and licked at the injury, her muzzle red with her own blood. *Poor thing. I wonder how long she's been here.*

Donovan raised the tranquilizer gun, and lined up the tiger in his sights. He hoped the poachers weren't close. It would be Evan's job to keep Amin and the porters safe while Donovan aided the tiger.

His finger grazed the trigger, ready to fire, when a low growl to his left made him pause. *That's not the snared tiger.* Slowly, Donovan lowered the rifle. He glanced at a dense thicket of reeds to his left.

A pair of yellow eyes stared back at him.

Fear paralyzed Donovan's limbs, and his heart pounded. This was a bigger tiger, with a well-defined scruff around the face, which suggested a young male. He stared at the animal, unable to break eye contact as it silently watched him. It was a gorgeous beast, with an unusual swirling of marks on one shoulder. The power in that gaze was electric. And dangerous.

One pounce: that was all it would take for the tiger to kill him, and a grown tiger could leap about eight meters. Donovan glanced at Evan, who was still on the phone with the center. The rest of the team hadn't noticed the tiger yet; the foliage was in the way. He could try to tranq this animal as well. But then they'd have two tigers to deal with.

When he looked back, the second tiger was gone.

Shit. No help for it—I'd better warn them.

"There's another tiger—watch out! I'm going to try and put the first one to sleep," Donovan called back to Amin. No point in being quiet now; the louder they were, the more likely they'd scare away the extra animal.

Saying a prayer, Donovan raised the rifle again. He zoomed in on the fleshy part of the tiger's shoulder as she rested for a moment, panting. With a muffled pop, the dart buried itself into the flesh, the red tufted end sticking out. The tiger yowled and lurched to her feet, and then curled in on herself, trying to chew at the rope. But it was useless. The poachers used a tightly woven nylon cord, and the tiger's big fangs, so good at crushing bones and cutting arteries, were just too unwieldy to get through it. The cord would only cut her lips and gums.

"Tiger should be down in five minutes. Where's our backup?" Donovan scanned the jungle. No sign of the other tiger. Muttering, he strode back to Evan and took the radio headset, putting it to his ear. "Roark? We're bringing a young adult female in with us."

Roark was an old friend of his—he'd met Roark while in London at university, where they'd both studied biology and ecology. Donovan liked to hike through the rainforest and get dirty, but Roark preferred managing the rehabilitation center.

"Yeah, I heard you. There's a team heading your direction, but it'll take them at least an hour. You think you can keep it under until then? Perhaps make a stretcher of some kind?"

It was impossible for them to move the tiger any other way. "We'd better. There's another tiger nearby—possibly a sibling. The good news is the five of us should be able to carry the one we found."

"If you can, then get out of there. You're taking the Punjab trail? I can meet you along it on your trek back with some guys to help get you to the truck."

Good enough. There were days Donovan wished for superpowers, to fly or sense enemies nearby. Or his very own satellite camera to spy for him. "The poachers might be in the area as well. I'm hoping not close enough to realize they've caught something. Warn the men to keep their guns ready."

"I'll do that. Have you had a chance to examine the animal yet?"

Donovan glanced over at the tiger, who was sitting, panting hard. Soon now. It swayed, eyes drooping. "Not yet. I'll call to let you know if we need anything."

"Brilliant. Keep me updated. We'll prepare a holding pen for it. Hopefully it won't need to stay long. Our budget's tight enough for this month. The province seems to forget we're a nonprofit organization." Roark's crisp London accent made him sound cheerful, even though Donovan knew this stuff worried him.

Donovan's anger rose when he thought about funding and provincial politics. "Plus we've got the bloody hearing to attend tomorrow. Damned government and their greed." There was a soft *thump* as the tiger tried to stand up and fell over instead, succumbing to the drug. "Have to go. Over and out." He switched off the radio, returning it to Evan. "Try to put some kind of stretcher together—I have some spare tarp in my bag. And stay here until I give the okay to come closer."

With that, Donovan approached the snared tiger, coming within three meters of it. The panting had subsided into deep breathing, and the tiger's eyes were closed. *Good.* He scanned the nearby brush, looking for its companion, but the jungle was still quiet, and would probably remain so until all the humans and predators were out of the area.

Cautiously, Donovan pulled out his walking stick, stepping forward again. He extended it and poked the sleeping tiger in the side. No response. Nodding to himself, he put the aluminum walking stick back, then reached into his backpack for his veterinary kit, which included a simple ear thermometer, gauze, medical tape, and stethoscope. Crouching beside the tiger, he listened to its heartbeat. Steady and slow. Just as it should be.

Next he listened to its lungs, checked the rolled-back eyes, the teeth, tongue, and then moved to check the animal's injuries. The tiger was indeed female, sexually mature but young, and he didn't think it had ever given birth before. It looked to be in excellent health, except for the snare around the left forepaw, digging cruelly into the flesh. Bright blood marred the white fur, dripping onto the forest floor. If he didn't work fast, they'd soon have ants and other nasties to deal with.

He used a knife to cut the main line of the snare, then safety shears to carefully cut the cording from the wounds. She'd likely pulled a muscle or two while struggling. Once the cords were cut, he disinfected the wound and applied a bandage to it. That would have to do for now. He didn't think any bones had been broken. They'd know more after the animal woke up and began walking around.

"Let's get out of here," he said, as Amin ventured near with the makeshift stretcher. It wouldn't get them back to the center, but it should work until they met up with the other team. The porters set the contraption by the tiger's head, eyeing her nervously. Donovan waved them out of the way and went to stand next to her head, smiling at the way her tongue lolled. "Evan, we'll each grab a leg and drag her on. Don't worry. She's out cold."

Together, they pulled the two-hundred-and-fifty-pound tigress forward, enough so that her front half was on the stretcher.

Donovan adjusted the tiger so that her front paws were somewhat secured to the stretcher. It was going to be awkward, but they'd make do. "All right, everyone. Help me pull her. Pay attention to her eyes. If she starts to come to, I'll need to dose her again." He'd probably need to at least once, but it was risky using too much sedative on a big cat. No telling how they'd react.

As they began the laborious chore of dragging the tiger back to the center, Donovan felt the itch between his shoulder blades that meant somebody was watching them. When he looked, however, all he saw was the forest.

Chapter Two

Gunung Leuser National Forest, Sumatra
May 14, 2013

As the five humans dragged the injured tigress away, Kersen watched from high up in a tree, safely out of sight. Claws dug into the hard wood as Kersen yawned, long canine teeth flashing, and then he snorted as he almost inhaled a mosquito. *Stupid stress response!* His heart was pounding in his chest and his gut was churning.

That was his sister down there.

Once the humans were out of sight, he climbed down, loping over to where they'd left the broken strands of the snare. Smelling his sister's blood on the thin cords, he growled.

Why had he and Gemi been so careless? They both *knew* how widespread the snares were these days, how bold and clever the poachers were becoming. Bitari was going to kill him for letting humans take Gemi. Ever since their parents died, his older sister had been the guardian of the family, who were all members of the *suka siluman harimau*, their weretiger clan.

Where would they hide when the natural tiger population went extinct?

Kersen rumbled to himself, taking a moment to memorize the humans' scents. He'd heard Gemi's cries from across the valley, but he'd come too late. It should have been him cutting the ropes and freeing her. *She must have panicked and gone too deep into her tiger mind.* The only positive was she'd been taken by conservationists and not the poachers. But what if they decided to keep her? She'd be trapped in her tiger form indefinitely.

He couldn't allow that. *I have to free Gemi.*

The area was layered with scents, but it was the leader's that most interested Kersen. The man was a veterinarian or something. He'd likely stay near Gemi. Kersen could track him by his scent if he needed to.

Kersen took a deep breath, sniffing. At first he smelled only repellent. *Uck.* But beneath that, the man had a pleasant aroma. A touch of clove, or coffee, perhaps. Earthy smells. Kersen took another whiff, whiskers twitching. *Cinnamon. Great Brahma, I could lick the fellow.* He huffed. *How can I think of sex when Gemi is in danger?*

Well, the man was handsome, for one thing. White skin lightly tanned by the sun, brown hair in a cut close to the head, and a short, neat beard. The man had remarkable blue eyes that had held concern for a wounded animal—not something Kersen typically encountered.

Licking his chops and trying to dispel the pleasant warmth that had begun to stir within him, Kersen followed the trail. He kept low to the ground, mindful of any snares the conservationists might have missed, until he caught up with them near the Punjab trail. *Where are they taking her?* It was easy to stay out of the humans' sight, easy to remain unheard with all the noise they were making. The leader was speaking in English on his radio set. Kersen's English was rusty, taught to him by his grandparents, but he could make out most of it.

"What's your estimated time of arrival? Has there been any sign of the poachers in this area?" The leader's voice sounded tense. Again, that warmth spread through him, feeling like home, like safety. He wanted to run over there and rub his face against the man's leg. Mark him.

That's preposterous. He's not of the clan. I shouldn't entertain such thoughts about him.

Kersen huffed, falling back to make sure none of the men detected him. The jungle had been calm all day, so they probably wouldn't be alerted to his presence by other animals.

If he could only free Gemi before she infected anyone, they could escape easily. The village where Kersen's clan lived their human lives was to the west of here. There they'd be safe.

For centuries, the weretigers had lived hidden away in apparently human villages, but nevertheless were connected to the wilderness. They needed to shift at least a few times a month. This meant that it would be very difficult to hide themselves once the real tigers were gone; plus the tiger spirits inside were intimately linked to the land. Who knew what would happen to those tiger spirits if the forests disappeared? Of course, another danger to his kind was that a white foreigner like this leader might discover Kersen's people and spread news to the world.

Kersen shuddered to think what might happen then. It was hard enough being different from the rest of the world, having both a human and an animal spirit dwelling inside. It could be wonderful and terrible at the same time.

As a youth, he'd only seen the good side of everything.

Five years earlier

"Can we go hunting today, Father? I really want to go. I've been practicing all week!" Kersen leaned over a rickety chair in the dirt yard. Behind him was his family's bamboo and timber longhouse, built on stilts for the monsoon rains. Father was sitting cross-legged on the ground nearby, busily weaving a basket. That meant they'd be foraging for fruit. Kersen didn't want fruit, though. Having experienced his first real shift only a month ago, he craved meat more than anything.

His father chuckled, threading the straw through the firm reed frame. "Yes, Kersen. As soon as I finish this for your mother. She may want to take Gemi as well."

Making a face, Kersen kicked at the dirt. Gemi was twelve, while Kersen was fourteen—nearly grown up—yet he'd only been shifting for a few weeks when Gemi first changed. It wasn't fair that girls generally began shifting before boys, but that was nature. Shifting came with puberty. *Why did her first shift have to happen so close to mine?*

Kersen sighed. "I don't want to wait for them—Mother will want to change clothing and everything." The girls usually wore dresses complete with head coverings, and they didn't like leaving such things in the fields when shifting. Kersen was barefoot and shirtless like Father, the two of them only wearing jeans that were streaked with dirt and mud.

Father folded his arms, staring at him. "Kersen . . ."

Kersen immediately hung his head. Wasn't it enough that his father had agreed to take him? "Yes, sir. I'll tell them, and then I'll help you finish." He peeked up again. "Do you think we'll find a deer?"

There were several species of deer in the jungle, but they were constantly on the move. Sometimes the village men organized hunting parties. They'd kill two or three and bring the carcasses back to the village to barbeque on a big bonfire. Lately, however, things had grown tougher, and the jungle kept shrinking. Villagers who used to sell meat and bone tools to outsiders now struggled to support themselves. It wasn't only the *siluman harimau*. The human villages were also suffering.

His father shrugged. "If Allah is willing. We'll see."

Kersen made a face as he climbed a ladder up to the house. His family actually traced their heritage back to Bali; his grandparents had been born there, and they'd been Hindu. Then they'd moved to Sumatra, when the last Balinese tiger was killed off by hunters. Kersen had been fond of his grandparents, who'd died when he was ten, and he still preferred the Hindu gods. The locals here were Muslim though, so Father and Mother were too, though Father wasn't very devout.

In the main room of the house, Mother was busy cutting vegetables on the tiny counter by the wood stove where she'd cook the chicken and rice. Bitari was helping grind the spices. She was tall at sixteen, with a square jaw and black hair held in a single braid, pinned up.

Kersen hovered near the door. "Father's taking me hunting after he finishes the basket." He held off mentioning Gemi and Bitari, despite his words to Father. *I don't want Bitari to come. She's bossy.*

Bitari whirled, staring at him. "He's taking *you*? He didn't say that this morning. Why wouldn't he take all of us?"

Kersen jutted his lip out at her. "I have to learn how to hunt. It's important that I learn." He dared her to argue. While all the villagers farmed, the tigers inside them demanded meat, and all were expected to contribute to the hunts. There were times the village was all but deserted as the inhabitants sated their urge to follow Nature and roam the jungle.

Crossing her arms, Bitari pursed her lips at him. Gemi paused in the action of washing vegetables, watching. Kersen's mother sighed. "Here's an idea. After dinner, we can go as a family. Bitari, if you keep an eye on your sister, then Father and I can show Kersen how to hunt monkeys, since he's keen to learn that. But everyone will need to stay close. Things aren't as safe in the jungle as they used to be."

Kersen wanted to grind his teeth. Monkeys? That didn't sound nearly as exciting as learning how to chase down a deer, even one of the tiny muntjaks. But when Mother decreed something, there was no going around it. He'd have to be satisfied that he was hunting at all today. "Yes, Mother." He returned outside to help Father finish the baskets. The sooner household chores were done, the sooner they'd go.

By the time the chores and dinner were finished, the sun was beginning to set, and cries of monkeys and wild birds filled the air. Fields surrounded their village, but Kersen's house was only a few hundred meters from the rainforest, not kilometers.

The urge to shift was upon him. He tugged at his father's shorts, stomping his feet in impatience. His father looked at him with a smile, and ruffled his hair, sending it into his eyes. "Soon, son. Your mother's changing into her casual clothing." Even as he spoke, Bitari and Gemi came out of the house barefoot, wearing only some old T-shirts and shorts. It was better than walking to the jungle naked, and they'd find somewhere to hide their clothes before shifting together.

Kersen ran to grab Gemi's hand, ignoring Bitari's glare. "Come on! We'll wait for everyone at the edge of the field." Let the adults meander; he needed to run. Gemi laughed at him, and with that, they took off, little puffs of dust on the ground rising from where their feet fell.

He let go of her hand as they reached the old wooden fence that separated the fields from the village proper, leaping over a low spot where a board had fallen. In other villages, he imagined the children would be warned against running through the fields, for fear of cobras or other creatures. For him, they weren't a problem. He could smell them, hear them in the brush.

The change was so close, he could feel his teeth lengthening. Kersen rumbled deep in his throat, a tiger's purr. The scents of freshly turned earth and rice sprouts filled his nostrils. He didn't run too fast, letting Gemi keep up with him. But it felt good.

Gemi shoved at him playfully. He grinned at her and saw tufts of white fur appear along her jawline. She was skinny and narrow-faced with hair in two long braids down her back, which looked funny with the fur.

Bitari yelled, "Don't go under the trees alone! Father will kill you if you get lost!" Kersen risked a glance behind and saw Father had started to jog as well, smiling. Only Mother and Bitari were walking, falling farther and farther back.

Nevertheless, as they neared the end of the field, Kersen slowed, breathing hard. The sun had fallen below the trees, bathing everything in reddish light. He'd never entered the jungle at night before. But that was the normal time for tigers to be awake, wasn't it?

Gemi leaned on the fence, her black braids swaying in the breeze, her gaze intent on the shadows beneath the canopy. "It's dark in there, isn't it? Will we be able to see, once we're changed?"

Kersen followed her gaze, sniffing at the breeze. He was getting itchy and hot, as fur began to sprout along his arms. Perhaps they'd better strip. "I don't know. I suppose. We won't be much use, otherwise." He'd only been into the jungle twice before, and since Gemi had only started shifting last week, this would be her first time.

"Oh, you two! You'll be the death of me someday!" Father laughed as he finally caught up with them, panting. "I've sat around too much. This was a good idea. I can't let myself fall out of practice either, can I?"

Kersen and his sister exchanged looks, and Kersen shrugged, scratching his arms. "Sure, Father. Now can we change? I can't hold it back much longer."

Father nodded. "Off with the clothes. I'll stash them here by the fence. Now mind me—don't stray! Stay close to either me or your mother. Follow what we do. And if you want to catch anything, be patient! Monkeys have sharp eyes, and sharper ears, and they're smart.

The art of the hunt is learning how to move silently and get as close as possible. You'll see."

Kersen was already pulling off his shorts before his father finished speaking. Naked, he crouched in the tall grass, digging his fingers into the rich, dark soil. He closed his eyes, smelling it, feeling the animal inside. Another low purr rumbled in his chest. The night air cooled his skin, and then it was happening: the aches as his limbs shifted, some lengthening, others shortening. He cried out as his fangs grew and fur sprouted all over his body. The most painful part was the tail, going from having none to a long dexterous one that lashed back and forth. Then there were a few seconds of blackout as his mind adjusted to the new form—Father had said after Kersen's first shift that this was normal, and sure enough, the change was smoother now. He retained his memories and his personality.

Kersen opened his feline eyes.

He was crouched in the grass on the edge of the rainforest, next to a young tiger still yowling in pain—his sister. The smell of humans from the village was strong in his nostrils, warning him that he should move away. One scent stood nearby, but that was Father, sending off a confusing mixture of human and tiger. Even as Kersen looked up, his father began to change.

To witness the shift was always amazing, especially with Kersen's enhanced night vision. He watched as Father's head grew larger, the jaw more pronounced, the nose longer. Kersen stepped forward to take a sniff, as tiger-smell replaced man-smell. It was strange, being half aware, still thinking like a human in some ways, but with animal instincts that threatened to take over at times.

A growl sounded to his left, and small teeth tugged at Kersen's ear. He snarled back, taking a swipe at his sister's muzzle. With the twitch of her tail, she spoke to him mind to mind. *Come on! Want to hunt! Want to run! Come play!*

Kersen wanted to. But he remembered what Father had said, about waiting for everyone. *Play with me here!* He crouched and batted at Gemi, and she pounced on him. They wrestled, rolling in the grass, until new scents forced both of them to stop. Standing over them was the remainder of their little pack: Mother and Bitari, in tiger form. A few feet away stood Father, sniffing at the air, his body turned toward the jungle in alert watchfulness.

Follow us, Father sent. Keeping his body low, he loped into the forest.

Kersen would always remember that first time he entered into the jungle at night, how every smell, every sound seemed to jump out and grab hold of him. He couldn't remember everything they had done that first hunting trip, whether Bitari had helped out or played with Gemi while he had stalked with his parents. Kersen did remember that he hadn't caught anything. Neither had Father. Mother had managed to kill a tapir, but it had already been wounded.

He remembered the taste of fresh meat and blood that was still warm. The joy of that first trip would long sustain Kersen against the grief of what happened only a few months later.

Pushing away the heartache that came nowadays when he thought of his parents, Kersen crept a little closer to the men carrying his sister, intent on not letting them out of his sight. No way was he letting humans keep hold of his little sister. Forget the fact that Bitari would shriek when she learned he was leaving the jungle in tiger form. Sometimes he followed the rules. Other times, he determined it was better to break them.

This was one of those times.

CHAPTER THREE

Ketambe Conservation and Research Center, Ketambe, Sumatra
May 14, 2013

D onovan wiped at the sweat pouring down his face and blinked to clear his vision. It had been a grueling two hours, but they'd finally reached an area accessible by vehicles. The sight of the research center truck, waiting for them to load the wounded tiger, was a welcome relief, not only physically, but because he wanted to keep details of this rescue quiet, lest anyone try to steal the animal. The quicker they got the young female patched up and returned to the forest, the better.

A few times under the canopy he'd had the nagging sense that they were being followed. Not that he'd detected anything; he'd stopped the group twice, listening for a heavy footstep or the whiff of tobacco, a clue that might give away whatever it was that had been following them. But he'd found nothing. If they were human, they would know how to erase their tracks. If it was an animal . . . but that was daft. No wild animal would track a large group of humans with a wounded predator in their midst. Not even another tiger would be so bold or clever.

They'd upgraded to a real stretcher when they'd met up with Roark an hour ago, who had quick footed it with a couple extra helpers. With the extra men, it was easy lifting the tigress into the truck. Donovan climbed into the front passenger seat, letting Roark do the driving.

Twenty minutes later, they arrived at the animal research and conservation center. When Donovan opened the back door of the truck, the tiger was lying sprawled across the stretcher, still asleep. Donovan sighed in relief, and grasped the front handles, allowing Amin and Evan to take the other end. He walked backward in order to monitor the animal.

As they hurried toward the veterinary clinic doors, the tiger opened her eyes groggily.

"She's waking up! Hurry and clear a table. Then get the anesthesia ready so that we can put her under again. She'll need stiches at the very least. I also want a full X-ray scan," Donovan called out, arms straining to hold up his end of the tiger's weight. Roark ran ahead to carry out the instructions. If everything went smoothly, Donovan wanted to also tag and chip her. The more tigers they could track for research purposes, the better.

As staff hurried to clear the way, Donovan, Evan, and Amin carried the tiger into the hall. Donovan tried to keep one eye on where he was going and the other on the tiger. She sneezed—she was definitely waking. Fortunately she didn't yet seem fully coherent; her lids were still closed and her movements sluggish. They rounded a corner, and Donovan swore as Amin jostled the stretcher.

The tigress's eyes opened and fixed on Donovan's.

He had time to pull back one hand as the tiger raised her injured paw, but if he let go with the left hand, they'd have a very pissed-off wild animal falling off the stretcher. The tigress swiped at him, and Donovan winced as her claws broke skin, leaving three gashes across the top of his forearm. "Anesthesia! Quick!"

The tiger turned her head and bit him in the same spot, snarling. Even though she was half out of it, she managed to clamp down on his arm. Donovan braced himself for the pain; those jaws could break his bones. But instead, the animal only mouthed him and nudged him with her nose. Her rough tongue swept over the gash left by her claws, and sent a fierce stinging sensation through his nerves.

Donovan lurched, fearful that if he tried to pull away, she'd bite harder. Vet assistants surrounded him to help. One grabbed the free handle of the stretcher, while another eased the tiger's mouth open and fitted a breathing mask over her muzzle. The gas hissed.

The tigress yowled in protest and kicked with her back legs, but Amin and Evan were ready; they held on, and together the team hurried the tiger into the surgery and onto a large steel table.

The tigress blinked, swinging her head back to avoid the mask, but the assistants were used to this. They secured the mask and strapped on the pulse monitor, working efficiently to prep her. Donovan was able to let go of the stretcher handle and inspect his wounds. A few stitches and he'd be good as new, but he needed to clean the scratches and small punctures where her teeth had broken skin. Her bloody saliva wouldn't have done the cuts any good.

He'd been lucky. He could have lost his right arm today.

"Get that X-ray," he instructed Helena Sun, his primary vet tech, as he headed to the sink. They'd find out if the tiger had suffered any broken bones or internal injuries. Then if she was okay, he'd stitch up the tiger's left forepaw where it had been injured, and then himself.

As they prepped the tiger for the scan, Donovan turned on the water and stuck his arm under the flow. He winced as cold water flushed the wound, then braced himself as he soaped up. The sting was less than expected. However, strange pains had begun to shoot up his arm, almost like electrical pulses. Donovan shook his head. *Tiger must've hit a nerve.* He allowed an assistant to wrap his arm in gauze as the buzzing noise behind him announced the activation of the X-ray machine.

Amin appeared in scrubs to pull off Donovan's shirt and replace it with scrubs. As soon as he was clean and prepped, Donovan rechecked the animal's vitals and sighed in relief. Heart rate was right where it should be, temperature was good, breathing was good. The animal didn't appear to be in shock.

Roark appeared at his side, standing out amongst his smaller colleagues with his wider girth and his bright-red beard. "Got a holding pen ready for her. God, she's a beaut, isn't she? Glad you were able to reach her before the poachers." He glanced at Donovan's arm. "What happened?"

Donovan didn't even slow down, checking the tiger's muscle reflexes to make sure she was really under this time. "She woke up. Didn't appreciate me carrying her, I reckon." He stood aside as Helena began shaving the fur from the tiger's paw where it had been captured by the snare. An assistant stood nearby to clean off the blood. Donovan pulled out what he needed for the stitches from a set of drawers. "At least she doesn't look like she's in too bad a shape. We were lucky."

"Bad news about the bite. I swear, sometimes I think Mother Nature's put a curse on this stretch of forest. Wish it would work more against the poachers, though." Roark gently touched the fur on the tiger's haunch. "I've got a tag and chip prepared, so we can keep an eye on her after we release her. And for now, I'm putting her into our private records. We can decide later whether to announce the rescue on our website." He scowled. "I'd love to prosecute the poachers responsible for this!"

Donovan shook his head. "We'll never catch them. Fuck, it's hard enough to get the government to care about corporations coming in and illegally tearing down whole swaths of forest! However, we could generate some support from the aftermath of this incident. Post some pictures of her to our blog. Maybe we can get a few donations out of the exposure."

He paused as Helena approached him with the X-ray film on a light board. She looked relieved. "You released the snare just in time. There's a hairline fracture of the third metatarsal, and there will probably be bruising. Nothing that should keep her here for long." Her news helped to settle Donovan's nerves. He nodded.

"Thank you. If we bind up the paw and give her a week, she can be released after that." He took the X-ray from her to study it for himself, and then nodded at Roark. "Hear that? We won't have to go broke trying to feed her. Order enough meat for a week and take pictures for our newsletters. We'll make as much use of this as we can."

With the X-ray results to guide him, Donovan set to work on the tiger. They had a strict time limit while the animal would be out, and every second counted. He set one pin for the fracture, stitched up the gash from the snare, and put antiseptic on the shallow lacerations caused by the vines and roots of the forest and the tiger's desperate attempts to free herself. Some gauze, a liberal wrapping with medical tape, and she was good to go. He debated putting a medical cone around her head to deter her from licking the wound, but decided against it. She would be freaked out enough being in a cage. No need to traumatize her further.

Other than the injuries, the tigress looked like she was in prime condition. She didn't even have any skin parasites that Donovan could detect, and her teeth were in excellent shape. He finished his checkup, clipped a tag to her ear, and inserted a microchip in her left shoulder. The thing was so tiny, she'd never notice it. Now they'd be able to track her movements and get an idea of her territory size and behaviors. They'd also know if something happened to her.

"She's ready." The room spun. *Damn, haven't eaten today.* His arm was still throbbing with pain too, but that was just a nuisance. He only hoped he'd sterilized it before infection could set in. *I'll pop some antibiotics just in case.*

Roark returned from the front office. With the help of Helena and some of the other staff, they moved the sleeping tiger to a concrete pen about six by six meters long; not big at all, but it would be enough for the short duration. They laid her on the floor next to a large water dish and a raw chicken in case she was hungry, and then Roark gave her the shot to help her wake up, patting her head affectionately. Once she was moving around again, Donovan could observe how the injured leg was doing.

"We should name her," Roark quipped, as they shut the bars, locking her inside. They were in a wing of the building jutting out from the main research facility. Typically these cells housed smaller animals including orangutans and the occasional tapir. Sadly, too often when Donovan found tigers, they were dead.

Donovan rolled his eyes. "She'll be here a week."

"I'm naming her Kitty. Because that's what she is." Roark ducked before Donovan could punch him in the arm, grinning as he backed up.

"'Kitty'? Really?" But Donovan was smiling too. They had a healthy female they could track now. If Roark wanted to name her something barmy, then fine.

Roark shrugged. "Keeps it simple. Now go stitch yourself up! I'll be in the main office watching her from the cameras."

He walked out, leaving Donovan in front of the bars to watch as the tigress opened her eyes and yawned.

His arm throbbed to the beat of his heart, but Donovan couldn't seem to pull himself away. She really was gorgeous, and it heartened him to know she'd recover. The fact she'd injured him was just bad luck—no fault of the animal. He should have given her another shot of tranquilizer before they reached the research center and avoided the clawing. But he'd wanted to keep it to a minimum.

Thinking back on the incident, he swore that when the tigress had opened her eyes, for just a second she'd seemed *horrified* at her circumstances. As if she'd understood where she was and what was happening. Then after the swipe she had licked him almost like she'd been sorry. What had that been about? It was strange.

Undoubtedly my imagination. Satisfied that he'd done everything he could for the poor beast, Donovan turned away and headed back to the surgery room. *A few stitches and loads of antiseptic and antibiotics, and I'll be fine.*

The pain lancing up his arm begged to differ.

///

Border of Gunung Leuser National Forest and Ketambe, Sumatra

At the edge of the forest, Kersen changed back into his human form.

He was forced to steal a pair of shorts that were hanging out to dry at a little farmhouse, but didn't bother with anything else. There wasn't time—a truck had come to pick up Gemi and the men who had taken her from the jungle. Even now, Gemi could be waking up. She might panic and accidentally change to her human form. Worse, she could wake up groggy, and if still ruled by her tiger mind, she could injure or kill someone. Considering the repercussions, it would almost be better if she killed rather than wounded. All those who came into contact with her blood would be in danger of contracting the virus that made Kersen's people shifters, and if not monitored and taught to control their predatory natures, they could wreak havoc on the population.

Kersen ran along the side of the dirt road, keeping an eye out for tracks from the research center truck. It wasn't long before he found where the truck had turned off, and from there it was only a few kilometers farther to locate the research center. It was surrounded by a chain-link fence with barbed wire at the top. Wrapping some long, thick grass around his hands to protect them, he scaled the fence easily.

Once inside the compound, Kersen weighed his options. There were three main buildings and a smaller one with a tin roof, likely a garage or storage facility. The main building was stone block and had obviously been built by foreigners; it was raised on concrete blocks against floods, but only by a few feet. He spotted the truck that had transported his sister over on the side of the main building. The second building looked the most promising—it was long and heavily fenced with yard areas suitable for holding animals, and it seemed to jut out from the main building. The pens were fenced on all sides to prevent climbing or flying out of the enclosures. His sister could be in one of those, unless they were working on her injuries.

Dread tightened Kersen's gut. He hated the idea of her being hurt. The one good thing about this situation was that somebody was probably caring for her instead of killing her.

As he huddled against a lone tree by the outer fence, Kersen weighed his options. This was a private facility, so he couldn't merely walk in and ask to see the captured tiger, never mind explain how he knew it was there. He'd have to sneak in. There wouldn't be much cover to hide him, though. *Nothing but grass between the outer fence and the two buildings.* He spotted three security cameras: two on the main building and one on the second building. Two of them faced toward the road and the electric gate near his position. The camera on the animal-enclosure building faced toward the side of that building, probably to watch for anyone trying to gain access to the animals.

Like himself.

Kersen blew out a frustrated breath. How was he supposed to break his sister out of here? If anybody was monitoring those cameras, they'd see him long before he reached the building. Approaching as a tiger wouldn't be any better. He'd end up in a cage next to Gemi.

The clock was ticking. Being captured here might be better than listening to his older sister screaming at him. She wouldn't care that it was each shifter's responsibility to avoid the traps set by poachers;

they'd learned that from the very first foray into the jungle. But family was the most important thing. You didn't leave family behind.

He crawled on his belly, hoping that the grass would keep him out of sight. *What happens if they spot me?* Since this facility was run by Western foreigners, he doubted they'd take a shot at him. *At least I hope they won't.*

Inch by inch, he crept forward, looking for movement. He didn't even have a clear idea of how to get in. *This is madness.*

Precisely as that thought struck him, an alarm blared from the main building. "Intruder alert! This is private property. Vacate this area or face criminal charges per the Aceh Provincial statute 251.5." In a man's firm voice, the warning was given first in Indonesian, repeated in English, and then in Acehnese. Fear rippled down Kersen's back, and he almost started to transform right there.

He clamped down on the urge. Heart hammering, he tried to think rationally. *I could run to find Gemi, and risk being shot or arrested.* Or he could run away and try again after dark.

After all, they won't kill her. They're the good guys. He wished he could believe that.

A figure emerged from the main building wielding a pistol. It wasn't the handsome man from the jungle. He yelled, pointing at Kersen. "You there! What are you doing?" Kersen jumped. His English was pretty good, but the man had a funny accent and a red beard that muffled his words.

This wasn't going to work. Though he might be able to dodge the fat guy, the other one, the doctor, was in there. He seemed like the sort who could keep pace and outmuscle anyone. Kersen stood up slowly, his hands raised. "My pet," he said, because it was the only excuse he could come up with. "You took my pet."

"What?" The man looked bewildered, which wasn't surprising. "We're a research facility. Wild animals. No pets. Now go away. Otherwise I'm calling the police, understand?" His Indonesian was very clear. He'd obviously been in the country for a long time.

Kersen took a deep breath and let it out. Panicking was not an option. Bitari was going to kill him, but he saw no other choice. "I'm going," he told the man. He backed up slowly, so as not to give the man any reason to shoot. Once he was outside the perimeter, the hum of an electric motor filled the air, and the gates shut. He'd have to wait for nightfall, and try again with Bitari's help.

Ugh. Now I have to tell Bitari. She'd be waiting at home, worrying.

He headed back the way he'd come. As soon as he reached the jungle, he shifted into his tiger form and began running north toward his village.

CHAPTER FOUR

Ketambe Conservation and Research Center, Ketambe, Sumatra
May 15, 2013

Donovan ran through the forest on four legs.

Scents assailed him on every side—rich smells of soil and moss, sharp green smells of broken leaves and foliage, the musky scent of an animal. It felt good to run. It felt good to be at one with the jungle.

Stars shone overhead, and yet in the darkness Donovan could see every vine and tree trunk, every ant crawling on the forest floor. Water dripped from an orchid plant, loud in his ears. He felt at peace for the first time in his life. He belonged here.

Up ahead, a tiny deer was standing in a clearing. Donovan slowed, feet digging into the mossy forest floor, and crouched low. He bared his fangs as he judged the distance between himself and a fine meal.

Then he pounced.

And nearly fell off the bed.

Sitting up shakily, Donovan glanced at the clock and groaned; his alarm hadn't gone off. Perhaps he'd forgotten to set it—he barely remembered falling asleep last night after taking some antibiotics and a painkiller. Apparently they hadn't done any good, because his arm was throbbing. Grimacing, he tore off the bandage to inspect the scratches. Sure enough, they looked angry red and infected. *Well bugger.*

He forced himself to get out of bed. Crap, he needed to dress up today. After popping a strong antibiotic and another pain pill, he pulled on black slacks and a short-sleeved gray shirt. He'd be damned if he'd wear a long-sleeved one in this heat, especially since he'd have to wear a blazer anyway. More antiseptic on the arm, and then he rebandaged it. *Not about to let a stupid scratch get in my way today.* Ironic that it should have come from the very animal he'd been trying to save.

Once he was fully dressed, he headed to the kitchen. Once there, he fumbled for his Tigger coffee mug to fill it with caffeinated goodness, hoping to shake off the fatigue. Roark was already there, dressed nicely as well, though his shirt was wrinkled and there was already a coffee stain on his sleeve.

"We had a bit of excitement yesterday after you caught that tiger." Roark filled his own coffee mug, a plain brown one with a chip. The man liked things bland and no-nonsense, which was probably a good contrast to Donovan's adventurous habits.

Donovan blinked as he took a sip. "Oh?" Had the tigress taken a turn for the worse? But no—if that were the case, Roark or one of the assistants would have woken him.

Roark nodded. "Warned off a poacher who actually tried to break *into* the research facility!"

Donovan choked on his coffee and stared at Roark. "Someone tried to break into the center? Were they carrying a weapon?"

"No. And he didn't get very far. But the idea! It's like we can't be safe anywhere anymore." Roark huffed, then stuffed a piece of toast in his mouth.

God, the last thing they needed was to start an all-out war with the poachers, like gang violence in America. And it didn't make sense. Poachers liked to work in secret, safe from prosecution by the law. Why would one attempt an obvious "crime" such as breaking and entering? Was this fellow that desperate for a tiger? This didn't bode well.

"He was young too—couldn't have been older than early twenties." Roark shook his head ruefully. "I could be blowing this out of proportion. Could have just been a kid trying to see a tiger or make mischief. Anyways, I scared him off. Things were quiet after."

"Had to be a local kid," Donovan agreed, and bit back a wince as he grabbed some toast, stretching both the bandage and the injury on his arm.

Not surprisingly, Roark noticed. "Your arm doing all right?"

"It stings a bit. I've taken Cipro. Should kill anything that came in," Donovan said.

Obviously concerned, Roark gently took his arm and turned it over, and Donovan had to force himself not to curse or cry out. It really fucking *hurt*. But there was no way he was missing today's meeting.

"I'm fine." This time he couldn't help the growl in his voice. *What's wrong with me? I usually have a better hold of my temper than this.*

Roark inspected the bandage and the skin around the large plaster, and Donovan had to take deep breaths to keep from retaliating. Roark's lips thinned as his eyes met Donovan's. "Once we return, I'm pulling this off and taking a proper look. We can't have you dying of septic shock on us, Donovan. Your mum would kill me, first of all."

Donovan snorted. "Like she'd know. She's busy on her own quest to save the world."

His stomach roiled. Trying not to grimace, he dumped the rest of his coffee. He'd stick to bottled water and rice today. *Can't afford to get sick. I'll take a nap later.*

"We'd better be going. No telling what traffic to Blangkejeren will be like," Roark said, clearly keen to change the subject. He cleared his throat. "Speaking of your mum, have your parents even told you where they've been lately?"

Definitely trying to distract me. But, at the moment, Donovan didn't care if it would take his mind off the pain. "Not a clue. I think last I heard, they were in New Guinea." He'd grown up pretty much all over, dragged along by his parents who were both scientists. Indonesia, Bangladesh, India . . . it seemed like every year his mum and dad had focused on somewhere new. And in each country they visited, they'd lived in one sterile flat after another, or sometimes only a tent, never knowing where they'd be going next. They'd always been working, and they'd sent him out to play with locals, to try to fit in as an outsider.

It wasn't that Donovan didn't love his parents. In some distant way, he did, and he was grateful to them for raising him to be intelligent and globally aware. But he couldn't remember his mum ever hugging him or his dad complimenting him. For all that they lived south of the equator most of the time, they weren't warm people. Both had been more obsessed with biological compounds or complex ecosystems than a messy, squalling brat.

Many times he'd ended up playing alone, or working with animals instead. Still, that had led to some happy memories, like how he'd cared for an Indonesian tiger cub here at this very center when he'd been ten. Even then he'd felt like he belonged there, with the tiny cub riding around in his backpack, or batting at the bottle when he tried to feed it. Now this research center was as close to a home as he'd found.

That was why he so needed to protect it. The forest was under threat, and without the forest, this center had no purpose. Today the Aceh provincial government was considering a bill that would allow corporations to utilize land within the boundaries of the Gunung Leuser National Forest, which was supposed to be a wildlife refuge. A Chinese paper company was petitioning for the right to clear a thousand hectares of land they'd supposedly purchased shortly after the tsunami disaster back in 2004, when the province had been desperate for cash. The laws here were too often ignored, in that lands set aside for a national park were frequently infringed upon by the local people and governments. The consequences to endangered species in these cases could be dire. Gunung Leuser was one of the last habitats for Sumatran tigers, not to mention Sumatran elephants, rhinos, and orangutans.

Stuffing the piece of toast in his mouth, Donovan followed Roark through the conservation and research center. Halfway out the front door, Helena caught up and updated him on Kitty's status. The tigress was awake and recovering well, although she was avoiding the injured foot. She'd eaten one of the chickens and was pacing the confines of her enclosure. Not surprising, since she'd never been in one before. More worrying was the fact she'd been scratching her ear, trying to remove the tag. At least she seemed to be unaware of the microchip in her shoulder.

"Keep an eye on her. Roark tells me we've had some trespassers. Let me know if anything unusual happens while we're out. You have my cell." She bobbed her head at Donovan's instructions. Meanwhile, he was already regretting the toast. It wasn't helping his nausea at all, and neither were the acrid smells of disinfectant in the center. He needed to speak with the cleaning staff. They didn't need to use such strong-smelling chemicals.

"You drive," he told Roark, climbing into the passenger seat. Once the Jeep was rolling, Donovan leaned back and closed his eyes. Okay, so he was feeling a bit off today. He couldn't let that deter him. He'd nap on the long drive and then get ready to face the bloody corporate lawyers.

The smells of jungle actually helped to calm his upset stomach. When he did sleep, he dreamed of tigers.

///

Aceh Province Council Chamber, Blangkejeren, Sumatra

After three hours at the hearing, Donovan was ready to slash the throats of every single bloody corporate bureaucrat and lawyer. The governor's position lately was that Aceh had the right to utilize natural resources within its borders, which included most of the protected national forest of Gunung Leuser. This meant that locals were free to make deals with foreign companies such as paper and palm oil corporations who wanted to clear large swaths of supposedly protected forest.

"The state of Aceh in the Republic of Indonesia recognizes that the governing of approximately ten percent of Gunung Leuser falls under the state and not the National Forestry Division," a middle-aged man stated in Indonesian, standing at the podium and rustling papers as if to make a point. His words were repeated in English by a translator; everything here today would be related in both languages, since Indonesia had many dialects.

Donovan shook his head, rubbing at his arm. Damned pain was giving him a headache. Who the hell was wearing so much perfume? And why was it bothering him? Stuff like that usually didn't.

Sitting beside him, Roark nudged his leg. "We're up soon, right?" The Aceh councilman was continuing to drone on about giving the people opportunities and the growth of the economy.

He leaned in close to Roark, and tried to ignore his rumbling stomach. Maybe he could have a nice juicy steak after this hearing. "The opposing side should give arguments soon, but we'll be a bit. First the head of the Department of Forestry is going to talk, and then I believe there'll be a few other speakers."

Roark shook his head as he listened to the council members. "It's all lies, this crap about opportunities. These paper and palm oil companies trick the local farmers into the subsidies they provide by planting near their land, and then instead the destruction to the forest leads to floods and major erosion."

It was a familiar point to the conservationists' argument, and Donovan nodded. "Wipes out the farmers' income entirely. But people always want to believe in the big-business dream."

The head councilman was still blathering on. Donovan sighed, wishing he were back in bed, or checking up on the tigress. This fight was important, but it felt so hopeless. The provincial council would probably vote with their wallets as they had too many times before.

While he'd been trying to stay focused on the arguments, he really didn't want to hear more. Donovan's gaze wandered, falling on the council members first—these people who would be deciding the fate of countless creatures in one of the most biodiverse areas in the world. They sat at a long table in front of the auditorium, facing the single podium with its microphone for public testimony. Slowly, Donovan turned his head to check the corporate representatives in their expensive suits, from several foreign countries. *Vultures, all of them.* They'd already been making their case, both this morning and for the last few days. As soon as Councilman Akbar finished his speech, then those defending the forest would get their chance.

On Donovan's side was a mixed bunch, including officials from the Department of Forestry, nature conservationists like Donovan, some locals not affiliated with corporations who had shown up to defend their land, and news reporters there to get the scoop. Donovan wondered if Akbar had any idea how the international news media would spin this story if more forest was destroyed. *They'll blast him.* It was his one comforting thought.

In the back row of the council chamber with the bulk of the locals, a young man who seemed to be staring directly at Donovan suddenly looked away. He was Indonesian with skin browned by the sun and short black hair. The fellow was young—perhaps twenty. His clothing was typical of a farmer or laborer: a homespun shirt and faded brown trousers, no tie. He stood beside a large woman, who was perhaps a few years older than him, in a patterned dress and a hijab, quietly speaking to her.

When the young man peeked over again, their eyes met, and a surge of arousal went through Donovan. *Amber eyes.* Why did they seem familiar? Donovan was staring, but he couldn't help it. The fellow was exceptionally beautiful. Fine structured cheeks, straight nose, and an almost angelic, boyish quality to the face. If the young man had been living in Delhi or even Jakarta, he'd probably be a model or an actor.

Don't forget the local laws. Homosexuality was not only frowned upon; it was illegal in Aceh. Donovan flushed and averted his gaze. If the bloke thought that Donovan was checking him out, that could put a serious kink in Donovan's plans to defend the wildlife preserve in today's hearing. And yet, Donovan couldn't help but risk another perusal.

The fellow was still eyeing him. Had they met somewhere before? There were no gay bars on the island of Sumatra, but even a white outsider like him knew where to find action when he had the itch. There were massage parlors, for instance. Perhaps he'd seen this fellow there? Somehow, he doubted it. The man appeared dirt-poor in his homespun clothing, yet even in the humble clothing, however, the man was attractively fit. Warmth stole down Donovan's collar, and his trousers grew uncomfortably tight.

Roark nudged him, and Donovan forced himself to turn away, though he longed to go and ask the young man a few questions. At the podium, Councilman Akbar had finished speaking, and the representative from the Department of Forestry was walking up, pulling a paper out of a manila folder.

"I think he has some internet hotshot who will also be giving a statement," Roark whispered, and Donovan winced; he seemed unnaturally loud. No one around them seemed to have noticed, however. "And then it should be our turn. Are you ready?"

Donovan's stomach churned, and he felt hot all over. "I guess I have to be." Truth was, he suspected he was coming down with something, but hell if he was going to let the Aceh government chop away another piece of his protected forest without a damned good fight. He would have forced a hospital to wheel him here if it had come to that.

The Forestry fellow began to speak about the tourism generated by the wildlife preserves and national forests. Donovan reached down to his briefcase and pulled out the speech he'd prepared, along with research about the effects of deforestation. Maybe he should have brought pictures of the tigress here to remind everyone the sorts of creatures they should be protecting. Perhaps that would have got people to wake up.

As the Forestry official continued, Donovan couldn't help himself. He craned his neck to search out the young man behind him again.

This time the man was watching the speaker, which allowed Donovan to ogle him further. That smooth dark skin was positively lickable. Donovan had always found the people from Southeast Asia attractive, perhaps because he'd grown up among them. Unfortunately, here in the jungle, the bloom of youth tended to fade quickly with the harsh environment and hard work of farming. Some even developed frown lines and a bad temper. But this fellow still had that bloom, and though he appeared to be angry, it was the anger of a man fighting for his rights, a hopeful determination. That was something Donovan could identify with.

Fire showed in those amber eyes, and it forced Donovan to listen to what was being said at the podium even as he continued to watch the young man. "If we do not do this today, if we vote the easy way and let the corporations carve out yet another little slice of our country's original preserved forest, then we are as a nation asking to die. This is our national treasure, this forest. We cannot merely give our treasure away. Once we do that, we will never be able to get it back."

Donovan's heart stirred. It wasn't the speech, although he agreed with everything the Forestry head was saying. It was the rapture in the young man's eyes as he viewed the speaker, the passion that matched his own. *I need to find out who he is.* Maybe he was a student at the local university, perhaps studying something like biology. Regardless, Donovan wanted to know more about him.

Just as he toyed with the idea of approaching the young man, Roark nudged him again. Donovan bit back a curse; Roark had nudged his wounded arm, which was hurting worse than ever. He cradled it, giving Roark a glare.

"Are we up next?" Roark asked. He frowned as he seemed to notice Donovan's gesture. Belatedly, Donovan realized some internet fellow had been introduced to discuss a petition that he'd put on the Web. He was describing the international attention it had received. Places like Chicago and Berlin were clamoring about protecting the forest.

Ugh, that meant Donovan needed to review his speech so that he didn't make a complete arse of himself. Sighing, he did so, half listening to the internet fellow. The results of the petition were surprising—ten thousand had signed already. Maybe they had a chance to stop this horrendous legislation after all. It wouldn't stop the poachers, but the animals could use a victory.

Applause followed the man's speech, and then Roark and Donovan stood to make their way to the podium. Donovan swore he could feel the young man's eyes on him as he walked, but couldn't verify that without falling over something. When he reached the podium, Donovan risked a second to look back toward the young man he'd been studying. Sure enough, Mr. Amber Eyes was watching him with an intensity that made him shiver. Clearing his throat, Donovan set his speech in front of him. The room seemed too hot, the rustling and murmuring too loud. He hated public speaking. The sooner this was over, the better.

He introduced himself and Roark, their research facility, and mentioned the key staff members. From there, he launched into a summary of the center's recent activities, including illegal clearings and plantings discovered, and estimated populations of the park's most endangered animals.

He'd debated whether to mention Kitty, since her case was more about poaching than illegal forest clearance, but found himself making a brief remark. "The danger to these dying species is real. Only yesterday my team rescued a live tiger caught in a poacher's snare. It's bad enough that poachers are illegally trapping and killing these animals, but if we don't protect their home, these animals really are doomed. A female tiger needs twenty kilometers of territory, and a male needs three times that size. What if this vote takes away this tiger's piece of the forest? What will happen to her then?"

Donovan paused, his gaze flicking to Mr. Amber Eyes. Had he imagined it, or had the young man just flinched? He continued. "The tiger is an ancient symbol that represents strength and power to the Indonesian people, but they're in deep trouble. We can't let these magnificent creatures disappear in our lifetime. Each time we cut into their forests, we bring them closer to extinction." He took a deep breath. "Don't let that happen."

Applause met his words, and that was good, because he was shaking all over and felt faint and overheated. All he wanted to do was get back to the conservation center and check his stupid wound again. Take some more drugs and a nap.

First, however, he had to wait for his partner. Roark spoke next—his speech gave further details about the impact to the environment from the commercial farming, particularly the impact on the soil quality and erosion. He also detailed the impact of deforestation on other species and how that could hurt the province. When he was finished, there was a spattering of applause from other ecologists. Donovan thanked the council for hearing their testimony.

That done, he staggered away from the podium and was grateful when Roark took him by the elbow to help steer him back to his seat. He sat down at once, and the noise just seemed to get louder and louder—the scraping chairs, the rustling papers, hell even the people next to him breathing. Plus everyone seemed to reek of sweat or cologne. What the hell was wrong with him?

Roark looked at him in concern. "Great speech. Are you okay?"

Donovan wiped a bead of sweat from his brow. "Hanging in there. I think the infection's set in. Bloody cocktail I took should have prevented it." Someone else was speaking on behalf of the forest, but he couldn't concentrate on the words. "I suppose it would be bad form to duck out of here early?"

"Probably." Roark shrugged. "When they break for lunch, we can leave. Just try to rest in the meantime."

Donovan nodded. Perhaps before they left, he could speak with that young man who seemed so familiar, and try to find out if they'd met before. It seemed daft. For all he knew, the fellow was simply a fan of the research center, or maybe had heard of Donovan.

But somehow, the connection felt much deeper than that.

CHAPTER FIVE

Aceh Province Council Chamber, Blangkejeren, Sumatra
May 15, 2013

Listening to Dr. Donovan McGinnis was both inspiring and surprising.

It had been Bitari's idea to go to the council hearing, both because there was land included in the dispute only a couple kilometers from their village and because she'd suspected the head of the Ketambe Conservation and Research Center would be there—Dr. McGinnis, who had penned up Gemi. Kersen hadn't been sure if the man would come, but it made sense, given his work. Small wonder that the man headed the center: He spoke like a leader. Like a man who had lived in Sumatra for all of his life.

Kersen wanted to be angry at this doctor with white skin and a faintly British accent who had admitted to taking his sister. He wanted to find out if Gemi was all right, if she'd bitten or bled on anyone, and if they were going to release her soon. But when Donovan looked at him, all thoughts flew out Kersen's head. Those blue eyes—they held fire and passion.

That power sang to him.

It didn't hurt that the man already possessed a dominant nature; that was clear through how he moved, how he spoke, even how he appeared. Rugged and muscular with a scruffy beard and cropped hair, Donovan had looked more in his element in the jungle than he did in this cramped, stuffy council chamber, and yet he still commanded the room when he spoke.

When Donovan staggered away from the podium, Kersen noticed the bandage peeking out from the cuff of his blazer. *Oh shit. Please let that not be what I think it is.* He sniffed at the air, hoping for a clue, but there were too many people here. Because of the warm temperature, it was also difficult to tell if the flush on Donovan's face was from external or internal heat. In any case, Kersen feared he knew the reason for the bandage.

What if he's caught it? What do we do then? Mentauri and the clan elders would go crazy.

No use in worrying about it yet. They had work to do before tackling Donovan and retrieving Gemi. His aunt hated coming into town, so Bitari was contemplating making a speech on behalf of the villagers who lived on the edge of Gunung Leuser. Kersen didn't think it would do a fat wad of good. Humans were usually only about one thing: money. They weren't like the tigers who roamed free and wild, or the shifters, who wanted a balance. Let it not be said by the other clans in other countries, however, that his clan wasn't trying to save their homeland.

Kersen fidgeted as other speakers came forward. Donovan was slumped in his seat, almost asleep. He didn't appear to be feeling well, and Kersen couldn't blame him. The room was too cramped, and he'd just as soon be out of here to shift back to his animal form. *Or he could be showing symptoms of changing already. Gods, I hope not.*

By four it was apparent that there were too many speakers to fit in for the day. The council moved to allow more public feedback the following day. Bitari would have to come here tomorrow if she wanted to speak. The council ended the session for the day, and Kersen thanked the gods that he would finally get a chance to speak with the conservationist.

He blushed in surprise when Donovan rose and turned around, his eyes immediately seeking Kersen out. There was no denying the energy between them, the attraction. Did the British fellow prefer men? *If he does, how do I resist? He's a foreigner. He's not worth me risking my home and clan.* In any case, today their fates were merged because of his sister. Kersen smiled and walked over.

Donovan smiled back tentatively. He was still flushed, and he'd removed his blazer, the collar of his shirt damp with sweat. When he held out a hand, it was impossible to miss the plaster covering much of his forearm. "Have we met? I'm sorry. You look familiar somehow."

Kersen shook his head nervously. Maybe Donovan had been manning the security cameras at his conservation center and had seen Kersen trying to break in. But if that was the case, Donovan probably wouldn't appear so friendly. "I'm Kersen. I don't think we've met. I know about you and your center, though."

The handshake was firm, and afterward, Donovan held on, as if he didn't want to let go. A tingle crept up the back of Kersen's neck, and his heart began to beat faster. That urge to brush up against Donovan returned, even stronger than before. *Why is this happening to me?* He'd never felt like this, not around anyone, though admittedly, he hadn't had much contact with people outside his family and village. While there were a couple of other gay weretigers in the clan, they were old, in their sixties.

"Nice to meet you. I'm Dr. Donovan McGinnis—Do you live near Gunung Leuser?" Donovan leaned closer, and Kersen detected a faint scent of tiger. A cold fear blossomed in his belly, and he sensed why he was feeling so attracted to the man. Never mind that he'd liked the smell of Donovan before, in tiger form. This was different.

Unable to help himself, Kersen turned over Donovan's arm, inspecting the large plaster. "Um, yes. What happened here?" He tried to make a joke of it. "One of your pets bite you?"

Donovan blinked as if seeing the bandage for the first time. "Oh. That? Animal I was rescuing scratched and bit me. It happens." He pulled his arm away and looked at Kersen again, but his eyes seemed unfocused and drowsy as he breathed in deeply. Heat flared along Kersen's nerves—it was like Donovan was taking in his scent, a greeting among tigers. With alarm, Kersen realized he'd grown hard. Donovan blinked. "You really seem familiar. What village did you say you were from?"

"Kutekane," Kersen replied. It wasn't actually his village, but his people never gave outsiders the correct name. Better that the outside world didn't know about them at all.

"Oh yes." Donovan paused, licking his lips.

The pause was dangerous; Kersen let his gaze trail down Donovan's broad chest, where his shirt stretched across the muscled frame.

Then Donovan's earlier answer caught up with Kersen. Scratched and bitten. *Gemi.* With a growing sense of dread, Kersen added up the signs: the lethargy in Donovan's movements, his changing scent, that sizzling connection between them. *He is becoming one of us. What do I do? Do I tell the others?*

The urge to touch him was still too strong to resist. Kersen laid a hand on Donovan's arm and felt the heat of a fever even through the fabric of Donovan's clothes. This was bad. This was very bad. "Are you feeling all right?"

Donovan blinked slowly, and Kersen couldn't help it; though he was concerned, he imagined how Donovan might look that way first thing in the morning after some amazing sex, heavy lidded and groggy. The sexual tension between them seemed intense—did Donovan feel it too?

"I'm—" Donovan paused, shaking his head. "I'm feeling a little off at the moment. I think my scratches are infected, but I did take some medicine earlier." He patted Kersen's hand. "Don't worry. I'll be fine. I'm heading back now." His gaze traveled over Kersen. "Did you attend to give a public statement about the forest?"

"Oh—not me. My sister, perhaps." Forcing himself to let go, Kersen gathered his courage to ask the important question. "You said you rescued a tiger recently. There's something special about that tiger. I cannot say more here. Would you be willing to meet with me later?"

A smile that looked like a leer lit up Donovan's face. Had Donovan heard anything beyond *meet with me*?

"I'd love to. Lunch tomorrow?" Donovan stepped aside to let people pass them. His companion, the same fellow who'd shouted at Kersen yesterday, approached, his attention focused on something on his phone.

His friend could stop me before then. "Are you available tonight?" Maybe Kersen could get Donovan to understand that something was happening to him, that he needed to let Gemi go and come into the rainforest himself. Then, at the very least, Kersen would be able to get an idea about how quickly the changes were spreading through his body. Great Vishnu, what would happen if Donovan shifted at the conservation center, or in a place like this?

Donovan frowned, rubbing his forehead. "Not sure I'm feeling up to doing anything tonight."

Kersen fought the urge to grind his teeth or pace as he would in his tiger form. "It's important. And it's urgent."

For a moment, Donovan studied him, and Kersen wondered what he was thinking. Then Donovan nodded. "All right. Come to the center after it closes at eight. Roark can let you in."

Roark jerked upon hearing his name, and his eyes widened in recognition. "Aren't you—"

"I need to go," Donovan said, lurching forward, one hand still clutching his head. "Roark—please? I need to lie down for a while." He began walking toward the exit.

Roark glowered at Kersen, but Kersen kept a straight face, determined not to give himself away. Didn't the foreigners always think his people looked alike? Perhaps he could bluff his way through this.

With a growl, Roark turned away from Kersen and followed Donovan. "Sure. Let's get you some stronger meds, and I'll check that arm again. Whatever else is going on can wait."

Not if I have anything to say about it. If Kersen had to break in to check on his sister and Donovan, then he'd do it.

A shift in the air told him without turning that his sister was standing behind him. Kersen fought the urge to stiffen, and instead turned around slowly.

"Did you find out what they're doing with her?" Bitari spoke in a low voice, watching everyone clear the council chamber. With her larger girth she was an imposing woman, and others gave them wide berth.

Kersen shook his head, ignoring her glare. "Not yet. But Bitari . . . we have an even bigger problem. That man—Dr. Donovan? I think Gemi bit him. We may have a new tiger to introduce. And he's dominant."

Bitari threw her hands up, then motioned for Kersen to follow. The council chamber was empty now, leaving only a couple security officers to ensure that everyone left. As soon as they were clear of the building, she slapped Kersen in the back of the head. "Idiot! I knew this would happen! You should have been with her. You could have freed her before the men came."

Hadn't she yelled at him enough last night? Kersen bared his teeth at her. He didn't care if it wasn't as impressive in human form. She'd get the message. "Gemi's seventeen! When will she be old enough to be on her own? And I wasn't that far away, but the humans reached her first. What was I supposed to do? Kill them?"

Bitari rubbed her forehead. "No! But you shouldn't have let her roam so deep." She stalked off toward her truck, and Kersen had to hurry or risk being left behind.

He pulled on his seat belt as she started the engine. "I know," he said, as she put the gear in drive. The old rusted hulk of the truck lurched, the engine backfiring once before settling into a rhythm. They were poor, as far as human things went; after all, tigers had no need of trucks. Neither would weretigers, if the humans would just leave their land alone. "I told you I'm sorry that I wasn't there. I've scheduled a meeting tonight with Dr. Donovan. I'll find out if he's really infected, and what's happening with Gemi." His stomach churned with nausea. She must have been scared to lash out at someone like that. What if they'd amputated her foot? What would Gemi do then?

Bitari must have seen the misery on his face, because her tone softened. "You do that. If he really is one of us, bring him to the house. Explain the situation to him. I can't imagine he'd want to keep Gemi if he understood the risks." She tapped at the steering wheel erratically. "And if he's not infected or you can't tell, convince him to let her go. These conservationists—they always want to return the animal to the wild, yes?"

Kersen nodded. "It's what they say." Though they probably wouldn't release an injured animal. If he couldn't convince Donovan, perhaps he could at least find out where they were holding Gemi and try once more to break in. "I'll get her out, Bitari. I promise." He didn't make such promises lightly. If he had to risk jail, he'd do it. He couldn't stand the thought of Gemi pacing in some animal cage.

Bitari's face crumpled. Kersen reached over, squeezing her hand on the steering wheel. "It's going to be all right," he said, though he had no way of knowing that for sure. She nodded, but still seemed afraid; for once Big Bitari wasn't so tough. Time for him to step up and take care of things.

He only hoped Donovan McGinnis would let him inside.

CHAPTER SIX

Ketambe Conservation and Research Center, Ketambe, Sumatra
May 15, 2013

Donovan dimly remembered the drive back to the conservation center; apparently Roark had to yell to rouse him, and half support his arse inside. He sat in a chair in the office while Roark tore the plaster off his arm and poured rubbing alcohol on it. That hurt like hell, and he screamed. Evan and Amin had to hold him down.

Then Roark shot him up with some antibiotics, and the three of them helped Donovan to his bed. He passed out for a while, and when he came to, he was hungry.

Ravenous, actually.

He was still wearing the trousers from earlier, which were wrinkled, so Donovan changed into some workout pants and a T-shirt, hot and itchy all over. It was as if his skin didn't fit somehow. Roark and Evan were talking in the front office, but he didn't want to disturb them, so he took the back way to the kitchen and hunted for food—he craved protein of some kind. Meat. He found leftover chicken and wolfed that down, but it didn't begin to satisfy the emptiness inside.

There was something he needed to do, that he'd been asked about. What was it?

The tigress. Something important about the tigress. I'd better go check on her.

Keeping out of sight, Donovan headed to the animal wing of the center. He passed by the monkey and tropical bird cages, but paused when he heard the monkeys screaming and banging madly at the fence, and the birds flying and calling out in distress. What the hell was the matter with them? He rubbed his arm. The pain was gone now, so whatever Roark had shot him up with must've done the job. He continued on.

When he reached the tigress's enclosure, she was pacing back and forth, eyeing him murderously. Fascinated, Donovan watched how she moved with strength and grace in each step. A charge went through him, like the air before a thunderstorm. She was beautiful, powerful. He could smell her earthy musk.

Bloody hell. I don't even go for human females. What is wrong with me?

The tigress—he suddenly remembered what he was supposed to do tonight. He was supposed to meet with that local man, Kersen, who had said there was something special about this tiger.

God, I'm hungry. He could really go for a steak right now.

The tigress had eaten her chickens, so she must have been hungry as well. Her yellow eyes drew him closer, tracking him as she loped back and forth. She seemed to be doing just fine on her injured paw. Donovan walked up to the railing and touched the double fence. Some dim part of his brain screamed at him that this wasn't safe, but he ignored it. *Kersen's right. There's something special about this tiger. She doesn't belong in a cage.*

Donovan staggered, dizziness sweeping through him. There was something in his head, like music—like a radio station that was coming from far away, fading in and out. He needed to free the tigress. Then he needed to get her to the forest.

Blinking, Donovan tried to clear his vision. The tiger had stopped pacing, was standing right in front of him. They locked eyes. He saw the image of a young woman in his head, long black hair and an oval face. Donovan blinked again. The image left. *Shit!* He jumped back from the wire fence where he'd been standing face-to-face with a two-hundred-pound tigress. Even with the fence, she might have swatted him and caught him with a claw. What the hell had he been doing so close to her?

The perimeter alarm rang out, startling and nearly deafening him. The tiger's ears flattened to her skull, and she snarled, backing away from the fence. Donovan clapped his hands to his ears. Was it always this loud? His senses seemed off-kilter today, like they were four times as sensitive. He looked at the tigress in apology. "I'd better go find out what's going on."

Staggering, he headed toward the front office where the controls to turn off the alarm were located. Other staff seemed to be headed there as well, including Evan and Helena. As he passed by the surgical rooms, Donovan heard sounds of a scuffle and voices arguing.

"Told you he's expecting me! Let me go!" *That's Kersen's voice.* Donovan was almost sure of it.

"I finally realized who you are—you're the trespasser! You're after that tiger, aren't you! Get out or I'm calling the police," Roark yelled as Donovan continued down the hall, his heart thudding like he'd been running for the past hour. Sweat broke out on his forehead, and he itched all over. It felt as if something inside was trying to come up from the depths of him and break free. He staggered, his temples pounding.

Then there was a loud bang, like someone being knocked into a wall. Groaning, Donovan shook his head to clear it, and ran the last few meters into the lobby. Helena ran to the controls and shut off the alarm, thankfully. Roark, Evan, and one of their security officers were wrestling with Kersen, who was fighting back like a wild thing, black hair in his eyes. Donovan stepped toward them, meaning to break things up, when a wave of weakness swept through him. He staggered, falling to one knee, and Kersen froze, staring at Donovan in shock. Roark and Evan turned in Donovan's direction as well.

Donovan's teeth ached, and they seemed different somehow, larger. He opened his mouth, touching them gingerly. Light from the setting sun was shining through the front windows and seemed unnaturally bright somehow. Wincing, he raised a hand to shield his eyes, and barely saw Roark letting go of Kersen, his eyes wide with concern. "Mate . . . are you all right?"

Breathing easier, his strength slowly returning, Donovan stood up and blinked a few times as his eyes adjusted. "I'm fine," he said, but his voice came out lower than normal, almost a growl. The itch intensified, and he pulled at the bandage on his arm. It was too constrictive.

Kersen looked panicked. "Dr. McGinnis, you need to come with me now. Hurry!" He dove past Roark, darting for the front door. Shoving it open, he ran outside, and Roark gave a cry and gave chase.

Things were happening too fast. Had Kersen really been the poacher trying to break in? Donovan's head was spinning again.

I need to find out why he wanted to talk. None of this makes sense! Donovan sprinted forward, caught the door just before it closed, and hurtled himself forward. *Must run.* It wasn't just the answers he was seeking; something inside was demanding action, demanding the chase. Outside, the scents of the jungle assailed him—the earth and the vegetation and the overlaying stench of civilization from humans trying to carve out their existence. Kersen had already reached the compound gate and was climbing up and over it. Roark was shouting something, his face red, his belly bouncing as he tried to keep up, but it was clear he was struggling.

"I'll get him," Donovan said, but it was almost like it wasn't him talking. Something was calling to him, and he couldn't have stopped if he wanted to. He ran past Roark, past the guard chasing Kersen, and though the other guard was hurrying to open the gate, Donovan didn't slow down. He climbed up and over just as the young man had, amazed at his own speed, despite the fact that his jaw ached, sending pain through his skull. His clothes were stretching, threatening to tear.

What's happening to me?

He landed in the brush on the other side. Kersen was running across open fields toward the jungle, pulling off his shirt as he went and exposing a beautiful tribal pattern across his shoulders and upper back. He was also barefoot.

Cripes he's fast! Where was Kersen going? This was insane; Donovan should stop and return to the conservation center and talk to Roark.

Some new scent drifted to him on the wind, one that seemed familiar, though he couldn't remember actually ever smelling it before. Donovan slowed, sniffing. Ahead of him, Kersen slowed to a jog, glancing over his shoulder back at Donovan.

That was an invitation, if Donovan had ever seen one. He ran a little faster, but then something sharp cut into his lip. *My teeth— they've grown.*

Donovan stopped, bending over and breathing hard. The two of them were in a cassava field now, away from the main road and buildings. The jungle was a few kilometers to the west where the red glow of sunset was fading to purple. He glanced back the way they had come. *What the hell am I doing out here? I should go back. I need to lie down.* But then a blinding pain went through him and he fell to his knees in the soft earth.

Kersen's voice drifted to him. "Come, Dr. Donovan! You need to reach the jungle!"

Donovan staggered to his feet, still fighting against something, some urge inside his body. The closest thing he could compare it to was an impending orgasm. His head pounded, and he was ready to explode.

Kersen ran up and grabbed his hand, pulling hard on it. "It's not much farther. You can make it. You must do this."

Up close, Kersen's smooth skin and lickable smooth chest tantalized him. Donovan stared into his eyes, lurching forward as Kersen coaxed him along. He wanted to speak, wanted to ask what the hell was going on. But he didn't seem to be able to make his mouth work right.

Kersen smiled encouragingly, as they began to jog again, still holding hands. "That's it. Faster. We need to get under the trees. Otherwise they will see us and may shoot at us."

"Wha'?" Even getting that single word was an effort. Running was becoming more difficult too; the pain flared up Donovan's spine and down his legs. It felt like he was fifteen again, muscles cramping and aching during his largest growth spurt. The trees were closer. But he wasn't going to reach them before whatever was happening took over.

"The tigress." Despite their increasing speed, Kersen seemed barely winded. *What on earth does he do for a living?* "I told you she was special. You're about to become like her and like me. You may not remember much, your first time."

Special? Become like her? This was crazy. What was Kersen saying—that she had a disease or something? Perhaps that was why the bite had ached so much. Donovan skidded to a halt. If he was sick, he needed to get back to Roark. A fresh wave of pain struck him, making him fall to his hands and knees.

God, what's happening? He tasted blood, his tongue brushing against frighteningly enlarged canines. He screamed as pain in his tailbone engulfed him; it seemed to stretch *outward*. Hands grabbed at him—Kersen's hands, tearing at his shirt, pulling his sweats down. *Help me, please!* A series of cracks echoed in his skull.

He blacked out.

"Cripes, you're doing this now? Out here?" Kersen spoke loudly, though he knew that Donovan couldn't hear him, wouldn't comprehend even if he did. Donovan was still rolling from side to side in the field, fur sprouting out all over. Kersen barely managed to snatch off the man's shoes before his feet were replaced by paws. He wasn't able to save the man's underwear; it tore as the human pelvis grew into a much larger feline structure. In seconds it was over. Instead of a veterinarian, he had an adult male Sumatran tiger before him.

We'll tear it all. The only thing he could do now was lure Donovan into the jungle and stay near him until he shifted back. That could take hours. *And I still don't know if Gemi is okay.*

"I can't believe you went and got yourself bitten by my sister," Kersen told Donovan, who was struggling to stand up, clearly groggy and disorientated. Groaning, Kersen pulled off his trousers and shoes. He'd have to leave everything here in the field, another inconvenience.

There was scarcely time to stash their things under one of the plants before Donovan regained his feet. A low growl made the hairs on the back of Kersen's neck stand up. *Brilliant. A dominant male. If I shift, he'll probably fight me.* No other choice, however. If he stayed human, Donovan was likely to kill him.

Kersen bent over and let the change take him, his vision wavering as it shifted from human to animal. Shifting was as easy as breathing now—well almost. It was still painful, but he'd learned to do it quickly. When he finished, Donovan had taken a step back, likely startled by Kersen's transformation. When it was complete, Kersen saw that he was the smaller tiger, but not by too much. He huffed a low greeting, hoping Donovan would understand.

Donovan snarled at him. He crouched low on his forepaws, hackles raised, and bared his teeth. Kersen couldn't stop his heart racing. Donovan was going to fight, as male tigers did, for territory.

I can't let that happen. Kersen turned tail and ran for the forest.

CHAPTER SEVEN

Gunung Leuser National Forest, Sumatra
May 15, 2013

K ersen thanked the gods that he knew the forest like his own
backyard.

He ran as fast as he could, leaping over fallen trees and mud
pits, scrambling through the dense foliage where tall trees had been
cleared. Behind him the other tiger crashed through the brush, close
on his heels. Good thing Donovan was still ungainly in his new form.
Kersen hoped that the man would retain some of his wits, but that
wasn't likely during his first shift. For the moment, Kersen had an
angry animal to deal with.

They couldn't run forever. He needed a place to turn and fight.

At least he'd managed to lure Donovan away from humans and
civilization. It would be nice if he could get Donovan all the way to
his village and have help from the other weretigers. But they'd never
make it.

So instead, Kersen ran deeper into the jungle, praying that
he didn't come across any poachers or snares. Night sounds cut
off sharply as the smaller animals heard the approach of two large
predators. While he could see fairly well in the dark, he couldn't see
long distances, especially in the thick underbrush. Was there a clearing
nearby? *Please let there be.*

Donovan tore through the trees, growling as he grew closer. At
any second he might leap for Kersen's throat. Kersen screeched to a
halt. *I'll make my stand here.*

Whirling, Kersen snarled, watching for the attack. He had one advantage: the fact he could think both like a tiger and like a human. *And you're so handsome too. It'd be a shame for me to have to kill you.*

Donovan leaped for him, jaws agape.

Kersen rolled on his back, kicking his legs out as the larger tiger landed on him. *Can't let him bite my neck.* If this was a territorial skirmish, then all he had to do was wound Donovan enough to convince him that this was his land.

Snarling, Donovan snapped at Kersen's shoulder. Kersen clawed at Donovan's white-furred belly and managed to flip him over to one side. He scrambled to his feet to take advantage, but Donovan was just as fast. *Listen to me! You're a man, not a tiger!* Kersen sent the strongest message he could, hoping that Donovan could hear his thoughts even if he wasn't a clan brother, and could comprehend the words.

Ears flat against his skull and shoulders hunched, Donovan bared his teeth. He circled Kersen, tail lashing from side to side, but did not pounce. That was hopeful.

I am not your rival. We could be brothers. Of course, Kersen wanted to do things to Donovan that were not brotherly at all. Still it was better for the tiger to regard him as a sibling than a threat.

Donovan swiped at him, teeth bared and claws extended. Kersen flinched back and felt the brush of air as the large paw narrowly missed him. Despite Donovan's attack, however, Kersen was encouraged. Donovan hadn't tried to pounce on him again. If nothing else, it seemed Kersen was keeping him off-balance with his mind-speaking; a dominant tiger should have been trying to pin him down and hurt him. *It's strange, I know. I'm here to help you. Trust me.*

Taking a step back, Donovan shook his head like there was a bug in his ear. Hope surged through Kersen. So Donovan could hear him, even if he couldn't make sense of the words in his animal state. Kersen might live through this yet. *That's it. I'm a friend,* Kersen sent to him in the most calm, most reassuring tone he could imagine.

He wished he could rub his face against Donovan's shoulder. That would show Donovan that he was friendly. But he dared not move, lest Donovan see it as a sign of weakness, or worse, an attack. All he could do was hold still, his heart pounding in his chest, waiting.

Donovan huffed and leaned forward, sniffing. Kersen continued to hold still, which grated against his tiger instincts. Holding still was weak—perhaps. It was also one of the bravest things he'd ever done.

Growling softly, Donovan circled Kersen as if daring him to fight or flee. The space between Kersen's shoulder blades itched; his ears tracked Donovan's movements behind him until Donovan was in sight again. Truly, he made an exquisite beast with his massive jaws and large canines. Donovan snorted, and then batted a paw at Kersen, dropping his front half in a crouch, his tail swishing.

You want to play! Happiness replaced fear. Kersen straightened and stepped forward, ears perking.

Donovan pounced on him.

For a second, Kersen felt the brush of teeth at his throat, but then they were rolling in the underbrush, Donovan's paws wrapped around Kersen in a wrestle hold. The bite had merely been a gesture, and now Donovan began licking at Kersen's jaw, soothing the sting. Kersen yowled, swiping back at Donovan, but gently. His weak protest was ignored.

He likes me. Thank you, Brahma, and any other gods listening.

Kersen relaxed as Donovan continued to groom him, moving from his jaw to his ear, and then to his face. Would the man be horrified if he remembered this later? Kersen hoped not. For now though, he was simply glad the tiger hadn't decided to kill him as a potential rival. The grooming felt rather nice, actually.

Then Donovan's stomach growled.

Donovan pulled back, shaking himself all over. It seemed grooming time was over. Now the question would be whether he knew how to hunt, or if Kersen would have to show him.

Slowly, Kersen took a few steps, lowering his head to sniff out the forest floor, to see what kinds of creatures had been by recently. Monkeys. Some wild pigs. Even deer, but that scent was old. Maybe they could track down a pig for the two of them. *I'm hungry too.*

Donovan circled the clearing, head turning one way and then the other, so Kersen brushed against him to get his attention. He'd only hunted with the aid of mental communication with fellow shifters, and he wasn't sure he'd be able to coordinate with the other tiger. Still, he had to try. Donovan was hungry thanks to his changed physiology, and Bitari might not be home yet. It was Kersen's job to keep an eye on Donovan until he shifted back, probably after he fell asleep.

Then he'd see where things went from that point.

With a soft growl, Kersen brushed Donovan with his tail, and then began following the pig scent. Donovan's ears perked. *Good,* Kersen sent to him. *Now follow me.*

He led Donovan deeper into the jungle.

May 16, 2013

Donovan woke to something wet dripping onto his face, something hard digging into his back, and something warm in his arms.

He was lying naked on the jungle floor; above him, a cluster of orchids attached to a tree trunk were dripping water onto him. A root was the thing digging into his back. And in his arms was the local man from the council hearing. *Kersen.* He, too, was naked, and asleep, his head resting on Donovan's arm, his legs entangled with Donovan's. His soft cock was pressing against Donovan's thigh.

"What the—" Donovan jerked away from the young man, panic seizing him. Kersen opened his eyes, glanced down, and scooted back hastily. With the dark skin, Donovan couldn't be sure, but he thought the fellow might be blushing.

Remembering his own nudity, Donovan grabbed a palm frond to cover himself. "Where the hell am I?"

Kersen rose slowly, both hands upraised as if to steady Donovan. "You're deep in the Gunung Leuser National Forest. Do you remember how you felt yesterday? Do you remember anything?"

The young man didn't seem concerned by his own lack of clothing. Donovan scanned the area, but he didn't see his clothes anywhere. Instead, he noticed a dead and gutted wild pig, not far from the two of them. He looked down at himself to find that his hands and chest were bloody. Heart pounding, he touched his face, only to find more blood caked and dried there. What the hell had happened? Had he killed the pig?

"I wasn't feeling well at the hearing." Donovan remembered that at least, and remembered meeting Kersen and his sister. Kersen had talked about the tiger they'd rescued. That there was something special about her. "I was supposed to meet with you to discuss the tiger we saved. Things started to go fuzzy—I took a nap." He'd been dreaming again. Dreaming of being a tiger. He glanced at the carcass. "I think I'm going insane."

Kersen reached out toward him, but Donovan avoided contact. *This doesn't add up. That pig was definitely killed by a tiger. Or two tigers.*

He glanced back, trying to find some sign of deception in the other man, but there was only sincerity in Kersen's gaze as he spoke. "You're not going crazy. Do you remember what you did when you woke from your nap? You heard your friend and me arguing?"

Donovan tried to think back, but it was muddled. He recalled standing in front of the tiger in the enclosure, like they were communicating somehow. Then running and witnessing Roark slamming Kersen against a wall. More running. "It's hazy. I do remember you and Roark having it out."

He wished Kersen would put on clothing, cover himself. This was a crazy conversation to have while bare-arsed. Kersen sounded so rational, but he, too, had flecks of blood on his chest. It wasn't right that it looked sexy. "I chased you. Didn't I?" He couldn't even remember why he'd done that.

Kersen smiled. "That's right. I ran off on purpose, so that you'd follow. You were starting to shift, becoming a tiger. That would have been dangerous for your friends."

Complete insanity. "Impossible. You drugged me." It was the only logical explanation. He rubbed his head. "A man can't simply turn into a tiger. There's the huge difference in mass, just for starters. It's not scientifically feasible."

"This isn't about science, and I didn't drug you. How could I? You felt ill after the tiger hurt you. Right?" Kersen's eyes were earnest, concerned.

Sputtering, Donovan began to pace. "Yes—the wound was infected. I had a fever." That would explain the dreams. *Racing through the jungle, hunting a deer. And his teeth sinking in . . .*

He remembered his teeth aching like the dickens. Remembered them *growing*.

"Do you remember pain? Like all of your bones were breaking, and then resetting? What about fur—did you notice that on your arms? How do you explain that?" Kersen followed him relentlessly, still calm, still so certain of himself. If he'd drugged Donovan, why would they both be naked? It couldn't be a kidnapping; Kersen didn't have a weapon, and he seemed just as vulnerable as Donovan in this remote location. That didn't add up.

Sitting down lest he faint, Donovan nodded. He *had* been feeling strange the whole day, not just after meeting Kersen. The teeth. God, he remembered his teeth cutting into his lips and the agony of growing a tail. "I don't believe in magic." This was madness! And yet here he was in the middle of the jungle, with a dead pig and a naked man.

Kersen shook his head, a little smile on his face. *He seems so young and innocent. Too young to pull off a prank like this.* It would have taken a great deal of planning, coconspirators, resources far beyond what most locals possessed. "You don't have to believe in magic for it to work, Doctor. My people have been shape-shifters for hundreds of years." Taking a deep breath, he let it out slowly. "It was your misfortune that you crossed paths with my sister as you did, that this happened to you. I came too late to free her—you saw me when you were about to tranquilize her."

Donovan's brows drew together. *Shape-shifters?* "Wait. You're telling me that you—" Those amber eyes, staring at him through the foliage. That sense of familiarity when he'd first met Kersen. "The tigress I rescued. There was a male tiger nearby." *It's not possible. There's no way that it's possible.*

Yet Kersen smiled as if he knew exactly what Donovan was thinking. "Yes. That was me. The tiger you rescued from the poacher's snare is my sister. Her name is Gemi."

Kitty was Gemi? "Your sister?" Dizziness wracked him again. "How is that possible? She's a tiger. She's been a tiger the whole time. We have cameras monitoring her." Roark would surely have mentioned a tigress turning into a woman.

Kersen groaned. "Yes! Because you have her trapped in a cage. We don't reveal our secret to strangers. Especially foreigners like you." He wiped his face with his hands. "We're not like your myths of werewolves—the moon has no effect on us, and we can change at will. Our ancestors discovered the secret of transforming from man to beast centuries ago. Legends say that there was a group of shamans who performed rituals, asking the gods for the power to transform into beasts. The gods granted them their wish. Our ability is passed down each generation through our blood, but we have to be careful. What's in our blood can be transferred to other people. That's how we've been able to survive, marrying normal humans and making them like us."

Passed through blood . . . the scratch. Donovan remembered the tiger swiping him with her injured paw, blood on her muzzle as she mouthed his wounded arm. "It's like a virus?" Reality was splintering around him like shards of glass from a broken window pane. He shuddered—those dreams of being a tiger, of running down prey. *It's too coincidental.* Turning around, Donovan checked the area more thoroughly. No roads. No trails. And he easily outweighed Kersen by several stone. The fellow couldn't have dragged him here, not without leaving some signs like broken foliage and drag marks. There was nothing like that.

Things were starting to add up. But he didn't like the answer that was forming.

He turned back, and Kersen shrugged. "It's a little more complicated than that. But yes, it behaves like a virus. We have a ritual for new members when the clan agrees to let them join. The husband and wife cut their palms and press them together. Then they each kiss and taste each other's blood, sealing the bond and sharing the gift of shifting. From there, it doesn't take long for adults before their first transformation. Their children, however, don't acquire the gift until puberty."

Donovan was finding it hard to breathe past the panic. He needed to get back to the research center. Either he needed to warn the police that he'd been kidnapped by a madman . . . or he needed to make sure the tiger they were holding didn't infect anyone else. "Why can't I remember?"

"Because your brain cannot handle the transition." Kersen stepped closer, laying his hand on Donovan's arm. This time Donovan allowed it. He sounded so honest, so reassuring. Donovan stared into his face. This couldn't be. Yet he couldn't detect any hint of deception from Kersen. Whatever the truth was, this man truly believed he could shift form.

Kersen continued. "It will get better. Next time, your mind will start to accept the reality and won't try to protect itself by erasing the memory. Soon after that, you'll be able to merge your tiger brain with your human brain. You'll be able to think like a man while you are a tiger." He smiled encouragingly. "It's pretty awesome, really."

"I don't want to be a tiger," Donovan found himself saying, like a whining toddler. He had a doctoral degree in veterinary science. He saved tigers. He didn't *become* them.

Kersen squeezed his arm. It felt good; it felt grounding. Donovan leaned in closer and caught the whiff of Kersen's scent. He couldn't be wearing cologne—they'd both been sweating out in the jungle. And yet he smelled wonderful. Donovan's groin tightened despite the panic going through him. More confusing was an incredible urge to push Kersen to the ground, to see fear and respect in his eyes. To *claim* him.

I'm not like that. I'm not some domineering arsehole. Why am I having such cravings?

He didn't even know what time it was. The hearing should be continuing today. Was he missing it? "I need to get back. Roark is probably pissing himself, worrying about me. Plus I'm supposed to be at the hearing." Not that he was scheduled to speak. And not that Roark couldn't handle things on his own. Donovan just wanted to know the vote.

Kersen frowned. "That's not a good idea." He glanced over his shoulder. "I must bring you to my village and introduce you to our clan elder." Sighing, he dropped his hand, and Donovan missed the contact immediately. "When you are in control of yourself, when we are sure that you won't accidentally shift and hurt anyone, then you can return to your old life. We know we have an ally in you. Your work is important."

"How long will that be?" Already Roark could have called the police. There could be a manhunt for Kersen and perhaps his older sister as well.

Kersen's amber eyes met his. "I do not know. It is different with each person. And you were not born to it."

Donovan sensed with all his heart that Kersen was being truthful. Though he still couldn't accept that this was even possible, that he'd really become a tiger. Right now he needed to get out of the jungle and back to more familiar settings. At least a village would be a step in the right direction. "What about our clothes?"

Kersen smiled. "Do not worry. I have clothing at my house." He glanced up, possibly to gauge the time, but the dense tree cover above shut out the sky. Closing his eyes, Kersen breathed in deeply, turning in a slow circle. Donovan watched him, mystified. He couldn't help but take in Kersen's body: the lean torso and slender legs, the intricate tattoos, the dark rich skin, which was nearly hairless. All except for the trail down from his belly to his cock, which was nestled in black curls. Donovan flushed, hoping Kersen hadn't noticed him ogling. Fellow had a nice arse too, round and supple. Again, he imagined taking the man down, but this time for an entirely different reason. *Get a grip. This isn't the time to indulge in fantasies.*

Kersen opened his eyes and turned back to Donovan. "Follow me. It's going to be a bit of a walk to get there." He smiled apologetically. "I'd have us shift, but . . . control. For now, we'll have to walk as humans."

Donovan blew out a breath. What choice did he have? "Fine."

It was going to be a long fucking day, between his terrifying situation, and the lure of this sexy stranger.

CHAPTER EIGHT

Unnamed Village, Aceh Province, Sumatra
May 16, 2013

They reached the village as the sun climbed to the midpoint above them. Emerging from the jungle into the rice and sugar fields, Donovan paused to gaze at the tiny village with wonder on his face. Kersen smiled, trying to imagine what the settlement must look like to the foreigner. The longhouses were traditional, made of wood and daubing and raised a few meters above ground against flooding, with dirt paths in between them.

At the edge of the fields, Kersen reached into a wooden box and handed Donovan a sheet to cover himself. His own nudity didn't bother him. Donovan pulled the cotton fabric around himself, giving Kersen an embarrassed smile.

It was a shame to cover that athletic figure. Kersen had ogled him earlier, hopefully without appearing to. Donovan's chest was lightly sprinkled with reddish-gold hair, which Kersen itched to rub his face against. Even more, he wanted to reach under that sheet and explore the impressive organ he'd felt against him in the night. But just because Donovan was a shifter now did not guarantee that the clan would accept him. And if they didn't, then Kersen couldn't risk allowing a mating bond to develop between them. If he did, he'd be ejected from the clan as well, because a mated pair couldn't be torn apart. As valuable as each shifter was to the clan in terms of providing for the village, it wasn't like Kersen mattered that much to the clan's breeding pool. His sisters were worth more in that regard.

Stepping away from Donovan, Kersen motioned to his longhouse. "That one's mine. I do not know if you will fit my father's clothing, but it will be better than mine." The familiar pang hit his chest. "He died about four years ago, along with my mother. My older sister Bitari may be home, or she may be at the hearing." He hoped she was at the council meeting in Blangkejeren, which was a three-hour drive away. Then he'd have Donovan to himself for the rest of the day. But he needed to introduce Donovan to Aunt Mentauri before other clan members caught sight of the stranger in their village. He shuddered to think what her reaction would be.

Donovan nodded, his posture relaxing somewhat. "Lead on. I'm ready to get into some clothes." He glanced at his bloody hands. "And a shower."

It didn't take long to cross the fields and reach the house. Kersen hurried up the ladder to verify that the place was empty. The silence reminded him that Gemi remained captive, still trapped in her animal form. Nodding to Donovan, they headed into the house and to the bathroom.

Kersen allowed the man to wash in private while he dug up some clothing that might fit. He found a loose pair of home-sewn trousers and a white muslin shirt. Donovan would look like a native. Well, except for his skin of course.

Next Kersen pulled on some of his own clothing, choosing an older pair of trousers in case he had to shift again. He wished he could take Donovan back to the conservation center so that they could release Gemi immediately, but they'd covered a lot of ground last night as tigers, so it would be a bit of a drive. And it was risky. Donovan and his friend might fight over what had happened. Donovan might return to his tiger form. And then where would they be? Back in the jungle.

Shortly after Kersen had finished gathering clothes, Donovan emerged from the washroom, appearing more like the posh foreigner Kersen had met at the council hearing. He seemed more confident as well, which could be a bad thing, if he reverted to thinking that this was all a bad dream. Kersen gazed at him sternly. "I'm going to wash. Don't go anywhere." The man was probably hungry for human food. "There should be instant noodles and leftover chicken in the kitchen. Help yourself."

With that, he hurried to wash himself, not neglecting to brush his teeth. He wanted Donovan to feel comfortable around him. To be honest, he wanted to curl up as close to him as he had when they'd been tigers. *Stop that. Bad idea.* Anyways Donovan undoubtedly preferred females, which would be good because the *siluman harimau* could use fresh breeding stock. The main issue with the clan accepting Donovan would be that he wasn't Indonesian, and worse, he was a Brit. His people tended not to trust certain countries. The British in particular had too much history of taking over other countries and exploiting them.

Once he had cleaned off and dressed, Kersen joined Donovan in the small kitchen. The man was nibbling on some chicken at the table, looking awkward in the tiny foldout chair. "I'm not that hungry. But this chicken's amazing."

Kersen laughed. "Bitari made it. She's a very good cook." He grabbed a bite himself, glancing out the window to see anyone about on the dirt road below. There was no one in sight. "It's time to meet my aunt. Are you ready, Doctor?"

"As ready as I'll ever be." Donovan didn't sound enthusiastic, but then if Kersen had been in a similar predicament, he probably wouldn't be either. With a sigh, Kersen nodded, waiting as Donovan pushed back from the table. Together, they headed out the door.

"Are you sure your aunt's home?" Donovan scanned the nearly deserted streets. It seemed strange that no one was in the village today. Had they all gone to see the hearing? Or were they all in the forest right now as tigers? *That's a creepy thought.*

Kersen had already knocked twice on the rickety front door of what looked like an abandoned traditional Indonesian longhouse. This village was unfamiliar—he'd been in and out of most of the villages near the Gunung Leuser National Forest, but he couldn't recall this one. He had a feeling it wasn't on any map.

It was almost like some kind of otherworldly energy hummed under the surface here, beneath the dirt roads, hovering in the humid air. So far the only people he'd spotted were some children playing in a ditch, their feet bare and dirt on their clothing. They seemed normal enough, and yet as he and Kersen passed, all four of them stopped and stared at Donovan as if he were an alien with three heads. Was this village that isolated? And because he was a stranger? Or perhaps that he was white?

Or could they sense that he was, as Kersen said, a tiger?

"Oh Aunt Mentauri's home all right." Kersen folded his arms as he waited. "She may have been out hunting last night, since it didn't rain. After hunting, we usually rest."

Hunting? As in bringing down a wild pig, as they had supposedly done last night? Donovan wanted to ask further, but as he opened his mouth, the door opened. A middle-aged woman answered, her dark eyes immediately scrutinizing him. She had sun-weathered skin, shrewd eyes, and a large mole on her face. By the bright patterns and the sleek fabric of her hijab, blouse, and skirt, Donovan guessed that she had some money to blow on fashion. In contrast to the modern clothing, she wore a necklace that appeared to be made of small bones. Monkey, perhaps? He wasn't sure he wanted to know.

Her lips pressed together in a scowl as she took in Donovan and then Kersen. She said something in Indonesian, too quickly for Donovan to understand.

Kersen translated. "She's asking why I've brought a stranger to our village. I will explain to her—hold on." He went into a long speech. Donovan understood more this time; Kersen said that he was an animal doctor and he worked to protect the jungle. But there were still parts that Donovan couldn't translate. He suspected it was about the changing-from-man-to-beast thing.

When Kersen finished, Mentauri tilted her head at Donovan, piercing him with her gaze. She grabbed his chin so fast that he jumped. A decidedly *nonhuman* growl vibrated at the back of his throat. He blinked hard.

I did that?

How had he done that?

Mentauri's lips curled into a little smile. She turned his face to one side and then the other, as if staring into his head. Under her inspection, Donovan started to feel hot and dizzy again, and he itched like something was crawling under his skin. He wanted to bear his teeth and take a swipe at her. That wasn't normal either, was it?

She cackled, letting go. "Very new, you?" she asked in heavily accented English. Donovan glanced at Kersen, unsure how to respond.

"Yes," Kersen said, again in Indonesian. He and his aunt spoke more, with Kersen growing more agitated, and Mentauri wildly gesturing. Eventually, she rose up and boxed Kersen's ears like he was a little boy. Donovan winced. Then Mentauri threw up her hands and went inside, leaving the door open. Apparently that was their invitation to enter.

"I explained how this happened to you," Kersen said as he led Donovan into a small living room with a futon couch that might or might not double as a bed. Mentauri sat down in a wooden rocking chair, still scowling.

Donovan settled carefully next to Kersen, lost as to how the conversation had ended. "Can she fix this?" From everything Kersen had said so far, it didn't sound like a reversible change.

Kersen shook his head. "You cannot undo what has been done." He sighed, fidgeting, then asked Mentauri a question. Donovan thought he heard the word *woman* in there somewhere.

At Mentauri's lengthy answer, Kersen rubbed his knees, not looking at Donovan. "She says you should be welcome here, if you choose to live with us. First, we would introduce you to the other clan elders, and they would have to vote to allow you to join the clan. You might need to establish your rank among the other dominant tigers. If that goes well, she can also find you a wife." He smiled, but it didn't reach his eyes. "I'm sure all the girls will be excited. As I said earlier, it is rare we have new blood in the clan."

The talk of establishing rank and dominant tigers was disturbing, but the last bit was the worst. Donovan blanched. A wife? How was he supposed to respond to that one? "I . . . No. Tell her I'm not looking for a wife." *God, this day is just getting worse and worse! Am I supposed to simply give up my house and career and live here in this tiny village? What does she mean about rank or dominance—or votes, for that matter?*

Kersen stared at him. "Why not? Don't you want to have children some day?"

Donovan couldn't run, and he couldn't hide. Again, that itchiness came over him, starting with his tailbone and moving all the way up to his arms and chest. In vain he scratched the spot where the tiger—Gemi—had bitten him, then behind his ear. It didn't help. "I don't date women. Period." Would Kersen get the message? Donovan hadn't said he actually slept with men. As long as he didn't go that far, he shouldn't be offending them.

Mentauri folded her arms, asking something. Again, Kersen translated for her. "You are celibate for religious reasons?"

Donovan glanced at Kersen, but the man wasn't looking at him. Was that a blush? Donovan took a deep breath. If she wanted the truth, she'd get it. "No, I'm not celibate." If she couldn't figure that one out, then there was no help for her.

Scooting farther away, Kersen related the message. Donovan sighed inwardly. He should have expected that, right? Still, it niggled at him. Mentauri laughed, however, and he gawked at her in confusion.

"*Maka kau boleh kawin dengannya,*" Mentauri said, pointing first at Donovan, and then at Kersen. With an obvious blush this time, Kersen shook his head.

What the hell? Donovan wanted answers, bugger it all.

Kersen said something back to her, and it sounded like he was arguing. She waved dismissively, and pointed at Donovan again, repeating the words.

"What's she saying?" At this point Donovan didn't care what they thought of poofters.

Swaying, Kersen closed his eyes. "She says you should be with me, then."

"Excuse me?" Was that some kind of strange punishment for Kersen, since he'd brought him here? Or did it mean what Donovan thought it did?

Rubbing his face, Kersen slowly opened his eyes, and Donovan realized it was embarrassment on his face, not disgust. Mentauri commented in Indonesian, but Donovan didn't bother to glance at her. His focus was on Kersen. "She says you should be mated with me, because she knows I also do not ... date ... women. It is not unheard of in the clan. As long as one of us can perform with a female enough to make a child to carry our genes, the others do not care."

Blood rushed to Donovan's face as well. So the old auntie was matchmaking the two of them already. Donovan cleared his throat. "Tell her I'll certainly take that into consideration." At the moment he wanted to avoid upsetting her, especially if she was a clan elder. Kersen's proximity was like a searing flame now though, and he had to fight the urge to move away too. "So what happens next? I still need to check in with the conservation center. As I said, Roark's probably having kittens by now."

Kersen nodded and smiled tightly. "I must rescue my sister also. Let me speak with Mentauri about it." He did so, at length, leaving Donovan to watch the two of them, wondering how an entire village could possibly be . . . what, weretigers? How many of them had been captured on camera? *Oh God.* He'd microchipped Kersen's sister. Had other shifters been tagged?

Not in a rush to tell Kersen about that.

As Kersen spoke, Donovan allowed himself to look him over again. He'd been attracted to Kersen from the first, even though he'd been feverish from the tiger bite and apparently heading for whatever ride he was on now. Still, the man was handsome. Donovan had never considered settling down before, but if he did commit to someone, he could certainly do worse.

But I don't know him! I don't even know which side of the bed he likes sleeping on. He could be a complete arse. Or he might think I'm one. And what happens if one of us turns into a tiger in the middle of the night but the other one doesn't? Would I hurt him? Would I have to live in this village so that I don't endanger normal humans? Worse—would I have to keep a low profile because of their secret? I'm not sure I could do that. My mission is too important.

Oh, but the attraction was strong. The bad thing was he'd seen Kersen naked—well what he'd seen hadn't been bad at all. Quite the opposite. But having seen Kersen naked, it was too easy to come up with fantasies of him lying in a bed, with Donovan on top of him. Of what he might look like, sound like, being fucked. *Bugger. What am I supposed to do? He's cute, yes. But this is madness.* Thanks to Kersen's aunt however, that was all Donovan would think about now.

"Donovan?" Kersen brought Donovan out of his thoughts. He fought hard not to blush. He was in a bind here, after all. There were more important things to consider than what his cock wanted at the moment.

"What did she say?" Donovan was proud of the fact that his voice didn't waver, and he managed to keep his eyes on Kersen's face.

Kersen appeared troubled. "She thinks there's no help for it. I need to take you to your conservation center, and you must speak with your friend. You need to tell him that you will be away for a bit, perhaps a week or two. And you need to convince him that the tiger must be released back into the wild immediately."

A week or two away. And then he could return to work? At least they weren't asking him to abandon his profession, then. "I thought you said I shouldn't go because I could shift into a wild animal at any time." The idea was still crazy. Yet he'd woken up in the jungle naked. As resourceful as Kersen was, it didn't seem plausible that the man had carried him there, and there had been no signs of a vehicle.

"I know. I don't like it. But we cannot risk leaving Gemi there another night." Kersen stood. "Just promise me one thing, Dr. Donovan. If you feel as you did yesterday—if you feel dizzy, or hungry, or especially if your teeth start to hurt and your skin itches, tell me. We may have to run for the forest again." He took a deep breath, letting it out slowly. Then he smirked. "At any rate, we'll stop to get our clothing back. I imagine you'll be happy to return to your Western style."

Meaning jeans, of course. Donovan chuckled. "Yeah. And please, call me Donovan." If they were going to get as friendly as Kersen's aunt wanted, they should be using first names. He nodded at Mentauri. "Thank you," he said in Indonesian.

She nodded to him. "You're welcome. Good luck." She rose and retrieved her keys, offering them to Kersen.

After saying their good-byes, Donovan and Kersen climbed into Mentauri's truck for the drive to Ketambe.

Hopefully Roark hadn't called the cops already. And hopefully he wouldn't go berserk at the news Donovan was about to bring him.

CHAPTER NINE

Ketambe Conservation and Research Center, Ketambe, Sumatra
May 16, 2013

Donovan and Kersen reached Ketambe by early evening. They drove to the farm where Kersen had hidden their clothing, and fetched that first. Then Kersen made Donovan take the wheel to drive up to the front gates of the conservation center. If Donovan looked like he was in charge, then perhaps they could avoid the worst of the trouble when Roark saw Kersen again.

As soon as Donovan punched the intercom button, Roark's voice sounded out, loud, clear, and panicked. "Donovan? Is that you? What the hell happened yesterday? Are you all right? Hang on—I'll get the gates." With the hum of electrical power, the gates slowly opened, and Donovan pulled Mentauri's truck forward, parking it near his Jeep.

He glanced at Kersen sitting nervously beside him. "Let me talk to him." He opened the door and walked toward Roark, who'd emerged from the center, arms outstretched and ready to either hold him back or give him a big hug.

"Donovan! Where the devil have you been? We've been frantic here, trying to figure out where you went!" Roark grabbed Donovan up in a fierce embrace, but then he backed off when he noticed Kersen. "And what is he doing here? Have you gone mad? He tried to take a tiger from our protection!"

Quickly, Donovan held out an arm to block Roark. "Hold on. Let me explain. We need to sit down somewhere, all three of us. Did you send anyone to the council meeting today?" That was his first concern, even before Kersen's sister, even before his own concerns with this whole shifter business. While it might be a losing battle, he had even more reason to try his damnedest to fight against the corporate interests. They'd all be in a lot worse trouble if the Aceh Council gave away more of the precious protected lands.

Roark sputtered, but he shrugged. "I sent Helena. I reckoned we needed somebody there, and she volunteered. I've been holding down the fort and fielding questions about you all day from your staff." He began walking, and Donovan signaled for Kersen to follow. Roark ushered them into a meeting room near the front office and shut the door, taking a seat at the head of the table. "So talk. First of all, what happened yesterday? I thought you were going into septic shock."

Bollocks if Donovan knew how to explain any of it. He sat down slowly, and Kersen sat next to him, away from Roark. "Apparently the tiger we rescued the other day has some strange virus. I contracted it and became ill." At the alarm on Roark's face, he hurried to continue. "It's a blood-borne pathogen. You recall how she bit me?" He sighed, rubbing the still-healing wound on his arm. "Luckily, I don't think anyone else has been affected." He stared at Roark. "Have they?"

Roark seemed to consider, then shook his head. "No one else has complained of any symptoms. Should I quarantine our staff just in case?"

Donovan nodded. So far he wasn't too terribly off from the truth. If anyone else had acquired this shifter thing, best that they stay here, near the jungle. "That's a good idea." He glanced at Kersen. "How long would it take to show up in a person?"

Kersen nibbled at his thumbnail. "If they do not show signs within a week, they should be fine. Fever, dizziness, itching, and extreme hunger would all be signs."

He took a deep breath. Now came the hard part. "So besides that, Roark, I need you to do a few other things for me. Kersen is from the University of Sumatera Utara, and he's with a team that's been studying this rare disease. I'm afraid I'll be there for the next week or so. While I'm not having symptoms right now, they could return."

Kersen jumped in. "It is very important. Dr. Donovan could be in danger, or a danger to others. He must be isolated." He looked down as Roark scowled at him.

"Why isn't he in quarantine? How do I know you're who you say you are? This all seems fishy to me." Despite Roark's obvious anger, Kersen remained sitting with his eyes lowered, not answering. Roark's gaze returned to Donovan. "So where will you be if I need to contact you?"

It was unlikely Roark would buy the story Donovan was about to tell him. But what choice was there? Roark would never believe the truth. "I'll be at the university medical center in Medan." He thought furiously. "The only reason they let me come today is because the risk of exposure is small—bodily fluids only, as you remember. Also, I told them you'd want to speak with me." That much was true.

Roark rubbed his face until his beard stuck out. "This is highly irregular. I don't like it." He sat back frowning but thoughtful, and Donovan allowed himself to feel a glimmer of hope. Maybe this would work after all. "What about this tiger? Are they sending a team to collect her?"

Donovan braced himself. "Kersen and I are collecting her immediately. We'll use one of the center's crates for transport. Don't worry—I'll bring the crate back when I can."

His friend's eyes seemed about ready to pop out of his skull. "What, the two of you? What about vet staff? Carriers? She weighs a bloody eighteen and a half stones, if anything!"

Donovan glanced at Kersen, but he looked unconcerned. That made sense. If the tigress really was his sister and had a human mind, she'd walk in or out of the carrier on her own. They wouldn't have to carry her.

Except of course, we need to get her in the back of the truck to begin with. "They have staff waiting for us," Donovan said. The lie tasted sour in his mouth.

Abruptly, Roark stood and began to pace in the small room, head bowed. "This . . . this isn't normal. What kind of idiots would handle an endangered animal like that? It's like it's some big government secret or something . . ." He stopped and looked at Donovan. "Is it? But that doesn't explain—" He pointed at Kersen. "He doesn't fit this at all. He's too young to be representing some university medical research team."

Donovan couldn't argue. If he'd been in Roark's place, he would have been ranting too, and saying the same things. He took a deep breath, his temples starting to pound. "Roark . . . sit down. Please." According to Kersen, he was supposed to keep calm, but if this went on much longer, that wasn't likely.

The silence that followed was louder than Roark's bellowing. After a minute, he sat down with a huff, his bushy brows drawn together. Donovan reached out to touch his hand. "Friend, you're going to have to trust me. I'm aware this isn't normal. Believe me, when I can, I will tell you everything. This is me, Roark. You know I'd never, ever hurt a tiger. Please, let me have her."

Roark pulled his hand back, and Donovan winced, but Roark only covered his face, leaning forward. "Donovan, you're a good bloke. Are you in trouble? Give me something here."

Donovan felt like a heel—Roark sounded so concerned, and here Donovan was lying to him. "Yes, but not the sort you might be thinking. The virus is no joke, mate. That's all I can say right now." Donovan absently scratched at his arms. The room seemed to have grown hotter as well.

Kersen half rose from his seat, his brows drawing together. "You're scratching. We need to get you out of here."

There was nothing fake about the concern in Kersen's voice, and Roark's eyes widened. "You two are serious."

"Deadly serious," Donovan told him. He stood up and swayed. Something in the room smelled good. His stomach rumbled.

Instantly, Kersen grabbed his arm, guiding him toward the door. The young man glanced at Roark. "Will you help us? If we do not hurry, I may have to return without Donovan. He will not be able to assist me. I don't want to chance that this could happen to another of your staff members."

All hesitation left Roark's expression. "Let's do this, then. I'm not releasing an animal to a kid. Donovan, are you going to be okay?"

Donovan couldn't help but look over at Kersen, who nodded slowly. "He'll be fine if he can keep calm. Stress makes it worse."

Bloody great. And here Donovan was stressing like mad. He took a deep breath, letting it out slowly. Roark was correct; he needed to be here for the transfer of the tiger, whether or not it might possess a human mind. "See if you can find a crate and some people to help carry it. Kersen and I will back up the truck to the animal-loading area."

Allowing Kersen to usher him out, Donovan concentrated on remaining calm, on staying focused. His skin itched like dozens of ants were biting him. Roark headed toward the back of the center while Donovan went to Mentauri's truck. He leaned against the warm metal of the frame, trying to compose himself. "Kersen, what's happening?" *Am I going to change into a tiger here?*

Kersen leaned in closer, looking into Donovan's eyes. The young man inhaled, and Donovan swore he was *smelling* him. "You're struggling to control your form because you feel nervous, threatened. Try to relax. Your friend seems willing to cooperate. If we can get my sister, we'll drive back to my village and release her. Then the three of us can hunt tonight."

Donovan nodded, but just the idea of going through the change again sent chills through him. Hunt tonight. Did that mean he had to kill and eat some hapless creature of the jungle? And tomorrow? What of the city council hearings, and making sure more of the wildlife preserve wasn't sold off to farmers and corporations?

"Will I ever be able to control this, and have a normal life again?"

"Breathe," Kersen ordered, setting his hands on Donovan's shoulders. Donovan's teeth began to ache. *Are they growing yet? They cut into my lips before.* The change must be near for him to be actually remembering it. He obeyed, taking a deep breath. *I need to stay human.*

Somehow he'd accepted that this was really happening. That it wasn't just some big hoax.

He stared into Kersen's eyes, so dark, so intent. So very human, as were the hands on him. Donovan could smell the young man's sweat, the faint musk of his skin. The next surge that went through wasn't fear or hunger, but lust.

Kersen's voice steadied him. "Yes, you will gain control. And you'll be able to continue being an animal doctor and conservationist." He remained still, watching Donovan with an almost shy look on his face. That look fed something dark and savage inside Donovan, that wanted to pin Kersen to the ground and claim him like some prize. It felt like a rising tide, unstoppable.

Then, without warning, Kersen kissed him.

Lust and confusion in equal parts assailed Donovan. He groaned because it felt so *good*, the softness of Kersen's lips against his. His body immediately reacted, a new desire and yearning filling him. He grew hard, which would have been embarrassing except that he could feel Kersen's erection against his hip as the man leaned in closer. Kersen's hands rested on his chest, fingers splayed as if unsure whether to push him away or pull him closer.

Kersen made a soft sound, almost like a mewl. He started to draw back, but Donovan pressed forward, grabbing Kersen's waist and nibbling on his lip. The good news was he felt totally human again. The bad news was he wanted to take Kersen, right here, right now. *Going to seize him and hold him down, make him mine . . .*

Roark's voice coming from the animal pens warned Donovan that he had Gemi to think about. *Since when did I start to go all Neanderthal? I'm not some domineering arsehole. Am I?* At any rate he couldn't let Roark see them like this. The man barely accepted Kersen as it was.

Breathing hard, Donovan forced himself to take a couple of steps back. He pointed a finger at Kersen. "We're going to discuss this later."

For now, they had a tiger to transport.

Climbing into the truck, Donovan started the engine to bring it around to the rear of the center where Roark would be waiting.

CHAPTER TEN

Unnamed Village, Aceh Province, Sumatra
May 16, 2013

It took them nearly an hour to move Gemi into the truck. Getting her into the crate was easy, as Kersen could have told them it would be if he'd dared. She took one look at Kersen and trotted on in, obviously happy to be leaving her pen. Then two men helped Roark and Donovan carry the crate; Kersen thought they might be the same men who'd been with Donovan in the jungle. It was hoisting the crate into the back of his truck and securing it that was the hard part. Twice Roark stopped them and argued about her safety, about how ludicrous what they were doing was.

Kersen didn't know what kind of relationship Donovan had with the center's manager. They seemed to be good friends, but by the end they'd nearly broken into a fight. It was only when Donovan suffered another dizzy spell that Roark finally relented.

Donovan drove, but they'd only traveled about a mile before he pulled over, panting heavily.

"It's happening again." He groaned, clutching at the steering wheel. Sweat was pouring down his face, and he was white as a sheet and trembling.

Quickly, Kersen touched his arm. "Donovan, look at me." His own pulse quickened, but for different reasons. He had his sister, and something was happening between him and Donovan. That kiss. Just the thought of it warmed him from the inside out. He'd dreamt a kiss could be like that, but he'd never expected it. Gemi used to go on about romance that could make a girl swoon, make her toes curl, but he'd never believed that. Nevertheless, one kiss and he'd wanted to strip Donovan naked and take him to bed.

He almost pulled his hand back as fear struck him. *I can't let that happen! If we bond—if we mate, I could be stuck with him permanently. Even if he decides to leave Sumatra, or if the clan rejects him.* But, oh, the urge was strong. Kersen rode the wave until it passed, forcing himself to remain calm, to focus only on the moment. The attraction between them could wait for later.

"Donovan!" Donovan finally looked at Kersen, and there was despair in his eyes. *He feels his change coming.* That was good, in one way. It meant his human mind was becoming more accepting of the tiger spirit inside. It was possible he might be able to remember things with his next shift. Still, they had kilometers to go to get back to the village. They could leave the truck and enter the jungle again—all three of them—but that would mean another rough night and additional delays tomorrow. Like Donovan, Kersen wanted to know what was happening with the council hearing. He'd hoped to learn more this evening when Bitari returned.

"Breathe easy," Kersen said, taking Donovan's hands. His skin felt feverish to the touch, which was expected. There were no signs of fur sprouting, so that was something.

"I don't want to change yet." Donovan's voice cracked.

Panicking wasn't going to help anyone. Rubbing Donovan's palms, Kersen asked, "Do you want me to kiss you again?" As dangerous as it might be to give in to his body's wants, they had few options. Gemi was stuck in the crate. If Donovan changed, Kersen would have to work fast to free her, assuming he'd be able to without help, before shifting. Hopefully Donovan knew his scent enough not to consider him a threat in the meantime. Or food.

Donovan glanced at the back window of the truck. Then he nodded.

As Kersen leaned in closer, Donovan leaned in as well. Their lips met, and this time there was no shock, no hesitation. Donovan claimed Kersen's mouth almost ruthlessly, delving deeper with his tongue.

Groaning, Donovan bit at Kersen's lip, nibbled along his jaw, before returning to his mouth. His fangs hadn't dropped, so he wasn't too far gone. But the purr at the back of Donovan's throat didn't belong to a human. They were treading on thin ice here.

On a whim, Kersen reached lower and flicked his thumb over Donovan's chest, finding a nipple to tweak. Donovan twitched and moved away, and Kersen realized the big fellow was ticklish.

"I'm okay, for the moment," Donovan said in a breathless voice that sounded as needy as Kersen felt. "What the hell is wrong with me? I'm not like this. Not usually, anyway."

Kersen flushed; he wasn't typically this aroused, this passionate either. "You have a great deal of energy flowing through you right now, because of the tiger spirit making a home within you. The tiger feeds your animal instincts to eat, hunt, and take a mate." He scratched the back of Donovan's neck where it was hottest. As long as Donovan remained in human form, Kersen was doing something right. *Here I am, trying to keep my distance, and yet how else can I keep him from shifting? I wish we could sit and kiss like this for hours. But of course this isn't the time.*

As Donovan relaxed, breathing slower, Kersen couldn't help but chuckle at their predicament. "Luckily for us, we only have sex in human form. That is why I'm using it to help you stay with me. I cannot put another tiger in the back."

Donovan took a deep breath, glancing over his shoulder. "Right. Mating instincts, eh?" He shook his head. "I'm not ready to believe I'm being influenced by animal instincts, but it doesn't matter. Buckle up. I'm driving as fast as I can to your village."

Nodding in relief, Kersen obeyed.

It took about two hours to reach Kersen's village. By then the sun had set, and stars lit the sky above. From the ground there came only faint twinkles from lights in the small cluster of houses. *His home is like another world, so cut off from civilization.* Donovan still couldn't find any GPS data for the place; it seemed to be nameless. But it was certainly real. This time when he pulled up to Kersen's house, he noted a vehicle that hadn't been there before: an old truck with rust spots and a large dent in the side. Donovan glanced at Kersen as he parked Mentauri's truck over to the side of the house.

"It's my sister, Bitari, back from the council meeting. We can ask her what's been going on there." Kersen gulped, and spots of color showed on his cheeks. "I'll have to explain about you. Us."

Donovan opened his mouth, but Kersen didn't give him a chance to ask questions; he unbuckled his seat belt and opened the truck door, before hurrying out. On the porch was the squat, grim-faced woman he'd met yesterday. *Oh joy.* Dread filled him at the thought of trying to make nice with someone who already seemed to hate his guts.

He climbed out of the truck slowly. *Can't get angry or stressed—have to keep calm.* Though if he changed now, it wouldn't be as big a deal. Kersen and Bitari could open the animal crate. Still, he wanted to know the news of the council hearing. Bitari and he were on the same side, despite the fact that he wasn't sure they were going to get along.

Bitari climbed down from the porch and approached them, glaring at Donovan. From inside the crate, the tigress growled, scratching at the sides.

Donovan held back, uncertain what to do, while Kersen worked at the latches of the crate.

"Is that safe?" None of them answered.

He watched as the tigress paced back and forth, her head down, lips curled back. Her paw was still bandaged, but she didn't seem to care. If Kersen was wrong, if all of this was just some crazy fantasy or that wasn't really his sister, what would happen? Donovan couldn't recapture a wild tiger by himself. And if Roark found out he had done something so stupid, not even their friendship would save him. Roark would have to report it.

Kersen opened the first latch. Bitari hustled over and opened the second one. Before they could unlatch the third, the tigress rammed the door, growling and snarling. Donovan dove for the cab of the truck before he remembered this wasn't his Jeep, and his tranquilizer gun was still back at the conservation center. *Should've brought the blasted thing!*

The tigress yowled, still trapped. Bitari slapped it on the nose through the metal grate as she struggled to get the last latch open. "Patience, Gemi!" she growled, and Donovan marveled that her voice really did sound like a growl. She managed to get the crate door open, and the tigress leaped out, landing on the ground and stumbling on her wounded foot.

He stepped out of the truck again, watching the three of them. "She's still hurt."

As he spoke, the tiger began to change. First she *shrank*. He never would have believed it if it wasn't happening right in front of him, but there was no denying it: the animal was diminishing before his eyes, the legs elongating, the great paws becoming small and delicate. The fur vanished, leaving bare skin. He didn't even see what happened to her tail. She cried out, and then there was a naked woman lying in the dirt, with bandages that were falling off her left hand because they were too large.

Bitari gathered the woman into her arms, throwing her skirt over the lower half to cover her. Kersen knelt next to her, saying, "I'm sorry," over and over in Indonesian. Donovan knew that phrase well enough, since he used it whenever he couldn't understand the locals.

The woman's nudity reminded him of another thing he'd forgotten at the research center—clothing. Donovan removed his shirt and handed it to Kersen. "She can use this, or I can grab something of hers if you like." It was awkward, standing while everyone was on the ground. *I don't belong in this family picture.* The notion tugged at a familiar empty spot in his heart, painfully.

The young woman stared up at him with wide frightened eyes. What would it be like to be stuck in an animal form inside a cage? At the moment, Donovan was probably lucky that Bitari wasn't trying to kill him. When she spoke, Gemi's voice was soft but clear. "You rescued me. Who are you?"

Kersen looked up at Donovan as well. "He's the man who saved you from the poacher's snare, Gemi. He's a doctor at the conservation center in Ketambe." He paused and then faced Bitari. "And now he's one of us. Gemi's blood has turned him."

Bitari stared at Donovan in shock and horror. "No!" Half turning, she snarled at Kersen and struck him across the cheek. "This is what your foolishness has caused! I told you never to leave her alone!"

Rage! Protect what is mine! Before he was even aware of what he was doing, Donovan was on all fours, and a deep growl was coming up from his belly. *That did not sound normal.* All his efforts to stay human, and this had undone him. He could actually feel his hackles rising, feel his claws forming.

"Bitari!" Kersen cried, but there was no stopping the change now that it had begun. Donovan cried out as pain enveloped him, starting from the bones outward. Would he know himself this time? Or would the three of them have to deal with a wild, irate tiger?

The pain escalated; he felt his fangs growing, felt an unbearable ache in his tailbone that must be his tail, felt the heat flaring brighter and brighter. *Kersen, help me!* He tried to say it, but it emerged as a whimper.

Then he blacked out.

Kersen wanted to scream at Bitari. He'd managed to keep Donovan with him, in human form, for the entire drive back, only to have Bitari make one stupid move and undo it all. His sister seemed appalled by the results of her actions, sitting there staring with Gemi trembling in her arms. He rose to his knees, putting himself between his sisters and the rapidly forming tiger writhing in the dust outside his home.

"He doesn't have control yet—he doesn't even have awareness when he's shifted!" That was the worst-case scenario, of course; after last night, it was possible Donovan knew Kersen's scent whether he was human or tiger. Hopefully. Kersen didn't want to shift and spend another night in the jungle, but it was probably unavoidable. Still, this time he'd wait and see how Donovan reacted, see if he knew him or not.

Tatters of clothing hung from Donovan's feline frame—they hadn't had a chance to undress him, though at least Gemi had his shirt. He seemed even bigger than last time, but that was likely because Kersen was sitting on the ground less than a meter away. Amber eyes focused on Kersen, and the tiger bared his fangs, shaking his hindquarters to remove what was left of the trousers.

"Easy, Doctor," Kersen said, praying that Donovan understood him.

"He's beautiful," Gemi whispered, holding still. Bitari kept quiet, though Kersen suspected her instincts were screaming at her to shift. That wasn't an option for Gemi with her injury and exhaustion though.

The tiger's lips relaxed; he seemed confused as to what to do next. His nostrils flared as the tiger took a sniff of Kersen. Considering the kisses they'd shared earlier, Kersen's human scent would be on the tiger as well, and the animal probably recognized it. So far, it wasn't clear what kind of mind was driving: man or beast.

Stepping forward, the tiger licked his lips. Kersen continued to hold still, aware that he'd never have time to shift if Donovan attacked him. Yet his instinct told him that it was okay. If he kept Donovan's focus on him, hopefully Bitari and Gemi could sneak away.

The big tiger walked right up to Kersen and sniffed at his hair, whiskers brushing Kersen's forehead. *Calm*, Kersen told himself. The key was to remain calm.

Calm, he received a faint echo of thought from the tiger, so faint that he suspected Donovan was more beast than man. But at least this time there was some awareness.

"Bitari, take Gemi once I lead him away," Kersen said in a low voice. He offered his hand for the tiger to sniff. The animal bared his teeth at the movement, his massive head low to the ground. He took a whiff, and then gave Kersen's forearm a big lick, rubbing his cheek against Kersen to transfer his scent. Well that settled it. While yesterday Donovan might have considered him a rival, today he was clearly a playmate. At least he wasn't food.

Kersen moved closer, then dared to scratch between the tiger's ears. Gemi eased herself out of Bitari's lap, scooting backward. Bitari began easing away as well, very slowly. Despite legends of the fantastic healing abilities of shifters, they were vulnerable to injury and bacterial infections. Shifters were more resilient than humans, but not by much. Kersen only hoped his sisters didn't startle the animal.

The tiger twitched when Kersen's hand made contact, but allowed the petting, huffing softly. Kersen simply needed to distract Donovan and lure him back to the jungle. Once Bitari and Gemi were safely away, he'd shift and lead Donovan toward the jungle. From his own experience, Kersen figured Donovan would spend at least a few hours as a tiger. With luck, he could keep Donovan close to home for that long, and they could return here once Donovan shifted back.

Cuddle. Play. The signals from Donovan were murky, but the fact that he was sending anything at all was a vast improvement. Kersen grinned, scratching harder and then going on hands and knees to rub his shoulder against the tiger's muzzle. Suddenly the tiger wrapped both paws around Kersen and flipped him onto his back, mouthing his hand, but by the gentleness, it was obvious this was only play behavior. Kersen had succeeded last night; either Donovan's tiger-self saw them as litter brothers, or maybe his aunt was right and it already saw him as a mate. They were the only possible explanations for this play session.

He'd never played like this before, as a human with a shifted tiger. It was thrilling; Donovan outweighed him by fifty kilos and could snap his arm in two or crush him. Yet here he was, nuzzling Kersen's stomach, paws splayed on either side of him.

A rustling in the grass behind him told Kersen that Bitari and Gemi were moving farther away. He grabbed Donovan's snout like he would a puppy's, shoving the tiger's head to the side with a grin. A great paw came up to bat his hand aside. The swipe was powerful, but it was clear the tiger was holding most of his strength back and keeping his claws retracted. Thank the gods.

"Let's steer you closer to the jungle," Kersen said in a quiet, friendly tone, rolling so that the tiger would have to turn away from the house to follow. He caught a glimpse of his sisters creeping toward the ladder before the tiger "pounced" on him. It wasn't much of a pounce, though it did knock the wind from Kersen, and left him on his back with the tiger on top, licking at his ear.

He allowed the licking for a moment, just to give Bitari a chance to get up the ladder with Gemi. Then Kersen heaved at the big muzzle and wriggled out from underneath the tiger. He removed his shirt and kicked off his shoes, then got his trousers off before he began to shift. Donovan seemed to know what was going on, because he didn't try to keep playing but only watched on with interest, head cocked.

Once Kersen finished shifting, he gave Donovan a hard swat. *For making me babysit you*, he sent via thought, but he wasn't angry. The man had done a pretty good job at controlling himself as a new *siluman harimau*. His tiger form needed time to establish itself, and his shift could only be delayed for so long.

At Donovan's growl, Kersen dodged aside to avoid another frisky attack. So Donovan's tiger wanted to play? He'd give him play.

With an answering huff, Kersen took off toward the jungle, Donovan fast in pursuit once again.

CHAPTER ELEVEN

Gunung Leuser National Forest, Sumatra
May 17, 2013

When Donovan came to his senses this time, it was dark. Once again, he was naked and curled up against Kersen. Beams of moonlight pierced the canopy of the jungle above, making spots of silver on the forest floor. They were lying in a soft bed of leaves, with no sign of a recent kill nearby, and no blood, thankfully. Donovan's arm was wrapped around Kersen almost protectively, and the young man's head was resting on Donovan's chest as he softly snored.

A peculiar ache tugged at Donovan in the center of his chest, near where Kersen's head rested. Donovan found his free hand venturing up to pet at Kersen's short black hair, tousling it. *I'm growing fond of him.* When was the last time he'd let someone get close enough to make him feel anything? Back at university, was all Donovan could recall. Since then he'd kept himself so busy with the animals, busy with work, that he hadn't thought about relationships or his personal life. This desire to watch over someone—that was new. He'd only experienced that connection with animals.

Mentauri's mention of him being with Kersen had made Donovan's heart pound, half in fear, half in excitement. Even now, such notions made him dizzy with possibilities he'd never imagined before. He shook his head. They'd been thrown together because of circumstance, because Donovan was destined to turn into a tiger whenever he lost his temper. He remembered a lot more this time. Bitari had slapped Kersen. That had enraged him. He'd wanted to smack her so hard, to tear into her throat and rip through her jugular, to feel the warm blood spill over his tongue . . .

It was good that Kersen had distracted him. He recalled that part, playing with Kersen. It had been like being a little child, full of wonder and curiosity, somehow himself and yet not himself. After that, his memory had grown dim. But he remembered changing, and what it had felt like being a tiger, even if only for a few moments. Supposedly next time he'd remember even more. Maybe he'd be conscious for the whole duration.

So perhaps eventually he'd be able to control this thing, like Kersen did, and have a normal life. But what was he supposed to do with Mentauri's talk of using him as valuable breeding stock? That was awkward, but he had to consider her need to protect her kind. Cripes, he dealt with endangered animals. He knew all about genetic diversity and breeding populations. It could be said that these weretiger people were just another endangered species, affected by habitat loss. So he supposed he could at least donate some sperm.

None of this meant that he had to spend the rest of his life with Kersen in his village. If he wanted, he could continue working as a conservationist and veterinarian, just as he always had, and no one would be the wiser.

Except that suddenly such a future felt empty. And lonely. The more he was coming to know Kersen, the more Donovan liked him. Unlike Donovan, Kersen had strong familial ties. And not only did Kersen care about his family, but he'd clearly do anything to protect them. He was courageous and responsible and tenacious too.

It's pointless to worry about the future and being with him. I don't even know if he likes me. He might think I'm a complete prick.

There was a lot to consider regarding his prospects, and soon. All of it was underlined by this overwhelming instinct to stay with this young man he'd only just met, and claim him.

But all that would have to wait. Donovan's bladder wasn't going to let him lie around any longer. Gently, he disentangled himself and walked off only far enough for modesty's sake, before taking care of things. It felt bizarre to be in the jungle with not a stitch on him. Adam and Steve, and all that.

When he returned, Kersen was awake and watching him with curiosity.

Heat prickled up the back of Donovan's neck. "Hello again. We've got to stop meeting like this."

Kersen snorted, smiling. "Yes." He looked Donovan over, and there was desire in his gaze. The heat traveled from Donovan's neck to his chest, right down to his groin. Blinking, Kersen's eyes met his before he shyly lowered his gaze. "Um. Did you remember more this time?" He wasn't rising, so Donovan sat down next to him where they could talk face-to-face.

Now their nakedness didn't bother him quite as much. He shrugged. "I remember changing. I don't remember much after that . . . except I think I pounced on you? Like we were playing." A rustling in the trees made him glance up. "How deep in the rainforest do you think we are? I don't relish the idea of another barefoot hike through the jungle."

That brought a laugh. "My house is less than a mile away." Kersen sat up and hugged his knees, and silence fell between them. *He was so open and caring with me yesterday. So why is he awkward today? Is it simply concern for me?*

Kersen rocked back a little, his lips pressed together, and then finally asked, "Are you ready to go back to the village? I promise Bitari will behave herself. I will make sure of that."

It would be wonderful to clean up and eat a normal breakfast; yet on the other hand, Donovan was alone with a man who was driving him wild with desire. Right here. Right now.

He found himself leaning in closer. He wasn't sure what it was, but something about Kersen just smelled so good. It was like Donovan's senses were extra receptive where this young man was concerned. "Sure." Donovan closed the distance and kissed Kersen.

Kersen made a noise, but it wasn't a protest—more like an exclamation of surprise, and then need, as he kissed Donovan back, opening his mouth to Donovan's questing tongue.

Unlike when they'd kissed in the truck, Donovan had no intention of stopping. Having Kersen to himself, naked, was too much of a temptation. He nibbled at Kersen's bottom lip, growling softly— thankfully it was a human sound on this occasion. Wrapping a hand around Kersen's waist, he pulled him closer, his other hand trailing down Kersen's chest to find a nipple to play with. Kersen's breath hitched, and he arched into Donovan's touch.

Doubt we'll be getting to the house any time soon. The timing was undoubtedly horrid. There were two women back at the house expecting them to return. But ever since that first kiss by the truck—hell, ever since he'd first laid eyes on the fellow, Donovan had wanted Kersen. Now he had him, and the man's responses were driving him crazy. His mouth left Kersen's only to nibble down his throat, then lower, finding a nipple to suck on. His fingers teased the other nipple, bringing it to a hard peak, and then trailed down the flat stomach to Kersen's thighs, spreading them.

"Donovan," Kersen said, but Donovan wasn't sure if it was a plea or a warning. It didn't seem to be a complaint—not by how Kersen's hips jerked as Donovan licked his way down to Kersen's stomach. He couldn't wait to get to the root of Kersen's desire, to taste the man. A tiny corner of his brain wondered what was happening, why he was so desperate. Taking control like this wasn't his style. But as Donovan wrapped his hand around Kersen's rigid cock, every thought left him, and it seemed the natural thing to do.

"Please." Kersen moaned, his head falling back, his hand grabbing at Donovan's shoulder. Donovan took a second or two to lick at the pearly drops of pre-come. Then he swallowed the head, sucking it, and swirled his tongue around the glans. His own cock was so hard it hurt, but what he wanted was to hear Kersen screaming with pleasure. To taste his seed. *No, I want even more. I want all of him.*

After swallowing as much of Kersen's length as he could, Donovan came off. "I want to fuck you." He gazed into Kersen's dark eyes, needing Kersen to know just how much he wanted him. Kersen groaned desperately. Again Donovan took Kersen down, deeper this time, until the head hit the back of his throat. Too bloody long since he'd had a good shag, or much of anything. Kersen tasted amazing. When Kersen's member twitched, Donovan moaned, deep-throating the young man over and over, almost frantic with need.

"Donovan— I can't— I need—" Kersen's short fingernails scrabbled at Donovan as the young man squirmed. *Right there with you.* Sighing, Kersen rolled onto his back, allowing Donovan all the access he could hope for.

Donovan hadn't planned to suck him dry, but when Donovan sensed that Kersen was close, he came up only far enough to taste him as the first hot splash hit his tongue. Kersen keened, shuddering as his orgasm took him, still holding a fistful of Donovan's hair. Donovan didn't let up until there was nothing left, until Kersen pulled away.

For a horrifying second, Donovan wondered if he'd gone too far. He looked into Kersen's face, and the only thing he saw there was a need matching his own. Before Donovan knew what was happening, Kersen turned and sprang on him. Now it was Donovan on his back in the damp leaves, and Kersen on top, straddling him.

Donovan wanted to say that he didn't know what was happening, that this was all a lot more intense than he was used to. But to say he didn't want this was a lie; he wanted this badly. As Kersen bent forward to kiss him, Donovan abandoned any thought of speaking, losing himself in the sensations of lips and tongues and teeth, in the taste and smell of the young man. Kersen wrapped his fingers around Donovan's shaft, giving him a slow stroke, and Donovan moaned into the kiss, his hips jerking in response.

Kersen murmured into his ear, "I want you to fuck me Donovan. But not like this—not here. Will you let me take care of your needs? I don't have a lot of experience, but I want to try."

Shuddering, Donovan nodded. The fact that Kersen wasn't experienced only made him that much more attractive to his possessive side. *You're mine.* But that was a crazy thought. They barely knew each other. As Kersen continued to stroke him slowly, Donovan forced himself to say the words out loud. "Yes. Please."

Kersen shot him a grin that was pure joy. Then it was Donovan's turn to cry out as Kersen took him into his mouth. There wasn't much artifice to it, but Donovan didn't care. Kersen's mouth was warm and his tongue felt amazing, and it was all Donovan could do not to grab him by the hair and thrust in deep.

When Kersen began to play with Donovan's balls, he feared his head would explode.

"Won't last," Donovan warned, but that only seemed to spur Kersen on. Stroking Donovan with one hand, he focused all his attention on the head, bobbing up and down as he sucked and licked. Donovan's climax began to build, and he was powerless to stop it, as he had been powerless to stop his change.

"Cripes!" Donovan yelled, just before the pleasure broke over him. He emptied his balls, and Kersen drank it down eagerly, until Donovan was spent and woozy, staring up at the pre-dawn sky through the canopy. Kersen crawled back up to lie next to him, and Donovan wrapped an arm around him, pulling him closer.

I should say something. But what the devil was he supposed to say after sex like that? He settled for holding Kersen firmly, and trailing his knuckles over his smooth chest, feeling the man shiver.

A few minutes later, the words came to him. "I hope there's a bed with some privacy somewhere in your village. For our proper first time." This was enough for the moment. But God, he wanted to fuck Kersen until they both couldn't move any more.

Kersen laughed. It was a good sound, and Donovan found himself chuckling as well. Rising up on one elbow, Kersen contemplated him. "I'm sure we can find something." He paused, looking Donovan over with an almost heartbreaking vulnerability. "Are you really attracted to me, Donovan?"

Donovan blinked. How could Kersen possibly ask that question after what they'd done? Not to mention the kisses in the truck, and the long stares before. "Yes, I am." He wondered if he needed to elaborate further. Roark had told him before that he was a hard man to decipher. "I'm not good with emotions. But, oh, I wanted you the first time I saw you in the council chamber."

It was too dark to tell, but Donovan had the feeling that Kersen was blushing. "I was looking at you too." Kersen moved in closer, pressing up against Donovan. "I like the work that you do. It gives me hope. You are an honorable man, Doctor."

"Don't call me that." Donovan placed a finger under Kersen's chin so that he could kiss him again, languidly this time. "Donovan. Or 'D' if you don't want to bother with all those syllables."

Kersen sputtered and then laughed. "D. It seems so . . ." He shook his head. "So casual. You foreigners." He said that with fondness, resuming their kiss.

They were clearly going to have more than a few cultural differences. At the moment, though, Donovan didn't care. It was tempting to lie in the soft leaves with his limbs entangled with Kersen's and taste him over and over. Donovan felt himself stirring again even as he forced himself to end the kiss. "We'd better get back to your house. As much as I'd like to do this all day, I need to know what happened with the provincial council."

Sighing, Kersen nodded and pulled away. "I, too, would like to know the news. And I'm hungry." He paused. "What will happen if the council votes in favor of the corporations?"

There was just enough light to see the worry on Kersen's face. A fierce protectiveness for him came over Donovan, surprising in its intensity. He laid a hand on Kersen's arm. "Then we'll lose another chunk of the rainforest. I am going to fight for every last square meter."

Kersen nodded. "I will help in any way I can. Come. It will be light soon. We'll go to my house, wash up, and eat. By then, my sisters will probably be awake."

It was Donovan's turn to sigh. He desperately wanted to do more with Kersen than simply shower and eat. For now, it would have to wait though. He stood, brushing off leaves that had stuck to his bum. "Lead on."

Chapter Twelve

Unnamed Village, Aceh Province, Sumatra
May 17, 2013

Kersen's clothes were right where he'd left them, next to the truck by his house. Donovan, unfortunately, had torn his trousers, and had given his T-shirt to Gemi, which left him with only a sheet from the clothesline to wear as a sort of sarong. Thankfully, his shoes had popped off during his transformation. Kersen knew what a pain those were to replace. Donovan picked them up and shoved them on his feet, sighing. Silently, Kersen watched. *I should reassure him—but how?* He settled for giving him a smile.

The house was blessedly quiet as Kersen led Donovan up the ladder to the porch and front door. Bitari might hear them coming in, but if she knew what was good for her, she'd stay away. Kersen threw a reassuring look over his shoulder, and they went inside.

"I should have packed a suitcase while we were at the center," Donovan whispered. "I have my own house, but I sometimes sleep at work so I keep an extra set of clothing there."

That made Kersen chuckle. They'd been a little preoccupied with getting his sister out.

"I know men in the village who can donate clothing," Kersen whispered back, but he wondered if their clothes would fit. Donovan was more than a head taller than most of the clan and broader in the shoulders. He took Donovan's hand and led him past the tiny kitchen and dining area to the bedrooms. At least as the only male in the family, Kersen had his own room.

Donovan stayed by Kersen's side as he put away the few things scattered on the floor, including the notice of the council meeting. He avoided looking at Donovan's face, afraid of what he might find there—never before had his home seemed so shabby. This wasn't some rich foreigner's mansion. They only had cloth curtains for doors and simple mattresses for beds. He'd always lived here, first with his parents and then with his sisters. Now suddenly, privacy would be an issue, and having only curtains wouldn't suffice. Donovan cleared his throat. "Toilet is down the hall, correct?"

Kersen nodded, glad he could offer something. "There should be water to wash. Bitari fills it every night." As Donovan turned to leave, Kersen couldn't stop himself. "Perhaps when things settle down . . ." He bit his lip to keep the question inside, where it belonged.

"Yes?" Donovan paused, staring back.

Why couldn't he keep his mouth shut? But the feeling of Donovan's mouth on him, the kisses in the truck and then under the starry sky—they'd been amazing. Kersen wanted this. He wanted to begin something with Donovan, something more than a one-night stand.

He scratched his head, fumbling. "I could visit you at your house. When things are safer." *Can I have him and my family too? Would he understand how much they mean to me?* The two needs warred within him, almost making him dizzy.

"I'd like that." Donovan smiled. Then he tiptoed past Gemi and Bitari's room to head to the washroom. Kersen sat and waited. His inner tiger was crying out at him, but not to be let out to play, oh no. His tiger wanted Donovan to claim him. As a mate.

Kersen closed his eyes and groaned. How was this supposed to work? Himself and this British doctor who probably made more money than ninety percent of the Indonesian population and who up until now had been a confirmed bachelor? He didn't know anything about the man other than that he liked rescuing tigers and fighting for wildlife conservation. *If I allow myself to get close to him, I risk everything if the clan doesn't accept him. I could be cut off from my sisters, my aunt, and everyone I know. What would I do then? Would I work for him? I'd be lost and adrift.*

It wasn't long before Donovan returned, cleaner and looking much happier. Kersen handed him another pair of trousers along with the shirt that Gemi had thoughtfully left by the front door. He blushed. "I don't have underwear that would fit you." For himself, he grabbed a fresh pair of clothing, ready to rinse off the dirt and sweat from the jungle. It was better to keep moving. That way he wouldn't be tempted to misbehave with Dr. Donovan again.

"No worries," Donovan replied, pulling on his shirt.

Already Kersen could hear soft footsteps against the wooden flooring and the soft murmur of voices, signs from the other room that Bitari and Gemi were waking. Kersen groaned. "I'd better wash up. I'll be as quick as I can." He hurried for the washroom before either of his sisters could beat him to it.

He took only five minutes to rinse down, but that was all he needed; they had always been careful to conserve water. When Kersen emerged, his sisters stood waiting for him. Bitari had her arms folded over her chest and a guarded expression on her face. Gemi had a new bandage wrapped around her hand. She seemed troubled too.

Before either of them could say anything, Kersen rushed forward to hug his younger sister. "I was worried about you."

Gemi stiffened for an instant, then relaxed and hugged him back. "I was worried about me too." She glanced at the curtain hiding the view of Kersen's room. He could practically hear her unspoken question.

Nodding, he stepped toward the curtain. "Yes, the doctor who saved you is here. Doctor McGinnis? Will you meet my sister Gemi?"

Donovan emerged, nervously straightening his clothes. His beard was scruffy and his hair unkempt, but Kersen could not deny the elegance with which the man carried himself. It had to be that UK education. And, oh, but he looked incredible, standing there with a T-shirt showing off his sculpted chest and trousers that only went to his muscular calves. A doctor he might be, but he was no stranger to physical labor. Kersen hoped his sisters didn't notice the scratches from their earlier sex play.

Smiling, Donovan reached out and shook Gemi's hand. "Pleased to meet you—officially, Gemi. Please call me Donovan."

After shaking hands, Gemi started to play with her hair. "Thank you . . . Donovan. For saving me from the poachers." She glanced at Kersen before gazing back at Donovan, and Kersen had a fresh flash of guilt that he'd left her alone in the forest.

Donovan looked down, blushing. "You don't need to thank me. I have a passion for saving tigers. I just didn't know . . ." His color deepened. "Well, I didn't know I had anything other than a tiger in our facility."

Bitari glared at Kersen. "If we had been doing as we should, Doctor, this would not have happened to you or Gemi." She stepped forward, and Gemi stepped back, her head bowed. Bitari thrust her hand into Donovan's, shaking it vigorously. "I apologize for my anger at you. Today and yesterday."

Donovan frowned at her, his brows drawn together in confusion. "Understandable, I reckon. I'm sort of invading your world, aren't I, with this change . . ." His gaze roamed over Kersen with an intimacy that couldn't be hidden.

Heat rushed to Kersen's face. He struggled for words, feeling everyone's eyes on him. "No, you're not. It's a shock to us, certainly. We have tried very hard not to spread our gift to outsiders. But perhaps it was a good thing." He couldn't help the flush of desire going through him, thinking about those glorious kisses and his time with Donovan on the bed of leaves. His aunt could be meddlesome, but she must have seen something between the two of them. Now that connection was becoming more obvious, and probably to his sisters as well. Not that he cared if they knew. He'd admitted to his sisters that he preferred men when Bitari had pestered him about finding a wife. They hadn't spoken of it since, but Bitari seemed at least tolerant of that aspect of him.

Bitari stared at Kersen. "How can this be a good thing? He knows nothing of our ways, our customs. What is to stop him from telling all the other doctors and whoever else he's connected with?" For once she didn't sound angry so much as afraid. Kersen could sympathize. He'd felt the same only two days ago.

Now he felt differently.

"He loves the jungle, just as we do. He loves the tigers." Kersen nodded to Donovan. "True, yes? I saw it when you spoke to the Aceh Council, defending our land."

"Absolutely," Donovan said without hesitation.

Kersen turned back to his sister. "Besides, he has already kept our secret. We had to lie to his friend at the research center to free Gemi. Donovan could have said something. He didn't." It was important that he convince Bitari now and that he have her on his side. Later they would have to make a case to the rest of the clan to accept Donovan as a clan member. The other dominant males would be the hardest to convince. They had killed to protect the clan's secrets before. Kersen bit back a shudder.

Donovan nodded. "I know I look like a bloody Brit. But I've spent most of my life outside of the UK. I grew up in places like India, Thailand, and yes, Sumatra. This is more my home than anywhere else because I spent some of the best years of my childhood here. I earned my degree to learn how to save the rainforests, and all the things that live in them. The Sumatran tiger has always been one of my favorite animals."

He glanced at Kersen before continuing. "I'm still trying to adjust to the idea that some of the tigers I've been studying may have actually been shifters. And yet Kersen tells me that your kind have existed for hundreds of years?"

He's trying. He's really trying. Though Kersen tried to keep his elation back, he couldn't help grinning. "Yes. Perhaps even thousands of years. Back to the time of Buddha, or the Vedas."

Donovan seemed impressed. "Right, then. To me, that means you are natives to this jungle as much as the wildlife is native. I'm committed to preserving as much of that as I can." It took Kersen a moment to understand the big words. Preserving? That meant keeping safe, didn't it? By Donovan's tone and the determined look on his face, Kersen thought so.

Bitari took several deep breaths, letting them out slowly. She glanced at Kersen, and then back at Donovan. "Brother, are you going to babysit him? Did you speak to Mentauri?" She tapped her foot impatiently.

"Cripes, did we ever," Donovan said.

At almost the same time, Kersen said, "Of course we did." He couldn't help peeking at Donovan as he answered the other question. "We have not decided where Donovan will be staying for the long term.

I've invited him to stay with me for now." He couldn't possibly say they were going to stay together after Donovan gained control of his abilities. What if they learned they weren't compatible after all? Or what if Donovan checked out the others in the village and found someone else? At least Kersen could be up front about his invitation. It was too soon to commit to anything else.

Donovan, however, showed no hesitation whatsoever. "And I've accepted. So yes, I'm staying here while I adjust to things." He rubbed his lip, his gaze traveling between Kersen and his sisters. "Kersen . . . your aunt seemed fine with me, you know, about my preferences. What about them?"

Kersen wanted to slap himself—they should have discussed this before walking into the house, but they'd been busy gawking at each other. It was a good question. What if he had to keep Donovan from shifting again, as he had before, through touching and kissing? And what if things did develop further? His sisters deserved to know.

He scratched the back of his neck, which had grown hot. "They know that I cannot be with women; it simply does not work." Steeling himself, he peered at Bitari. "Dr. McGinnis is like me in this way. Mentauri thought we might make a good pairing." The heat traveled to his face, and even down his chest. *I'm glad I never had to have this conversation with our parents. But I wish I could have gotten their advice.*

She humphed, focusing Donovan. "What do you have to say about that?"

If Donovan was nervous about being put on the spot, he didn't show it. His voice was calm and respectful. "I think your aunt is an observant woman. Yes, I'm attracted to your brother, but anything that happens depends on what he wants. I've already invited him to visit my home some time. Would that bother you?"

The tension flowed out of her shoulders, the lines between her brows softening. She inspected Donovan seemingly with more curiosity than fear now. "Hmm. I'm not sure yet. I suppose we will find out how that goes."

Gemi nodded, rubbing at her bandage. "I hope it works out. I want you happy, Kersen. I know it's been lonely—for all three of us." She smiled, and Kersen breathed a sigh of relief, which Donovan echoed. That seemed to close that matter for the moment. Still, he'd hoped for more from Bitari. *What did I expect? We've never been comfortable talking about such things.* At least Bitari seemed willing to give Donovan a chance. That was an important step.

Turning, Bitari started walking toward the kitchen. "I'm making breakfast. We must talk about what happened at the meeting yesterday."

Donovan shot an urgent look at Kersen, then followed her. "Can I help you cook? I need any information you have. I may be stuck here, but I can direct Roark, my partner, on anything we need to do to sway votes."

Kersen wanted to return to his room to finish getting ready, but he was aware that Gemi was still standing near, holding herself, her brows furrowed. When he faced her, he realized there was a bandage on her ear. "Are you really all right? What happened to your ear?"

She frowned, her dark eyes flashing. "Your doctor tagged me. I ripped it out last night, after I cleaned up. I forgive him. I know he meant well, and he didn't realize what I was." She glanced at where Bitari and Donovan had gone. "Is he a good man?"

Kersen blushed, but nodded. He didn't trust himself to say anything further. From the kitchen came Bitari's voice ordering Donovan about, having him pull out dishes. He smiled. If Donovan could handle his sister's bossiness, then he might be ready for the stresses of being around other people after all. Bitari would no doubt give Donovan the information he was seeking, but she'd probably make him work for it.

Once he was dressed and groomed, Kersen joined them in the kitchen, setting the small table as his sister fried up eggs with pepper sauce. Donovan stood nearby, asking about the ingredients. As expected, Bitari held off on talk of the meeting until the food was ready and the four of them were seated at the table.

Bitari took a few bites before beginning. "Yesterday did not go well at the council meeting. The Aceh government refused to let some group from America speak. The council said that Aceh would not bow down to foreign interests." She shook her head, poking at her eggs.

Donovan's fork rattled as he slammed it down. "Bloody hell— what hypocrites they are! Bowing down to 'foreign interests,' when they're bending over backward for foreign corporations with cash.

I knew they'd pull something. If it doesn't have money attached to it, it's not worth a bucket of spit to them." He colored, picking his fork back up and taking a bite. "Sorry. They just make me insane."

"You're not the only one. They did allow some of the farmers to speak then. I tried to say how the companies affect villages in the area. After all, we have several clan members of the Batik tribe, and the province is always going on about preserving such cultures. But I'm not great at making speeches. It wasn't a very good argument, I fear." Bitari sighed. "Today's the last day for the public comments. Tomorrow they'll take the vote."

Donovan growled under his breath, and this time there was more than a human rumble to it. Kersen glanced at his sisters nervously. "Perhaps we shouldn't talk of it. It's not like there's anything we can do, right?"

The last thing he needed was for Donovan to become angry again and shift. They needed to introduce him to the village to meet the other *siluman harimau* so that he could be accepted into their clan, and he needed to be human for that. Once that happened, Kersen could spend time with him without fear of being expelled with him if a mating bond formed between them. Plus, there was another concern. If Donovan spent too much time, too soon in his tiger form, that might become his dominant nature, rather than the other way around. That was why Kersen's parents had always been so careful to monitor their children's shifting.

"You can't distract me from this, Kersen," Donovan said in a low voice, pushing his eggs aside. "This is what I do. It's what I live for." He growled, clenching his fists. "When will I be safe to be around people? I need to be at this hearing today. I might be able to work with some of the other wildlife rescue organizations, provoke more public outcry or something. We have to hit them hard now, before they take that vote." He glanced at the three siblings. "Unless you fancy the idea of bulldozers invading your village and carving up your forest. While the government may not know about this village, we're nevertheless in Aceh. Have you checked to see if this is part of the land under dispute?"

Bitari's tone was heavy. "Most of the land they want to use is east of us. But there is a part that comes within two kilometers of here. They would find us."

For a moment, Donovan was silent. Then with a scrape of the chair on the wooden floor, he stood up. "I'm going. Kersen can keep me from shifting. He's done it before. And I reckon that since I'm starting to remember more, I should start to gain better control. This is too important to miss. I need to speak to the others opposing this land deal. We have to find some way to sway the council's votes." He paced from one end of the kitchen to the other, which wasn't very far. "Do you have a phone?"

Kersen glanced over at Bitari, shuddering. It wasn't just the idea of Donovan going to a government meeting. There would be the drive, and then there would be no way to hide him if he shifted. Having loggers driving through their village would pale in comparison to the danger posed by Donovan shifting in front of a government council. He could only imagine how they would react—death by stoning was perfectly legal. Too often people condemned what they perceived as monsters.

Bitari stood as well. "I have a cell phone. We don't have a house phone; the only one in the village who does is Mentauri. Why? You really shouldn't go. You will destroy us if you fail to contain your tiger."

Donovan took the phone as she offered it. "I'm going to call Roark. He put up pictures of Gemi—sorry—when we rescued her. We were trying to gather international support, such as Greenpeace. The more international voices that are heard by the Aceh government, the more likely they are to listen. That's where the money is. They only speak in dollars and pounds." He huffed in frustration. "This couldn't have happened at a worse time."

Bitari snorted. "That's usually how magic works. It doesn't listen to our meager lives and schedules."

Unable to sit still a moment longer, Kersen stood. "Don't go, Donovan. Let your partner handle things, as you said he would. What can you possibly do that he cannot?"

"Well, he hates speaking in public, for one." Donovan began dialing. "Plus, he doesn't have all the contacts that I have. We're going to start a bloody Change.org campaign. Let the Aceh governor's office be inundated by emails from angry Americans. I'd pay to watch that."

He was obviously agitated, but that was to be expected. Kersen watched as Donovan paced, trying to detect any signs of a pending shift, but for now, he seemed to be in control. Cautiously, Kersen glanced at Gemi. This whole conversation was making him feel helpless. "Perhaps he's ready. Do you want to come with us? Or stay here and rest?" A part of him wanted to know all about her time in captivity, what it had been like. Another part of him wanted to forget that it had ever happened.

"I'm staying home," Gemi said in a low voice, hunched over her eggs. She ate them like she hadn't eaten in days. "I don't want anything to do with this."

A twinge of guilt wracked Kersen that he wouldn't be able to stay and keep her company. "Perhaps we should ask Mentauri. After all, it affects our entire clan."

Bitari opened her mouth, but Donovan was already speaking to Roark, his voice rising in volume as he spoke. "Hey, Roark. Yes, I'm fine. The tests are looking good, actually; I may be able to return to work in a few days. We'll see. Hey, mate. I know you're heading to the council meeting. I think I'm going to come as well. I'm convincing my doctors right now." He glanced over at Kersen and Bitari, with an expression that said he'd ignore whatever they had to say.

Kersen couldn't understand what Donovan's friend was saying, but he sounded pissed off.

"Yes, I'm fine. No, I'm not having those headaches any more. No, really, I'm fine. What do you mean see a 'real' doctor? Roark . . ." Donovan said, but Roark was apparently going off on some rant, because Donovan went so far as holding the phone at arm's length, scowling at it. He waited until there was silence before returning it to his ear. "You done? Now listen to me. I'll get plenty of rest later. At this time we need to put everything we have into influencing this vote. I need you to bring my laptop with you, my phone, and any contact lists we have for other organizations. I'll meet you at the council chamber."

Donovan glanced over at Kersen with a smug smile. He added, "By the way, I'm bringing that local fellow Kersen with me. Be nice to him." He winked at Kersen, then clicked off the phone.

Kersen waited for a hole to swallow him up, along with his flaming face.

Gemi giggled. "I like him."

Bitari gave a long-suffering sigh. "I suppose we're doing this. Dr. Donovan, if you expose our secret, I will personally hunt you down and drive you out of the clan, no matter what our aunt says. You had better keep control." She gathered up the dishes. "Let's go to Blangkejeren."

CHAPTER THIRTEEN

Aceh Province Council Chamber, Blangkejeren, Sumatra
May 17, 2013

Before they left Kersen's home, Donovan made a few more calls from Bitari's phone. He reminded Roark to put up footage from the tiger rescue on the center's website and Donovan's Tumblr account, ignoring Gemi's long-suffering expression. He then sent out a few well-placed emails, including a new Change.org petition. While he was doing that, Kersen ran over to Mentauri's house to inform her of the latest developments, both with the council hearing and Gemi's safe return. Kersen returned it with news that Mentauri would hold a village meeting the following evening. She expected Donovan and Kersen to attend.

There was a lot of traffic on the road, and by the time they reached the council chamber, all crammed together in Bitari's truck, Donovan was sweaty and his arms were itching again. He wasn't about to tell Kersen, however. Shifting while they were away from the jungle was simply out of the question. *Inner beast, you will obey me in this.* They managed to find one of the last parking spaces and exited the vehicle, hurrying over to the main building with the provincial council chamber.

When they reached the chamber, however, a security guard blocked their entrance. "The council is not taking further public comment today."

Hot prickles broke out on the back of Donovan's neck, and he reminded himself that he wasn't allowed to lose his temper. "Is the council taking a vote today?"

The guard shrugged. "I don't know. All I've heard is that they're full, and they won't be allowing speakers."

Donovan counted to ten. "You might want to tell the council members that there's a new social media campaign that is going to pull attention from all over the globe to our little province. I'm the one leading that campaign. They will want to listen to what I have to say before they vote on something that impacts the entire region."

The guard stared at Donovan as if he were speaking French. For a moment, Donovan had the sinking feeling that the fellow simply didn't care, and they were going to be stuck out here. Well, not if Donovan had anything to say about it. It had taken them three hours to drive here, and he wasn't leaving without doing something. Borrowing Bitari's phone again, Donovan called Roark to see if he had managed to get inside the council chamber, and wasn't surprised when the call went straight to voice mail. He left a message. Then he pulled up his Tumblr account and was pleased to see there were already over a thousand shares of the picture Roark had posted earlier. Smirking, he held the phone up to the guard to see. "We only posted that two hours ago."

Frowning, the guard leaned forward to check. After scrutinizing the webpage, he brought up his radio and conferred with someone in Indonesian, throwing glares as he spoke. Donovan was pretty sure he heard a curse word or two in there, along with "British meddler." *Yeah. That's me.* The guard listened to the reply, then with a huff, handed Donovan the clipboard where public speakers were required to sign in. "Hurry. They're already in session. You can enter when the current speaker finishes."

Perfect. Donovan smiled, filling out the line quickly, then returned Bitari's phone to her, wishing that he had his own back. Kersen was shifting his weight, and Bitari stood with her typical arms-crossed stance. "We'll be able to go inside in a minute." Donovan gave Kersen an encouraging look. "I'm fine. There's good stuff happening. They're all fools if they don't listen to this."

Kersen sighed, running a hand through his thick black hair. He seemed so lost, now that they were away from the jungle, and Donovan wondered how often he left the village. That brought other questions—where had he been schooled, and where did he work?

What were his hobbies? More importantly, could they find enough in common to have a relationship? The future was starting to open up for Donovan like a path in the woods, still dark and foggy, but he had glimpses of what it might be like with someone special in his life.

He took a step closer to Kersen, leading him away from the guard so they could speak privately. "So what do you want to do as a career, Kersen? I'm sitting here thinking and like a ponce I realized I barely know anything about you." At the shock on Kersen's face, Donovan added, "I don't even know the simple things. Like what's your favorite color?"

That got a laugh. Kersen rubbed his cheek with his knuckles, blushing. It was one of the traits Donovan found so endearing about him. "I like green. As far as work, most of my life has been about survival. My parents died defending us against a group of poachers one night when we were all in the forest in our tiger forms. That's one reason why Bitari was so upset with me concerning Gemi." He glanced over at the guard, who was still waiting at the door to the council chamber. "I might like to do what you do. Speak for animals. Protect the forests and land."

Donovan nodded, trying to think of how Kersen might be able to help at the center. "You know animal behavior. And you know the jungle well. You'd be good on one of our Tiger Patrols that I take out weekly, doing as I do, searching for poacher's traps and signs of animals. You could also scout for any illegal farming or clearing of the protected forest areas."

Kersen's eyes lit up. "I could do that. I'd love to do that."

This might work out after all. Although I'm not sure I want to be his boss. That wouldn't feel right. "I'll tell Roark to get to know you better. You two had a rocky beginning." He was about to say more when the guard cleared his throat loudly. Donovan turned to find the man signaling him.

He hurried over. The man opened the door, staring Donovan down like he was a bug he wished he could crush under his foot. "You may go in."

With a nod, Donovan headed into the council chamber, closely followed by Kersen and Bitari. It didn't take long to spot Roark, who was seated in the back row with a couple of empty seats beside him. Donovan quickly took a seat, but Kersen and Bitari hung back, standing. Donovan sent Kersen a come-hither look, but Kersen shook his head.

Fine then. Apparently he wasn't ready to be publicly associated with Donovan yet—either that, or he wasn't ready to face down Roark again so soon. Roark elbowed Donovan, handing him his tablet and phone. "Am I going to have to be quarantined for sitting next to you? And what bullshit are you going to feed me today to convince me you're really staying in a hospital? You look like a homeless man."

Donovan winced, glancing down at the shirt he'd been wearing since yesterday and Kersen's other pair of trousers. "Yeah, I should have asked you to bring me some clothing. I need to stop by my place later today. It was a rough night. But you're good, as long as I don't bleed on you."

Roark hissed under his breath. "I want an explanation. An honest one."

I'll have to see if they'd let me tell Roark. Otherwise he's never going to stop digging. "And you'll get one, I promise. After the vote is over," Donovan whispered, and then they fell silent because the council members were speaking, arguing the points from the last several days' testimonies.

Donovan's temper rose as the Aceh council members debated back and forth, talking about how the province needed the Chinese money for businesses and how the "responsible use of land resources" could better the common man. His skin was itching, which wasn't good, but he was helpless to go anywhere to calm himself until after they allowed another public comment. He glanced over his shoulder and saw that Kersen was watching him worriedly. Okay, so maybe this hadn't been such a hot idea after all. He was half man, half tiger now, and his wilder side wasn't having fun sitting around and listening to idiotic pandering.

Of course, that was the same opinion he'd had even before this crazy mutation. Only now when he wanted to kill something, he might actually do it.

Donovan's phone kept buzzing in his back pocket. He pulled it out, aware that he'd look like an arse, but he needed to see what was happening. His social media accounts were blowing up as people found the pictures of Gemi and retweeted or shared them to their contacts. Just as he returned his phone to his pocket, an official-looking man in a suit brushed past the door guards, walking quickly over to the council members' table. He bent to whisper in the chairman's ear, handing him a paper. Donovan fidgeted. What news could be important enough to interrupt a council session? Was it the fruits of his little idea?

Roark exchanged looks with him. "Here we go," he muttered under his breath.

The chairman read over the page, frowning. He glanced up at the audience and sought Donovan, locking eyes once he found him. Donovan grinned toothily, and a shiver went through him that had nothing to do with being cold. He could picture himself standing over the chairman, his fangs in the chairman's neck . . .

Uh-oh.

Donovan ran a tongue over his teeth, and sure enough, they seemed sharper, longer. *Cripes, not now! Not when we're so close.* He tried to think back to the morning with Kersen, how languid Kersen had been after coming in his mouth, how he had tasted.

The sense of urgency passed. His teeth stopped aching. Well, at least thinking about sex remained a way to stay human. Donovan took a deep breath, trying to hold on to that calmness.

The chairman cleared his throat and spoke into his microphone. "I believe we have a public comment from Dr. Donovan McGinnis, with the Ketambe Conservation and Research Center, regarding an international social-media campaign that apparently started up today. Dr. Donovan?"

Cold panic swept through Donovan. This was it. "Mr. Chairman," he replied, hoping his teeth didn't decide to grow again, that he could get through the next fifteen minutes or so without making a whole new meaning out of "fighting tooth and nail." He stood, doing his best to smooth his rumpled clothing. "I'm afraid I don't have visuals to show the council," he began, easing himself past Roark and heading for the podium, his voice carrying in the suddenly quiet chamber. "But if you're able to pull up the Jakarta news website, I think you'll see what I'm talking about."

He reached the podium, sweating under the scrutiny of the council. *Nothing different than the fifty other times I've spoken in public.*

Bloody hell, I've given enough lectures. There's nothing to be nervous about. Somehow he couldn't convince his racing heart of that. His skin itched. He needed to get this over quickly.

"I mentioned in my statement the other day that my facility recently rescued a wild tiger caught in a poacher's snare. I'm happy to say that last night we were able to return the tigress to the jungle—what jungle there is left, that is, in the Gunung Leuser National Forest. This tigress represents everything that we're trying to save by protesting against this proposed plan. If we protect the national forest, we protect all the animals that live within."

Donovan turned to face the council members. "Chairman, my colleagues and I have heard the arguments that land has value, and Aceh wants to make the most value off of its land. But consider this. Tourism is the fourth ranked source of income for Indonesia. The nationally protected forests here in Sumatra are one of the great attractions for those dollars. And yet you want to chip away at the forests. How much do you think you can do that before the species die out, and the tourists stop coming?"

Someone, perhaps one of the few supporters on the council, had managed to project an image onto the back wall of the council chamber. Donovan glanced up to find an image of Gemi in her tiger form in the cage, her paw bandaged up, along with a news article from Jakarta. "For those who can't read the English here, this article is saying that UNESCO is considering the removal of Gunung Leuser from their World Heritage list. This will be a huge blow to Aceh and tourism if it happens." There were comments lined down the page, some of them in all caps, furious at the Aceh government for not protecting their natural resources.

Then Donovan glanced at his bare arm. White hairs had spouted near his wrist. He quickly dropped his arms to his side. *I have to get out of here. Kersen, please help me!*

"I and my colleagues from around the world ask that the Aceh Province Council members observe carefully what impact their decision today could have on the Aceh Province. What kind of an economic, ecological, or even social and moral impact their decision may have, when considering whether to sell to foreign businesses one of the most important natural resources this province possesses.

Think well, council members. And remember that the whole world is watching." He gave a stiff bow and retreated, his skin on fire.

Roark stared at him with a furrowed brow, but Donovan couldn't spare him any words. He headed straight for the exit, shooting Kersen a look. He needn't have bothered. Kersen seemed ready to jump out of his skin, and before Donovan even reached him, he was making for the exit as well, clearing the way.

As they left the chamber, Kersen grabbed Donovan by the arm. "Men's bathroom," he said under his breath. Donovan was on board with that idea—at least he hoped they had the same one. It wasn't like they could snog each other in public, and as far as he knew, sexual intimacy was the only thing that would keep him human right now.

Kersen let go of him as they reached the facilities, standing aside for Donovan. Donovan rushed inside, uncaring of anyone watching. If he was lucky, they'd think that he had Traveler's Diarrhea or something. He'd claim as much, if the council called him back.

As soon as Kersen was inside, he quickly closed the door. The bathroom was empty except for Kersen and himself, thank God. At a nod from Kersen, Donovan followed him into a stall, locking the stall door behind him.

Before Donovan could say a word, Kersen's mouth was on him, kissing him fiercely. Kersen's lips were insistent, his hips grinding against Donovan's, pressing their erections against each other through the fabric. The itch had left, and the heat Donovan felt now was purely sexual.

Kersen's teeth nipped at Donovan's lower lip. Donovan nipped back, grasping Kersen's waist and then let his hands slide lower to cup arse, squeezing the firm muscles. Kersen moaned, thrusting up against him.

"Going to get us a bloody hotel," Donovan muttered, wishing they had more space than the tiny toilet stall. Government buildings were cleaner than most, but still. This was hardly ideal. He bit down on the side of Kersen's neck, sucking at his skin.

Gasping, Kersen nodded, his own hand working its way between them, rubbing against Donovan's trapped cock. "Brilliant idea. Only we have to wait. What if they call you back in there?"

"At the moment, I don't care. I want to fuck you so badly," Donovan whispered, pressing a finger in between the firm globes of Kersen's arse, rubbing down the crack. He froze at the sounds of voices outside the bathroom door, and reluctantly withdrew his hand. "We'd better return. Deal with the daft politicians."

Kersen was breathing hard, his hand hovering near himself, perhaps fighting the urge to finish off now. Slowly, Kersen took a step back. "You're right. Later." There was a note of pleading in his voice.

"Soon." Donovan nodded and let go of Kersen. Sighing, he exited the stall before either of them could lose control again, as he tried to think of numbers and figures to bring his raging wood down. The good news was that Donovan felt entirely human again, no danger of shifting. The bad news was he was hornier than hell.

Animal scat. Dead babies. To further distract himself, he set to washing his hands. A man walked in, proceeding to a urinal, and Donovan breathed an inner sigh of relief. Good thing they'd stopped. It was too dangerous to do anything here.

A moment later, Kersen flushed the toilet and emerged, washing his hands as well. They shared a glance.

Then Donovan and Kersen headed back to the council chamber to see if the gambit with the online campaign would sway the Aceh Council.

CHAPTER FOURTEEN

Aceh Province Council Chamber, Blangkejeren, Sumatra
May 17, 2013

onovan returned to the chamber, leaving Kersen standing at the back as he headed for Roark. Inside, Bitari threw him a look that was a mixture of unease and relief. *Probably happy I'm not running around the place on four legs.* He flashed her a smile, then took his seat next to Roark again, who eyed him dubiously and leaned over.

"Are you having sex with that man?" Roark whispered.

Leave it to his friend to cut right to the chase. Roark knew his proclivities, even if he didn't talk much of them. Donovan didn't want to embroil Roark too deeply with the whole shifter business—not unless he had to. "No. But I want to." There had been the blowjob, but he wasn't counting that.

Roark made an exasperated noise. "And give him this disease you supposedly have? Of all the times for you to get the horn for somebody. You're either lying about being ill, or you're endangering everyone." He sighed. "Still, that was a good speech. Not sure why you had to cut and run at the end of it. But they've been debating this question about losing the World Heritage listing since you left, because they know that has an economic impact. So that's hopeful."

Donovan listened in, and sure enough, the council members were arguing now, where before they had seemed ready to give a final vote. The audience appeared restless as well, which could be good or bad, depending on their side. He checked his phone again, and saw that the petition was continuing to be shared by more and more people.

Now the Aceh Council just needed to get a clue.

"We will be holding private discussion for the rest of the day, and tomorrow morning we will vote on this measure. We ask that the business parties who sponsored this action remain to answer questions. Everyone else, thank you for your time, and please depart the council room." The chairman finished his announcement, and the audience grumbled, gathering their things and rising to their feet. All except the representatives from the Chinese paper company and the palm oil companies.

Donovan swore under his breath. So the council was giving their private business partners one last chance to sweeten the pot.

He stood abruptly. There was nothing more he could do today; it was out of his hands. The worst thing now would be if he allowed his rage to endanger everyone by shifting, and if he thought about the council's case too much, that was what he would be. Enraged.

Roark stood up as well, blocking his path. His bushy eyebrows drew together in ire. "So? Spill it! This seems as good a time as any for you to explain everything to me."

Of all the hassles he didn't need right now—Donovan let out a frustrated sigh. "Roark. You're going to think I'm mental. And believe me, this is not the place for me to go mental." He furiously tried to think of some way out, some way past his friend's dogged determination. "What if you meet me tomorrow for lunch, at the research center? I should be able to clear things up by then." He waved a hand toward the floor of the council chamber. "It doesn't appear that they're going to allow anyone else to speak, so we can send one of the staff to take notes and update us about their decision."

Glowering, Roark's eyes bored into Donovan. He glanced over at Kersen and Bitari. "You've been feeding me a crock of shite, with that tale of yours about the tiger and the disease and all."

The surge of protectiveness that rose up for Kersen and his family startled Donovan. *I barely know him, and yet I'm ready to fight my best mate for him. Why?* He cleared his throat. "No, it's not shite. It's why I had to leave right after my speech." Even now he was feeling a bit warm, trapped inside his skin. Kersen had helped him before, but between the stress of the council and Roark's pestering, that inner beast was waking up again. "Feel my arm. Tell me there's not something off with me."

Roark opened his mouth to speak, but instead he reached over and took a hold of Donovan's forearm. Donovan hoped the white fur didn't reappear. Sweat was beginning to break out on his forehead.

Roark's eyes widened. "You're burning up! You should be in a hospital. A *real* hospital."

Donovan shook his head. "Can't do that. You need to trust me, mate. I've never let you down, have I? And I'm not going to. Give me until tomorrow, and then I'll show you something. I'll need you to prove to me that I can trust you as well."

He didn't give Roark a chance to argue with him, but hurried to join Kersen. Bitari waved impatiently and they followed her out of the chamber and to the truck. She climbed in, looking disgusted. "You two in back. I do not have to watch my brother being a woman to you, foreigner."

Kersen winced, and Donovan had to fight back another urge to attack Bitari and defend the young man. *These violent urges . . . I'm becoming a monster.* Keeping his mouth shut, Donovan sat in the back of the extended cab, and waited until Kersen was strapped in before taking his hand. He placed it on his crotch, wanting, needing that little bit of sexual tension to avoid the animal urges assailing him. "Bitari, thank you for driving. Can you drop us off at my place? We can take my motorcycle back to the village, with Kersen's directions."

Bitari sighed but nodded. "Yes, Doctor. Until you have control over your abilities, I think it would be best if you and I keep our distance." She glanced over her shoulder at her brother and started the truck. "You have this? You don't need my help?" In her eyes, Donovan caught a glimpse of the stress she must have been under, having to raise her siblings in a hostile environment. He felt for her, a bit anyways.

"I have this, sister. You don't need to worry about me." Kersen sounded calm and confident, and Donovan's heart swelled with pride. That taking ownership and carrying himself with dignity were two things he found very appealing about Kersen.

As the truck rolled out of the parking lot, Donovan met Kersen's amber eyes, letting himself fall into them for a moment. *I can relax now.* He'd done everything he could to sway the vote for the protection of the forest.

It was time to explore an area of his life that he'd neglected for a long time.

Donovan reached over, wanting, needing to know that Kersen was just as aroused as he was. When his palm encountered the firm bulge, Kersen's eyes fell closed, and his breath hitched as he pressed his lips together.

"Are you planning on telling your research center friend about us?" Leave it to Bitari to completely destroy the moment. Donovan bit his cheek, reminding himself that it was only a two-hour drive. He could restrain himself for that long, especially given the reward.

He withdrew his hand from Kersen's crotch. "Yes. He's been my best mate since we went to university together. We don't lie to each other. Also, Roark's a stubborn bastard. If I don't tell him, he'll find out anyways, somehow."

No sense in risking Bitari's temper, so he hastened to add, "You can trust him. He wants the protection of the tigers and the forest every bit as much as you all do. And he won't want to appear cracked, telling others about humans shifting into beasts. Once he understands everything, he'll be on our side."

She glared at him through the rearview mirror. "And how do I know that? How can you know that for certain? This is the same fellow who chased Kersen off, yes?"

Count to ten. Donovan took a deep breath and let it out. "Yes, because he thought he was protecting the tiger we'd rescued. And I know I can trust him because even now he's coming to me rather than calling the authorities. I've known him for years. Your secret will be safe with him." He grimaced. "Once he believes it, that is."

They drove for a few minutes before Bitari spoke again. "You had better be right about this. We have not survived thousands of years to be torn apart on lab tables. Our clan will do whatever is necessary to protect ourselves." Her tone hinted that he'd be best not to inquire further.

That didn't sound good. Luckily, he and Roark were both scientists. They knew how society worked, what the consequences of something like this getting out could be. Donovan couldn't imagine Roark ever consigning him to life as a lab rat. "I'm right. And I don't want to be on that lab table any more than you."

He let silence take over the rest of the trip.

Kersen's heart raced as his sister pulled the truck into the paved driveway of one of the nicest houses he'd ever seen, near the jungle at least. Donovan's place was like most houses in Sumatra, raised several feet off the earth. However, there the similarities ended. It wasn't a huge house, but it was new, and easily two or three times the size of Kersen's place. A pristine white staircase led up to the double front doors, which had a large brass knocker and a doorbell. Screens covered the windows to keep out the sun and some of the insects, and there were solar panels along the roof.

"Do you get all your power from those?" Kersen didn't know the first thing about how well they worked.

Donovan laughed as he climbed out of the truck. "Not all, unfortunately—it depends on the season. But there are days where I don't pull anything from the grid. I like living in a way that has a low impact on nature." He nodded to Bitari. "Like those of your village, actually."

She gave him one of her half smiles. Kersen grinned—the fact Donovan had received even that much from her said that she liked him. As Kersen exited the truck, she waved. "What time should I expect the two of you?"

"We'll call you," Donovan answered.

Kersen grinned at Bitari. "Yes. We will call." He took Donovan's hand, his posture a quiet declaration that Bitari had best let them be.

Bitari rolled her eyes. "Fine. I'll make extra rice and *gulai* for you to have later." She drove off, and Kersen couldn't help but wonder if she'd purposefully make the Indonesian curry too spicy for Donovan to enjoy.

"At last! I have never wanted to be alone so much in my life." Kersen groaned, leaning against Donovan as the dust settled. He noted that Donovan's house was off by itself, near empty farmland and the borders of the jungle. "So this is where you live?" Now that they were actually here, now that the last obstacle to their romantic pursuits, his older sister, had been removed, he didn't know what to do.

Thankfully, Donovan clearly did. He pulled Kersen up against him, grinding their hips together. "This is where I live," he confirmed, and then he was kissing Kersen, putting all the need and passion into it that neither of them had dared at the council building.

Their teeth clacked as Kersen kissed back with an almost frantic fervor. The scrape of Donovan's stubble along his jaw hurt, but in the most wonderful way. *I love kissing him. I've never been able to kiss a man like this.* Kersen's hands gripped Donovan's arse, feeling the muscles tighten. He sucked at Donovan's tongue, amazed at how good it felt, how right.

Before he could get a decent taste of him, however, Donovan drew back. "Inside. I want you in my bed." Grabbing Kersen's hand, he led him to the stairs.

"Yes." Kersen was dizzy with arousal, his cock threatening to tear through his trousers as he followed Donovan up to the front door. Donovan pulled his key out of the backpack his friend had given him, and let them both inside.

In normal circumstances, Kersen would have loved to get a tour of the place, but desire demanded that they hurry. He saw flashes of white walls and sparse furniture made of rare woods on the way to the bedroom. There were a few Indonesian touches as well, including a batik throw that was local and gorgeous photographs of tigers in the wild.

Kersen's heart caught in his throat—surely this was a sign that Brahma had intended for them to be together. Then they reached the bedroom, where a large bed in white cotton sheets stood, and Donovan was tearing at Kersen's clothing, pulling his shirt up over his head.

"I want to be inside you," Donovan groaned, his hands roaming over Kersen's narrow chest. His thumbs found Kersen's nipples and tweaked at them, squeezing.

Kersen moaned. It felt like his entire body was on fire. He'd dreamt of loving a man like this, but the only experience he'd had had been in secret bath houses, usually just quick blowjobs, or being bent over and taken with no preparation at all. He'd never imagined his nipples could be so sensitive.

"Yes," Kersen said, tugging at Donovan's shirt. They needed out of their clothing. He craved the feel of Donovan's skin against his.

Donovan helped him, stopping his caresses long enough to pull the shirt up over his head and to yank down the ill-fitting trousers. His cock sprang free, already hard and glistening with pre-come. Kersen tugged off the rest of his clothing as well, and then couldn't resist taking hold of Donovan's length, giving him a pull. Granted, he hadn't seen many cocks, but Kersen was sure that Donovan was the largest man he'd been with before.

"God, that feels wonderful." Donovan pulled Kersen closer. "Come on. Almost there. I swear I'm going to get a good look at every inch of you."

Kersen allowed Donovan to steer him toward the bed, letting himself fall onto it when the mattress hit the back of his knees. The sheets were wonderfully soft—softer than anything he'd ever felt before. Fitting the lush surroundings, Donovan looked like some sort of lustful demon, naked with his scruffy beard and piercing blue eyes. Kersen drank in the sight of him, noting several small scars, not including the most recent ones given to him by Gemi. Every mark made Donovan all the more attractive. He wasn't some soft city dweller. He was rough and accustomed to the land, like Kersen.

Eyeing him with a similar focus, Donovan grinned. "You're perfect. Absolutely perfect." He crawled onto the bed and between Kersen's legs, his head just above Kersen's stiff member. Kersen rose up on his elbows, wanting to see everything, to participate as much as possible. He sighed as Donovan ran a hand up his leg to fondle his balls, lightly massaging them, and hot desire swept through him.

"Let me see you too," Kersen said, even as he widened his legs further, allowing Donovan better access. He bit his lip when the pad of Donovan's finger brushed over his pucker. Too long since he'd had sex with anyone.

"You will." Donovan's voice was rough with need. He worked his way up Kersen's body, and yes, Kersen did get to see more, much more. Eagerly, he touched the soft curly hairs on Donovan's chest, so different from his own.

With a sigh, Kersen wrapped his arms around Donovan, pulling the man on top of himself to feel skin to skin, to feel the weight of him. He arched up, grinding against him, their cocks rubbing together obscenely. "Yes. Oh gods, forgive me. I want you so badly."

Donovan kissed him again, and this time Kersen just let him do as he liked, sucking on the sweet taste of him, letting their bodies writhe. His only fear now was that he'd come before they had a chance to do anything. Kersen grasped Donovan's length, stroking him, letting him know that while all this was wonderful, what he really needed was that cock inside him. Groaning, Donovan thrust into the tight circle of Kersen's fist, and not long after, he broke off the kiss and rose up to his knees. "Cripes—let me . . . let me find a condom."

He stretched toward a small night table, pulled the drawer, and rummaged through the contents. Meanwhile Kersen continued to explore Donovan's body, fondling large balls lightly dusted with hair—even Donovan's legs were hairier than his. Kersen loved the contrasts between them. On an impulse, he slid down to where he could get his mouth on that cock, to taste some of the nectar threatening to spill.

Donovan groaned again, as if in pain. "I want *inside* you—shite, but that feels good." His hips shifted wantonly even as he poured some lube over his fingers. Kersen took his cock deep down his throat, sucking hard. After another moment, he came up panting, and looked at Donovan. "Later, then. After you've fucked me?"

"Absolutely." Donovan pointed at the center of the bed. "On your back. I want to see your face."

Kersen complied, keeping his knees bent and spread apart. Donovan slid his fingers down the crack of Kersen's arse, rubbing lube over his entrance, sending little tingles up him.

"Has it been a long time for you? It has for me," Donovan confessed, as he slid the first finger inside, coating the passageway with lube. "You're tight."

Breathe out. Relax. "It— Yes. It's been a very long time." No need to go into the fact that he'd never done it this way, with this much attention to his comfort. Even though it was tight, his nerves sang at the intrusion, especially when Donovan's finger brushed over his spot. "Ohh." His legs trembled and his head fell back.

"That's it. You're doing great." Donovan added more lube and another finger, scissoring them. The stretch burned, but Kersen didn't mind.

"More," Kersen pleaded. "You need to hurry."

"I agree. But I'm not an arse. I don't want to hurt you," Donovan murmured, sliding his fingers in and out, until Kersen's nerves were screaming at him. It was so good, he didn't want Donovan to stop, but he needed more than just fingers. He breathed a sigh of relief when Donovan pulled his fingers out and rolled on the condom.

"You won't hurt me." Kersen tugged Donovan closer, then boldly took hold of the man's cock, positioning it, pushing himself against the blunt head. That didn't work, so he lay back, trying to relax.

"Fuck, but you're tight." Donovan hitched up one of Kersen's legs, hooking his ankle over a shoulder, as he pressed forward. Whether because of Kersen's excitement or nervousness, his body didn't seem to want to let Donovan in. "Close your eyes and breathe. There's no rush here." Donovan's voice was calm, gentle. He began stroking Kersen's cock again, and it all felt so good, between that and Donovan's member rubbing against his hole, seeking entry.

This time when Donovan thrust forward, the head breached the ring of muscle, and Kersen hissed at the burn and stretch.

"That's it," Donovan whispered. His thumb made little circles around the slit of Kersen's cock, and he played with the foreskin, moving it back and forth. Kersen saw stars as Donovan's cock sank in deeper, brushing over his prostate.

"Oh gods." Kersen grabbed Donovan's hips. With one more thrust, Donovan sank in all the way. Kersen had never taken someone so big before. Everything stretched to the point of pain, and yet it felt so good at the same time. He clutched at Donovan's arm. "Hold on for a moment. Let me adjust to you." If he sounded breathless, he had good reason.

"Right . . . yes . . ." Donovan groaned. He bowed his head, his forehead brushing against Kersen's cheek. "Not hurting you?" He shifted, and that was actually a good thing, because it eased the burn.

"I'm brilliant. You can move. Slowly, please, at first," Kersen panted, moving his hands to Donovan's back to feel the play of muscles as Donovan withdrew a little, then sank home again. It felt perfect, and Kersen sighed, taken away by the sensation. Quick fucks were nothing like this.

"That's it." Donovan did it again, withdrawing halfway, then gently thrusting in. "Let me add a bit more lube—you'll like it. Trust me." He pulled almost all the way out, drizzling lube—presumably along his shaft, on the rubber. This time when he thrust in, there was no resistance, only pleasure that seemed to resonate throughout Kersen's body. "How's that?"

"Don't stop!" *It's bliss, that's what it is.* Kersen's cock was trapped between them, aching for attention, so he slid one hand down to stroke himself, in time with Donovan's thrusts.

Donovan grunted and increased his pace, his thighs slapping against Kersen's arse, a look of intense concentration on his face. Even though the sensations were nearly overwhelming, Kersen indulged in watching him, how the tendons bulged in Donovan's arms, how his skin became red around his face and neck. Leaning up, he kissed Donovan, shivering in delight at the scruff of beard scratching his chin. They were so different from one another, and yet so perfect.

Pleasure began to boil inside him from the rub of Donovan's cock over his prostate, and from his own hand on his cock. "Close." Kersen forced himself to look Donovan in the eyes, wanting, needing the connection, even though it would be so easy to close his eyes and get carried away in bliss.

"Go ahead," Donovan urged him. He shifted a little to put all his weight on one arm, and added his other hand to Kersen's, stroking Kersen's cock. "Make as much noise as you like. It's just us."

That was all the encouragement that Kersen needed, and he gave a shout as the pleasure peaked. The first shot of come hit Donovan's stomach; the second spilled over both their hands, coating them. The orgasm went on and on, the most powerful Kersen had ever had. Though he'd emptied his balls, his cock stayed hard, thanks to the continued relentless fucking.

"Oh God. I'm so close," Donovan groaned, letting go of Kersen to use both his arms for leverage. He started fucking Kersen even harder, and Kersen reached down to fondle the base of Donovan's cock as it plunged into him over and over, then massaged Donovan's balls.

"Fuck!" Donovan swore, and then he was coming, thrusting in deep. Kersen moaned, feeling the pulses both through his hand on Donovan's sack, and inside him as well. His own cock gave a twitch, but it was too soon after the first orgasm. Donovan's face was red, the veins standing out on his throat. His eyes had closed, but that didn't matter. Kersen hadn't gotten to see another man climax before, not like this, face-to-face.

It was beautiful.

Donovan collapsed on top of Kersen, and even that was good, the come-slicked muscles of Donovan's lower abs sliding against Kersen's unflagging erection. Kersen wrapped both arms around him, and relaxed as Donovan held him in return. If every day could be like this, he'd be the happiest man alive.

I want to be with him. Brahma help me. I want to be with him forever.

CHAPTER FIFTEEN

Donovan's House, Ketambe, Sumatra
May 17, 2013

Donovan was content. It was an odd thing for him; typically when he'd felt content, it was after triumphantly saving an animal he'd been sure was going to die, or after a victory in protecting national parks. He breathed in the scent of Kersen's skin, the aroma of their lovemaking. Kersen was still hard, which was probably only natural. Kersen was nineteen, after all.

That had been some mind-blowing sex.

They both needed a shower, which gave Donovan an idea. He licked a circle around one of Kersen's brown nipples, sucking on the hard bud. Most of his weight was still on him. "You said you've had how many lovers?"

Kersen groaned, scratching at Donovan's back. That was nice too. "I don't know. Do quick encounters at the bath house count?"

"No." A flash of guilt went through Donavan. *I didn't realize he was so inexperienced. Bit late now.* "Let me ask a different question. How many boyfriends have you dated for at least a month?" He turned to the other nipple, determined to give it just as much attention.

"Oh," Kersen moaned, thrusting up against Donovan, his erection trapped between them. Donovan was still inside him, although any further movement now and he would slip out. It would be a bit before he was ready to go again. Kersen nuzzled him. "You're going to keep torturing me, aren't you? None. It was too risky to have anyone human, and I didn't know any gay *siluman harimau* my age."

There was a deep loneliness and ache to his answer. Donovan paused to look Kersen in the eyes. The brash, confident young man he'd met in the council chamber had been replaced by someone much more vulnerable.

Donovan kissed him, taking the time to tell Kersen without words that he cared. When the kiss ended, Donovan smiled. "Guess you'll have to get used to not being alone." He finally pulled out. "Come take a shower with me."

"Brilliant." Kersen sat up, wincing, and then grinned. "That was amazing. In case you couldn't tell by my noises." A blush was faintly discernable on his face as he got up from the bed.

"Oh, and I didn't enjoy myself at all," Donovan quipped, chuckling. He stood as well, then drew lazy circles on Kersen's skin with his fingertip. "You're still welcome to come live here, by the way. I can't imagine how you've survived living all this time with your two sisters."

Kersen inspected a bite mark on his chest, smirking. "It hasn't been easy. But I love them both, with all my heart. Bitari kept the household running, and kept us together after our parents died."

That sobered Donovan up. He'd pushed that fact to the back of his mind, and yet it had obviously affected Kersen deeply. "I know you told me some things earlier, but can you tell me more about that?"

Kersen scooted a little closer to Donovan, possibly unconsciously. "It was a trip into the jungle that went horribly wrong." He scratched at his neck in an almost feline fashion. "It wasn't like Gemi and the tiger snare. The poachers we encountered were hunting using high-powered rifles. Some tiger—a real one, not a shifter—had been killing livestock in Ketambe. The villagers hired the poachers to kill it, and then offered the poachers the tiger to sell to the Chinese medicine market." Rage flashed in Kersen's eyes. "I found this all out later, after my parents were dead. The poachers never were caught."

A lump caught in Donovan's throat. "That's . . ." Words couldn't encompass the horror. "There wasn't a way to charge the men for murder, I take it?"

Kersen shook his head. "We stay in whatever form we are when we die. It's not like the old werewolf movies where a shifter turns back to human." He took a deep breath. "Anyways, so what happened was the poachers found the five of us—two adult tigers, one male, one female, and three adolescents. Bitari was sixteen, I believe. I was fourteen. Gemi was only twelve."

"Christ," Donovan swore under his breath. He could only imagine. That received a shrug. "So the poachers found us, and they wanted us, the children. My parents attacked them. They were both shot and died, screaming in our heads for us to run back home."

Donovan winced, almost hearing the frantic shouts. "You must have been so scared."

"Actually I was furious. I didn't even have a chance to be frightened. Not until much later, when there was no food in the house and the rest of the village was too busy to teach us all that we needed to know to survive."

But there was one other thing to consider. "Your aunt helped the three of you, I hope?"

Kersen nodded. "Yes. My aunt Mentauri helped a lot. But it was still hard, and it was scary, the three of us in our home, when the monsoons came and we couldn't go outside for days at a time. We had to learn a lot of things very quickly. Like how to plan ahead." Kersen's hand moved down Donovan's back, over his arse, then back up again.

Kersen smiled. "That's all the past. I'm much more interested in the future. You said something about a shower?" He rubbed up against Donovan eagerly.

Donovan laughed. "Absolutely. Come with me. I'll keep you distracted while the water heats up."

Together they went to the bathroom. Donovan got the shower running, and then wrapped his arms around Kersen, kissing him. The kisses were longer and slower this time. With a sigh, Donovan slid a hand down to fondle Kersen's cock and balls as they sucked on each other's tongues. Kersen moaned.

As soon as the water was warm enough, Donovan guided Kersen into the shower. It was a tight fit for the two of them, but that was fine; he took the opportunity to stay pressed against Kersen, letting the spray wash over them. He lathered up his hands and then began washing Kersen's chest and back, ignoring his cock.

"I thought you were going to—" Kersen began plaintively.

"Shh—soon enough." Donovan raised Kersen's arms, one at a time, lathering his armpits and his arms as well. "Enjoy this for the moment."

He turned Kersen around, and gently washed his backside, allowing himself only a brief tug at Kersen's balls before washing his legs. It was awkward to go lower, so he allowed Kersen to wash his own calves and feet, loving the way their slippery bodies rubbed against each other. He was half-hard, not that he had any plans for himself.

As Kersen rinsed, Donovan started to maneuver himself down, eager to get Kersen into his mouth again, but a hand stopped him. "Let me wash you first. I've never done this before." Kersen grinned. "It's so simple. I like it."

Donovan chuckled and nodded. "Be my guest." He held still as Kersen took the soap and washcloth, sudsing up before he worked on Donovan's chest. Kersen's hands were sure and strong. He might be inexperienced, but he was hardly shy. Donovan sighed as Kersen washed his arms and back, arching into the touches. *Why didn't I allow myself something like this before?*

"I could get used to this," Donovan said, as Kersen ran the washcloth over his arse.

"This is a nice shower—but I wish it was even bigger," Kersen said, rubbing between Donovan's arse cheeks. Donovan couldn't suppress a gasp when the young man pressed a finger to his pucker. Would he want to switch later? Not something Donovan generally agreed to, but for Kersen? Maybe.

Kersen seemed to realize what he was doing and pulled his finger away. "Sorry. I was curious."

Grabbing his wrist, Donovan encouraged Kersen to return to his explorations. "Don't be sorry. I haven't let anyone top in a long time, but that doesn't mean never." He leaned in closer, rubbing Kersen's bottom. The fellow was probably sore. "Have you ever been rimmed?"

Kersen gave him a blank stare. "Have I what?"

Oh that was too good to be true. Donovan grinned as he carefully went to his knees, holding on to Kersen for support. "You'll see. Turn off the water. No need to waste it." It was tropically warm outside, and air drying would feel pleasant.

As Kersen turned off the water, Donovan licked the droplets off of Kersen's cock, starting from the base and working his way down to the head. He sucked and licked as if each drop was honey, and was rewarded with a low groan. Kersen's erection had started to flag, but he was soon rock-hard, sheathed in silken skin. Trailing his tongue over the hood, Donovan paused, teasing him. Then he took the head into his mouth, sucking with enthusiasm.

"Oh gods!" Kersen cried, steadying himself with one hand on the shower wall.

Donovan chuckled, which only made Kersen moan louder. Then Donovan took Kersen deep, giving him no mercy.

"Don't stop, please." Kersen's voice sounded strained.

But Donovan wasn't going to be done with him so easily. He came off Kersen's cock, licking his lips. "Turn around. I'm going to show you rimming first, before you come."

Kersen gave him a look that said he was daft, but he obeyed, placing both hands on the tiled wall in front of him. Donovan parted Kersen's arse cheeks a little, before leaning in close. He nibbled on the perfect round globes of Kersen's arse, loving how firm and muscled the young man was.

"What are you— Oh that feels good," Kersen stuttered, shifting his footing as Donovan nibbled in closer, licking the perineal area before moving up to Kersen's pucker. He gave it a firm licking and Kersen shuddered. "Oh! That—that—"

"That's rimming," Donovan finished for him, gleefully. Then he pushed his tongue in as deep as he could, tasting Kersen's flavor.

Kersen leaned forward, giving Donovan more access. "That's so . . ." he began, but his words dissolved into sighs.

Once Donovan was certain he'd driven Kersen nearly mad with his licking, he stopped. "Face me again. And you can put the water on if you like." Kersen had begun to shiver, though Donovan wasn't sure if it was temperature or sensation causing it.

Pupils blown and expression slack, Kersen turned and braced his hands behind him on the tile wall. "I can come this time, right? Please?"

Donovan grinned, shifting his knees to give them relief. "Yes. Then we'll sleep. It's been a long day." He reached one hand around to play with Kersen's balls as he slowly began to suck cock, working it deep into his throat. It probably wouldn't take long; Kersen's pre-come tasted strong.

"Mm-hmm." Kersen sighed, cupping Donovan's head with one hand. The touch was gentle, almost reverent. Donovan focused all his being on giving Kersen the best fucking blowjob of his life, working his tongue, his throat muscles. He gagged a few times as Kersen's cock hit the back of his throat, but that was part of the fun, wasn't it?

"Close." Kersen's voice was ragged, and he barely seemed able to stand.

Donovan didn't let up. Instead, he concentrated on the most sensitive areas around the foreskin and head, using his hand to stroke off Kersen, a hard, fast pace that he knew would send the man over the edge. Sure enough, Kersen cried out; his gentle hold of Donovan's hair became a tight fistful. Donovan drank down every last drop, making sure to thoroughly tongue-clean Kersen's cock afterward. Then with a groan, he stood up, rubbing his sore knees. Kersen grasped his arm, leaning against him. He looked utterly shattered, which was exactly what Donovan had been aiming for.

"Fuck." Kersen groaned, swaying. "Just . . . fuck." He laughed, breathing hard and maintaining a hand on the shower wall.

"Give me a few seconds to rinse off. Then we'll dry off and curl up in bed. I'm knackered," Donovan said, turning the water back on.

The water was a bit cold at first, but it soon warmed up. They finished washing, and then Donovan helped Kersen towel dry, before quickly drying himself as well. He hadn't enjoyed being with someone so much in a long time. Kersen wasn't just hot; with his mixture of exuberance and inexperience, he was adorable.

They sank into the bed in a tangle of limbs. Donovan fought to pull down the sheets even as Kersen tried to burrow against him. Soon they were spooning, with Kersen's head resting on Donovan's arm.

"This is nice," Kersen said, yawning.

It was better than nice. It was something that Donovan had needed for years. He just hadn't known it. "Sleep well, Kersen." A thought came to him. "What happens if I change in the middle of the night? Can that happen?"

Kersen pulled Donovan's arm a little tighter around him. "It is unlikely. You should start to gain more control over your form soon. If it does happen, you may tear the sheets a bit. I am not afraid."

The sheets were Egyptian cotton and rather expensive, so Donovan hoped not. But since Kersen wasn't worried about him shifting while asleep, he reckoned he shouldn't be either. "Night, then."

Closing his eyes, Donovan allowed himself to settle against this warm and caring young man. He couldn't help thinking about Mentauri, the certainty on her face when she'd pointed to Kersen and him. *Mates. Maybe that's not such a scary idea after all.*

He wanted that. He really did.

CHAPTER SIXTEEN

Donovan's House, Ketambe, Sumatra
May 18, 2013

A ringing phone woke Kersen, who found himself facing Donovan, their limbs entwined, Donovan's soft beard brushing against Kersen's forehead as he snored softly. Kersen couldn't help smiling. All his life, he'd wanted a relationship like this. *The village elders won't make me choose between my mate and my family, will they? I've been a good member of the clan. Never brought any trouble.* Yet the elders might see Donovan as trouble. Worse, there would be the other dominant males, who would want to see where the new tiger ranked. *I'll need to prepare him.* Later, he'd take Donovan back into the forest and have him try to initiate a shape change. For now, all he wanted to do was lie here like this and enjoy the feel of the man against him.

The phone continued ringing.

"Fucking hell, this better be important." Donovan groaned. He nearly squashed Kersen as he reached for the phone. "Sorry." Then he answered in a gruff voice. "McGinnis here."

Untangling himself from the sheets, Kersen sat up. Donovan was frowning, and Kersen thought he recognized the voice on the other end—Roark.

Donovan sat up abruptly. "You're where? What are you doing there?" He looked at Kersen in alarm and mouthed, *Your house.*

Kersen blinked. His house? But Roark didn't know where he lived. Nobody even knew that their village existed, unless they were looking at satellite pictures.

"Fucking . . . Okay. *Okay*. Roark . . . I said I'd explain everything. I'll be there as soon as I can. I'm home right now."

Roark said something in a thick accent, and Donovan winced. He closed the call and sighed. "I forgot that we not only ear-tagged your sister; we microchipped her as well, with a tracker we can access from our center. Roark decided to follow it to find me, and now he's wondering why the hell the tiger we rescued is in the middle of an unmarked human village." He rubbed his forehead. "We have to get to your house immediately. He's arguing with Bitari."

Terror swept through Kersen. He tore off the sheets, fumbling to find his clothing. "Shit! If Bitari doesn't tear him apart, some of the village dominant males might. This will ruin your introduction to the clan." He pulled on his shirt. "Hurry. They might kill your friend to keep our secret."

"I'm moving." Donovan crossed the room to a tall chest of drawers. Kersen was already dressed and tying his sandals as Donovan finished throwing on his clothes. Neither of them bothered with their hair.

Using Donovan's phone, Kersen called Bitari, but she didn't answer. "Isn't your car still at the research center?" he asked Donovan, handing him the phone back.

"I have a motorcycle. It saves on gas when I don't need the Jeep. Come on."

They hurried out of the house and over to Donovan's garage. The bike was a Honda Magna, and Kersen tried not to think about how he'd never ridden before as he climbed on, fumbling with the spare helmet. Donovan put on his own helmet and started the engine, revving it a few times.

"Hold on to me, all right? Don't forget to lean as I lean on the turns. We'll be fine." As Donovan began rolling forward, Kersen clutched him, his heart pounding madly.

The feel of Donovan's back against his chest helped to steady his nerves. He'd need his calm—Bitari could be in full frenzy by now. "Drive fast. But please, be careful. It won't do anyone good if we crash on the way there." Kersen spoke loudly, in the hopes that Donovan could hear him with his helmet.

"No worries. I wouldn't want to damage that gorgeous body of yours," Donovan quipped.

Kersen held on for dear life as they headed out.

It wasn't a long drive, thankfully, but it was a bumpy one, with many of the roads barely paved or simply dirt tracks. Kersen tugged on Donovan's shoulders to indicate when he should turn left or right. When he finally saw the unmarked signpost one mile from his village, he started to relax. Maybe they'd make it in time. Maybe Bitari or his aunt was handling things, keeping everyone from a violent solution.

Then he spotted the crowd in front of his house, including several men standing near the front, who were gesturing wildly and pushing back the other spectators. The hairs on the back of his neck rose with all that dominant energy. "Oh no." *And I'm heading right into that storm with a dominant male who isn't part of the clan.*

They rode up to the side of the house, and Donovan killed the engine. He pulled off his helmet as some of the villagers looked at them in curiosity.

Kersen hurried to remove his as well. "It is I," he announced loudly in Indonesian, waving. He couldn't see who was at the center of the crowd, but it was a good bet that Donovan's friend was in there somewhere. "We need to speak with the stranger. I have a new mate." He squeezed Donovan's arm by way of introduction. No time to decide if they really were going to stay together or not. If the others thought he'd willingly chosen Donovan, things might go better for everyone involved.

One of his neighbors, Anwar, turned, obviously sizing Donovan up. "A foreigner? How can this be?" Two women beside him were eyeing Donovan also, but skeptically.

Donovan leaned toward Kersen. "My Indonesian isn't so good, but I understood that. Are they going to have a problem with me?"

Kersen nodded quickly. To Anwar, he replied, "He is not like other foreigners. He understands the forest. Please let us through. We need to speak to his friend."

Anwar and those nearest to him stepped aside, and Kersen grabbed Donovan's hand to pull him forward.

Roark's loud voice cut through the air. "Donovan! Thank God you're all right! These people are insane!"

The rest of the crowd parted enough to let Kersen and Donovan through. As Kersen had feared, his sister and Mentauri were standing toe to toe with Roark, and all three of them appeared angry. At least no one had shifted yet. Kersen patted Donovan on the back. "Explain to him what he needs to know. I'll take care of my family."

"Happy to," Donovan said, then strode up to Roark. They spoke quietly in English, too fast for Kersen to understand. That was probably just as well. If he couldn't understand them, then maybe the rest of the village wouldn't know what secrets Donovan was divulging to his partner.

Kersen faced his older sister, who was standing next to his aunt. "Tell me what happened."

She glared at him and took a deep breath. Kersen braced himself. "So this *foreigner* sped into town this morning, scared all the livestock and the children, then began yelling about a hospital and a tiger with a disease. He kept asking about Dr. Donovan. I told him the doctor was with you, and that I didn't know anything about a sick tiger. He said he had a tracker on her, and she was inside our house! Kersen, this is what I feared. We were about to knock him unconscious and tie him up. The clan wants to discuss what to do with him."

Mentauri didn't look happy either. "You said your mate could keep a secret. That he wouldn't endanger us. This is not good."

"You're a traitor! You know we don't tell strangers," a woman behind Kersen exclaimed.

"That's right," another said.

"Who else knows?" a third villager, this one male, asked.

Kersen raised his hands to wave them off. "Donovan—Dr. Donovan—said that he'd forgotten that they'd implanted the tiger they rescued with a microchip, one that included a tracking device. We can fix this. Please, let Donovan talk to his partner. They work for the Ketambe Conservation and Research Center to keep the forest and the tigers safe. We have to trust them."

He couldn't help hearing one of the village dominants, Sabtu, muttering, "We'd be better off killing them both."

Kersen threw the man a scorching look. "No, we wouldn't." It was good they were all speaking in their local dialect. He doubted either Donovan or Roark would understand them with their knowledge of

Indonesian. "We would attract even more attention from the police. These are both well-known men. We must work with them, not against them."

Bitari grabbed Kersen's arm. "You are saying Gemi has a *microchip*? Where? Can they get it out?"

Yes, there was still that problem. "I will ask Donovan." Kersen glanced over to see how Donovan was doing with Roark. Roark appeared angry, but seemed to have settled down somewhat.

Turning to the crowd, Kersen cleared his throat and spoke in a loud voice. "Everyone, please listen! My sister was nearly killed by a poacher's snare, and these two men rescued her. Please, let us talk in private. We will make sure everyone is safe." He sighed. "Dr. Donovan McGinnis—the tall one—he is one of us now. He is with me. Please, for my sake, do not reject him."

As he waited for his fellow shifters to react, Kersen pressed a hand to his chest, feeling his heart pound. He'd never stood up to anyone in the village before. What had he been thinking, trying to convince Donovan to stay with him? The *suka siluman harimau* had always been a reclusive people, for good reason. Doctors and scientists could not be trusted. His people had seen how the world treated what they would perceive as a disease—fear and panic like with the Ebola outbreak in Africa and the swine flu in China, putting people in quarantines and studying them like lab rats. Then there were all the failed attempts at saving the rainforests of the world. Humans destroyed everything that they did not understand.

Kersen jumped as Mentauri patted his cheek. She stared at him measuringly. "You still believe he will protect our secrets? And his friend too? What assurance can you give us that this will not spread further?"

His heart stuttered. *I hope Roark hasn't told any more of his staff.* "Donovan's friend was going to find out sooner or later—they are close. Yet both have had every opportunity to go to the police or the news, and yet they haven't. We can trust them both."

The villagers around them grew quiet, obviously thinking that over. Mentauri gave him an encouraging nod and a smile. "You speak well, nephew. I have long said our tribe needs new blood, and your Donovan is a fine specimen." To the others, she said, "Consider his words—just look at that fresh male! Look how tall, how strong he is! I'd wager he makes a great tiger. He is a gift of strength we have needed. I dare anyone to say otherwise."

She stood with her hands on her hips, glaring at Anwar and Sabtu.

As the villagers paused to consider things, Kersen walked over to Donovan to see how his conversation with Roark was going. For now, the villagers seemed to be calming down, and that was a good thing. As long as they were talking and not fighting, there was hope.

"Roark, it's not as bad as all that," Donovan said, as his arms began to itch again. He was getting better at holding down the anger, the urge to shift, but he still wanted to throttle Roark. Of all the rotten timing!

Roark glanced at where Kersen was speaking to the crowd of about twenty irate villagers. "Not that bad? Do you see those blokes over there? I think they were talking about killing me!" He was sweating in the morning heat, beads dotting his upper lip and forehead. Donovan felt a bit warm as well, but that could be the tiger inside wanting to come out. It didn't help that he was ravenous.

"I told you that I'd speak with you. Why did you have to go looking for the tigress? I told you she had a rare disease, and she does. Only she's not precisely a tiger. She's like a werewolf, except that she becomes a tiger instead of a wolf. The pathogen that causes the shifting is carried by the host through blood and bodily fluids and can be transmitted through a bite or open wound."

Roark growled. "Shape changing. From man to beast. You do know that's scientifically impossible, don't you?"

This was too familiar. Donovan rubbed his forehead. "I do. And yet I woke up the other morning in the middle of the jungle, naked, with a dead pig near me that had been killed by a tiger. Explain that one to me. Not to mention that I saw our tigress transform into Gemi, Kersen's younger sister."

"How do you know that wasn't some hallucination, brought on by your fever? Or perhaps your friend there drugged you. I told you that you should see a *real* doctor in a real hospital. I'm sorry, mate, but

I can't simply take your word on this." Roark stepped closer, peering into Donovan's eyes, brows furrowed. Donovan glared at him.

"Fine. I'd like to see how you explain your microchip being magically implanted inside a human woman. I don't think Kersen or anyone else here could pull off such a trick."

Donovan paused, and Roark paced, pulling at his beard. He turned suddenly. "Take me to this girl, Gemi. Let me scan her. If I see that our chip is implanted inside her, then that might convince me." He squinted, looking Donovan over. "Or if I see you change in front of my eyes, that'd probably do it as well. But then what? You're going to live inside this tiny village for the rest of your life? Please don't tell me I have to avoid you during full moons." He snorted. "That'd be daft."

Donovan rolled his eyes. "No. It doesn't work like that. Granted, I'm not exactly sure how it works. At the moment, I change form when I lose my temper or become agitated."

"You mean like the bloody Hulk? Brilliant." He still didn't sound convinced.

It won't look good if I strangle him right now. It also wouldn't be good if Donovan's rising temper caused a transformation. "I suppose so. I couldn't remember anything the first time. I got a few snatches of images the second time. Kersen says that each shift, I'll gain more control and remember more, until I'm fully cognizant in both forms. I do know I became a tiger in front of Kersen and his sisters, and I didn't hurt any of them, so that's promising. But that's why I'm quarantined. Until I can get control over this, I'm a danger to others."

"And it's transmissible via blood and bodily fluids. You weren't lying about that?" Roark had stopped pacing and he'd lowered his volume, which meant things were getting through. Donovan loved him like a brother, but God could the man be a stubborn arse at times.

"That's right. No one else has shown signs, have they? Based on how quickly it affected me, I'm hoping I'm the only victim of this strange pathogen. It's not curable."

Roark sighed. "Half of me wants to drag you off to some reputable laboratory and test out this entire thing. For now, I'll settle on inspecting my microchip. Let me see this sister of your friend— your boyfriend? I heard him saying something about you being his mate, and I don't think he meant that in the platonic sense." Roark glanced over at where Mentauri was speaking loudly and pointing at Donovan. Donovan caught enough of the Indonesian to know that she was extolling his virtues in height and strength. *Just brilliant.* A blush crept up his cheeks.

"Did she say what I think she said? Fresh blood? As in . . ." Roark grimaced.

Donovan shrugged. "Apparently they have the same problem as our forest population of Sumatran tigers. Their breeding pool is too small."

Kersen was heading over, but Roark ignored him. "So what, you're supposed to be a breeding stud?"

"Something like that." Donovan didn't want to go into it. If this was what it took to woo the village into accepting him, then so be it. He could bed a woman or two, just as long as he didn't have to do that on a regular basis.

"Are things settled between you?" Kersen asked, as Mentauri continued to speak, saying who-knew-what to the villagers. Donovan wondered if next they'd be asking him for odd jobs, or veterinary services. Or money.

Roark scowled. "Not exactly. Donovan here promised me that I could check the tigress we microchipped. Who is apparently in human form at the moment." He paused. "They seemed pretty angry with you, earlier. I gather this is somehow your fault?"

Kersen flushed, and Donovan fought the urge to leap in for his defense. If Roark was going to accept Kersen, he'd have to do it on Kersen's own merits. "Somewhat, yes. The tigress you rescued is my younger sister. We were in the forest together, I let us get separated, and she ran into the poacher's snare. When Donovan helped her, she scratched and bit him, and she must have had her own blood on her claws or in her mouth."

"This is starting to give me a headache." Roark rubbed his temples and wiped his brow. "Right, then. Let's scan her and get this over with."

Donovan couldn't wait to get away from the others as well. He'd felt that strange electric current in the village two days ago, when he'd first met Mentauri. It had been bad enough then, the hum that had seemed to rattle his bones, but now it was far worse. It had to be having all these weretigers together in a small space, fired up and upset. *Or is it as Mentauri said about me being dominant? I don't know about weretigers, but in other species, introducing new members into a group, especially if they're dominant, can be dangerous. Even lethal.*

He was feeling hot again. This wasn't good.

Nervously, he put a hand on Kersen's shoulder, as a ripple of something fierce and violent passed through him. "I need to get away from all of your people. I'll come with Roark to see your sister."

Kersen's eyes widened. *What does he see? Or sense?* "Yes. Let us get you somewhere quiet. Calm." He took hold of Donovan's hand, and pulled him toward the crowd between them and his house with determination in his eyes. Donovan nodded to Roark that he should follow.

They were attempting to skirt around the others when a strong hand grabbed Donovan's other arm. He turned to find a tall, thin man with hard eyes and corded muscles holding him back. One look at him, and Donovan's hackles rose, and he itched again, all over.

The man spoke to Kersen in Indonesian. "Where are you taking them? We have not decided . . ." Donovan lost the last words, but he got the gist. Apparently neither Kersen nor his aunt had succeeded in swaying the village to their favor yet.

Even though he was much shorter, Kersen stood up to the man. "He is coming to my house. He is my *suami.*" Donovan was pretty sure the last word meant *husband.* He had a feeling, however, that it was something much more basic and primal in this context. *Mate. That word again.*

The man continued speaking, letting go of Donovan, but just when Donovan thought they were in the clear, the man pushed him, forcefully. A wave of dizziness struck Donovan, and his teeth began to ache. *Not good. Really not good.*

"Stop it! He . . ." Kersen shouted something back at the man, but Donovan was having a harder and harder time understanding the words. He only knew that he needed away from this person—this weretiger, who radiated power like a low sonic frequency, felt but not heard. Otherwise there was a real possibility that he'd try to kill the fellow. That couldn't be good for being allowed to live with these people. *Tigers. Whatever.*

The man grinned cunningly at Donovan and switched to heavily accented English. "He say you with him. You fight me and show you belong. We see who strongest."

Donovan groaned inwardly. A fight for dominance.

Just brilliant.

CHAPTER SEVENTEEN

Unnamed Village, Aceh Province, Sumatra
May 18, 2013

Kersen wanted to pull his hair out. Even though his heart was quailing, he stood before Anwar. "You can't fight him now! He has no control yet. You're asking for a blood match." This had nothing to do with mates; Anwar already had a wife. Village politics were at play here. Mentauri had told everyone that Donovan was strong, and therefore desirable. But strong also meant dominant, and now the other dominant males wanted to see where this newcomer would land in their clan hierarchy. The problem was that Donovan did not have enough control of his tiger to keep it from turning deadly. Anwar was rushing things.

We don't have time for this.

Anwar sneered at him like he'd done when they were both young; he'd always been the biggest and the strongest, and Kersen had usually ended up shoved into the mud after such looks. "You said he is starting to learn control. I have no fear of him. If he is truly your mate, you will find a way to communicate with his tiger soul."

After last night, that was entirely possible, but Kersen didn't want to test it. "Have patience. We must deal with Donovan's friend—then we can see about fights and tests of strength." This was his last chance to stop Anwar.

Donovan fell to one knee, panting hard. With all the testosterone in the air, it was obvious that Donovan was on the verge of shifting. Roark tugged at Kersen's sleeve, looking panicked. "What's wrong with him? What's all this about a fight? Are you the one in charge here?" His cell phone rang, and he picked it up, scowling. "Bloody hell." With an anxious glance at Donovan, he stepped aside to answer it.

What control Kersen might have had of the situation was lost. Bitari and Mentauri were arguing with Sabtu and Sabtu's wife. Other villagers had heard Anwar's challenge, and had gathered to watch. Anwar had already removed his shirt, handed it to his wife, and was working on his sandals, grinning fiercely.

Anwar was correct about one thing. If there was any hope of avoiding a disaster, Kersen needed to maintain communication with Donovan. He hurried over, helping to unbutton Donovan's shirt, and couldn't help but notice the white tufts of fur appearing on Donovan's forearms. "Do you understand why my clansman wants to fight?"

He received a glare. "I thought Mentauri said they'd accept me. Now I have to prove myself? Is that it?" Donovan pulled off his shirt before Kersen could get the last button, popping it off. "My teeth hurt. He realizes how stupid this is, right? What if I kill him? Or he tries to kill me?" He looked suddenly worried. "He can't kill me, can he?"

"Technically he can't. He would be in trouble because we are so rare. But you're not a clan member, so he may not feel bound by the traditional rules." Kersen had to be honest, though this wouldn't help Donovan's anxiety. He checked for Mentauri—she was standing behind the crowd of people that had gathered around Donovan and Anwar. She was shouting, but he couldn't hear her. Despite her authority, chaos had taken over.

Donovan groaned, clutching at his stomach.

Just as Kersen yanked at Donovan's shoes, Roark ran up, eyes widening in alarm at the two of them. "Donovan! Whatever's happening, you need to hear this!"

With obvious effort, Donovan stopped, his eyes wild, pupils blown. He was probably seconds away from shifting, and Kersen doubted Donovan would be able to pull back from it now. The tension in the air was even making his own tiger restless.

"What is it?" Donovan's voice barely sounded human anymore.

Roark hesitated, blanching, but continued. "The Aceh Provincial Council has made a decision regarding the Gunung Leuser National

Forest lands." He glanced nervously over at Anwar, who had begun to remove his trousers. Turning his back on Anwar, Roark faced Donovan again. "The corporations won. Aceh Province is opening up 150,000 hectares of protected forest to industries to become 'production forests and nonforest lands.'" Roark gulped, eyes locked on Donovan. "As far as I'm concerned, that means they'll be coming in immediately to start land surveying and chopping down trees. There's news that the companies are already sending out representatives to the locations to divvy up things and convince the locals of all the 'wealth and opportunity' they're going to bring." He spat on the ground. "Bollocks."

If Kersen had thought Donovan was pissed off before, the fire in his eyes at Roark's words put that notion to shame.

"No," Donovan whispered, the veins in his neck standing out. He staggered, fumbling at his jeans. "I'll kill them," he hissed, and fell to his hands and knees. Kersen hurried to help him shed the rest of his clothes before they joined the grave with the rest of the man's wardrobe. "I'll bloody kill anyone who . . ." Donovan's words were lost in snarls and growls.

Kersen glared at Anwar. "He won't be fighting you right now. He'll be too busy killing stupid foreign businessmen." He pulled at his own clothing in desperation. *I'll never shift in time to stop him.* Would Donovan have his human awareness this time?

Unfortunately, Donovan probably would have both the human intelligence to plan out his attack, as well as the tiger's instinct to protect territory and kill threats. Kersen couldn't imagine the doctor reacting in such a murderous way normally.

Anwar looked both alarmed and furious. "What does the foreigner say?" He pointed at Roark, and Kersen realized he hadn't understood Roark's English. "What is happening?"

Even as he undressed, Kersen spoke loudly in the local dialect so that everyone gathered would hear. "The Aceh Provincial Council has sold our protected forest lands to foreign businesses. Some of the land is not far from here. People are coming to mark out land they want to use, to cut the trees and plant sugar or trees for paper or palm oil. Donovan fought to stop this." Kersen swayed as his control over his form wavered. He could actually *feel* Donovan's rage.

It's done, then, whether we desired it or not. We're mated. A mixture of elation and fear swept through Kersen, but he couldn't spare a moment to dwell on it.

He continued, putting as much weight into his words as possible. "Donovan wants to kill the men who are coming. To protect the forest."

Beside him, Donovan was still shifting forms, gaining mass and muscle quickly, growing fur and fangs. Roark staggered back, his eyes wide and his mouth open in horror. "Fuck! What—fuck! He wasn't just having a laugh! It's real!" He was addressing Kersen, as if he could save him from this spectacle. But Kersen had no time for his shock.

He grabbed Roark's arm. "I need your help." What Kersen really needed was to shift, before Donovan ran off to do whatever he was going to do. "Do you know where the land is? Where the businesses are sending their men?" As closely as Donovan had been involved in this case, Kersen had no doubt that he knew exactly where the disputed lands were. His tiger-self might know that also.

Roark gulped, watching as the big Sumatran tiger shook himself after his change, whiskers twitching. Anwar hadn't shifted yet, but he looked ready to, studying Donovan's movement. A few women whispered about how big a beast Donovan was, how beautiful.

He isn't for any of you. He's mine. Kersen smiled grimly at the thought.

"Aye, I know exactly where it is. We've been following this case for months." Roark checked his phone again, opening an app. "Only two kilometers west of here, there's a section of forest included in the ruling." He glanced back at Donovan. "He can't really mean to kill them, can he? That'd take planning, intent. He's a *tiger*." He said the word with wonder.

Donovan growled, facing Anwar, who began to shift as well.

Fear made Kersen's voice shake, and he struggled to remember his English. "Wrong. He's a tiger with human intelligence, but not necessarily human morality. I have to change now. I have to stay near him." He risked looking away from Donovan to stare Roark in the eyes, to drive home his point. "Have my younger sister shift and follow me. You can track Gemi as you tracked her here. We'll follow Donovan and try to keep him out of trouble. Hurry!" He pointed over toward Bitari. Mentauri was shouting for the others to get back, to mind the children. Nobody was listening to her. At the moment, Kersen wasn't sure if this would be a fight or if Donovan would attack the clan in order to get free of the circle of spectators. For the moment, he seemed to be watching Anwar's transformation.

Roark nodded. Though he seemed scared, he hadn't bolted in terror. "Right. I may call in members of my team as well—not to join me! I think your people are wise to keep this a secret. But I may have other ways of stopping companies trying to invade your forest."

Kersen gave him a terse nod to show that he agreed. There was no more time. Anwar had finished shifting, and others were stripping down to change, either to help protect Anwar or simply because the energies were becoming too potent to control. With his own last shreds of restraint, Kersen called out to Bitari, "Tell Gemi to follow me! I'll keep watch on Donovan."

Donovan snarled and leaped at Anwar. Kersen winced, anticipating those fangs sinking into Anwar's throat even as Anwar crouched low, still dazed as he recovered from his shift.

Instead, Donovan jumped right over Anwar, charging into the crowd. Two men ducked away, and Donovan surged past them. Kersen groaned.

No fight for dominance today. Donovan must have joined his human and his tiger mind. He was going after the businessmen.

Shedding the last of his clothes, Kersen crouched and let the change take him. Donovan was fast. What if he couldn't catch up?

And, shit, what if the businessmen had guns or rangers with them? *What if they shoot Donovan? I can't let that happen. Wait for me, Donovan! Don't do this!* The pain was excruciating as he tried to force the shift, make it happen faster. Claws grew, his tailbone extended, and the itch all over signified the fur that was growing. From somewhere in Donovan's direction, Kersen faintly heard his mate's mind-voice.

I'll kill them! Not taking my forest!

Kersen yowled in worry. He looked up at Roark who was staring at him incredulously. By now the chatter of clan members inside Kersen's head threatened to drown out Donovan. He marveled again at being able to feel Donovan's rage. So what the other shifters said was true. When you found your mate, you knew. You just knew.

Donovan, stop! Murdering humans will only destroy us! They'll hunt us down and take away everything. This time Kersen's message was to everyone in his clan, as well as Donovan.

Bitari called to Roark. "You, stupid Englishman! Come over here. We are going to follow them with your truck and your evil tracking device."

At the edge of the crowd, Mentauri was walking back to her house, removing her hijab. She only ever did that to shift forms.

Kersen couldn't delay any longer. *Gemi, follow me!* He took off running, past a mother pulling her angry boys into a house, past a tiger barely old enough to shift and an older tiger attempting to hold it back, heading toward the jungle where he sensed Donovan. He caught small wisps of scent along the way, and kept listening for Donovan, but there was nothing. It was possible that Donovan had gone deeper into his tiger-self and lost his ability to speak. Earlier, Kersen had thought that dealing with a natural tiger was dangerous, but he suspected this mixture of man and beast was much worse. It wasn't like the innocent and fun-loving youths he'd known growing up, trying to control their inner beasts and having guidance from their elders. This unsupervised adult transformation was terrifying.

I'm shifting now, brother! Gemi's voice was clear and strong in Kersen's head. Mentauri was calling to the clan members, organizing who would watch over the children and giving orders to those who would be shifting, either to remain and defend the village or follow Kersen to deal with this dangerous intrusion into their privacy.

Kersen ran across the fields and along the outskirts of the jungle. Donovan was keeping to the fringes of the forest, probably because it wasn't possible to run like this in the entangled undergrowth within. While he couldn't see Donovan yet, Kersen caught more scents of him. Birds flew in agitation above, startled by the passage of two predators. Kersen crossed a dirt road, and cursed inwardly. He was never going to catch Donovan in time if he kept going like this. Tigers weren't meant for running long distances, but Donovan's anger seemed to be fueling him. As for Kersen, he already longed to slow down and take a nap somewhere.

Donovan, stop! Let's talk about this. Panting, Kersen was forced to slow to a loping trot as he passed into thicker brush between the villages and plantation fields. Mosquitoes buzzed along muddy ditches where trees had been cut years before. It was several kilometers to the next village, but there were a few service roads used by forest rangers. He didn't know exactly where the area that had been lost in today's council decision was located, but two kilometers wasn't far.

No response from Donovan.

I'm here, brother. Anwar is following farther back with some of the other males. Bitari is taking the human in her truck. Gemi appeared just behind Kersen, running through the tangled brush.

I can't keep up with him. What if he really does it? What if he kills someone? Years ago, it wouldn't have mattered as much, back when there were more natural tigers. It had been the law of the jungle then, that tigers sometimes attacked humans. With their population so low, however, the last thing the *siluman harimau* wanted to do now was stir up trouble with humans.

You've gotten lazy. We can do it. It'll be faster to follow the game trails, as he's probably doing. Gemi was smart. Confidence rang out in her mind's voice, bolstering Kersen's hope.

They took off again, sniffing out the pig trails that would be easiest to follow.

When they reached a field, it became easier to run. A minute later, Kersen spotted a quickly moving shape far ahead. *Donovan, stop! Please stop!* Kersen put all his worry into his telepathic cry, all his concern. He was only just getting to know Donovan, but the more he learned about him, the more he liked him and the more he wanted to learn. He wanted to spend lazy evenings in bed together, exploring each other's body. He wanted to teach Donovan to speak better Indonesian and to show him parts of the jungle that Donovan had never explored. He wanted to grow old with the stubborn fool.

From up ahead, there came the low rumble of a truck engine. Kersen smelled exhaust on the air.

I think there's a forestry road over there. Gemi sounded uneasy.

With a flash of orange, the tiger ahead of them disappeared behind a clump of brush. The loud rumbling intensified, and Kersen realized it wasn't just a single truck but several trucks, and they were stationary. That couldn't be good.

Coming up on you, a new voice rang out in Kersen's head.

Anwar. There might be more tigers with him, but Kersen wasn't sure if that would help or not. They hadn't yet accepted Donovan into the clan after all.

Let me try stopping him first! Kersen's lungs ached from running. His feet hurt, and his muscles were cramping up. He spotted the trucks: four of them, idling along a dirt service road. He couldn't tell for certain, but there was movement around the trucks.

Men.

CHAPTER EIGHTEEN

Somewhere along the borders of Gunung Leuser, Aceh Province, Sumatra
May 18, 2013

onovan crouched in the brush alongside the forestry road, watching men in work clothes and heavy boots setting up gear for land surveillance and digging holes to post signs in. Several trucks lined the side of the dirt road, including a bulldozer, a dump truck for carrying out debris, and a flatbed with a backhoe on top. They looked ready to destroy some prime rainforest topography.

They were all dead men, as far as he was concerned.

Donovan's whiskers twitched at the stench of human sweat, and his tail straightened, balancing him for the strike. He wasn't used to these added features yet, and they annoyed him, but a deeper part of him sensed that they belonged. That must be his tiger-self, as Kersen liked to say. That same deeper, more primal part sensed that the men and the trucks were a danger to his territory. *Kill the humans. They have hurt the tigers enough.*

Donovan! You have to listen to me. If you kill a human, they're going to hunt you. Us. Kersen's voice echoed in Donovan's head, and as much as he wanted to shut it out, he couldn't. What was even worse was the nagging worry and fear that came with it. Kersen sounded young and scared, and all of Donovan's instincts were screaming at him to protect his mate (*mate?*) and take him somewhere safe. But this might be his only chance to hit the corporation and send them a message that they weren't welcome here. By striking early, they might reconsider messing with this part of the forest.

Well, let them hunt me. Donovan growled low in his belly, his tail lashing. He'd pick off each and every one of the bastards the minute they stepped foot into his forest. If the poachers thought he'd been a pain in their arse with his rangers, pulling snares, they had no idea what they were in for now. It was bloody time that tigers fought back for their right to exist.

Hunkering down lower in the brush, Donovan watched one of the men walk closer with a tripod for his surveying device. He'd be checking the lay of the land so they could dig ditches that the company could fill with water and use to transport logs as they cleared out this section of forest. Then when they cut down all the rare hardwood trees, they'd burn the rest. Once the land was clear, they'd plant acacia for paper pulp or palm trees for palm oil.

And the wildlife would lose yet more of their scarce land.

These people deserve to die, Donovan thought at Kersen, not sure if Kersen would hear him, and not really caring. Why shouldn't he sink his fangs into the land surveyor who was so close at hand? But, no, he needed to target the supervisor first. Send their operation into chaos.

He'd always devoted his life to saving the wild. It looked like he might give his life for it today.

Donovan scanned the rest of the men and found one wearing a shirt and tie, holding a clipboard. That would be the site supervisor. The fellow was a little far to charge—and Donovan wasn't even sure how he knew what the distance for a good charge should be.

Kill the supervisor? Or the surveyor, since he's closer? Which one should I choose?

A rustle of movement behind him startled Donovan out of his thoughts. He whirled, ready to swat at whatever it was until he saw a smaller tiger with a gleam in his eyes and a familiar pattern on his shoulder. It had to be Kersen. His mind-voice confirmed it. *Neither. Stop this insanity, Donovan. This isn't the way to defend our land. You're not in your right mind at this time.* Another tiger crept into the brush behind Donovan, and this tigress Donovan recognized before he scented her.

Donovan bared his teeth. *Your sister? Why did you bring her?* They were going to blow his cover; the bushes were thick, but asking them to mask three tigers was a bit much. Warily, he turned to look at the surveyor, who had paused in setting up his tripod. The man might not have noticed them yet, but he had clearly sensed that something was off. The birds, of course. They'd gone quiet.

Kersen rubbed up against him in greeting. Donovan longed to turn and nuzzle him back, but he fought against the instinct. Kersen's mind-voice was insistent. *I brought her because I wanted Roark to track her and come and break up this party. Let him handle these humans. If you attack, they will stop at nothing to destroy us. All of us. You cannot win the war this way.*

Anguish filled Donovan. The surveyor had resumed setting things up, and his supervisor had taken a few steps closer. Maybe they'd chat before taking measurements. If they did that near enough, he could take them both out at once. *I tried to stop them the legal way, Kersen. It didn't work. Nothing but violence gets through to these people. I'll make it clear that it's just me, just one tiger involved in these attacks. I'll keep your village safe. I can't let them farm here—they'll find out about you.*

Perhaps Kersen tried to say something else, but Donovan was no longer listening. He watched as the supervisor came over to the surveyor, holding out his clipboard, speaking in Mandarin. Donovan sank low, his muscles tensed, ready to spring. *Let's see how fast this project moves without these boss-men.*

Baring his fangs, he attacked.

He was upon the supervisor before the man had a chance to blink. Crying out, the fellow tried to swat Donovan's face with his clipboard, but that was useless. Donovan knocked the supervisor down and pinned him to the ground with his paws on the man's shoulders. Leaning, he opened his mouth to take out the man's jugular, but then he hesitated. This wasn't like shooting a gun. It wasn't even like stabbing an attacker. This was gruesome murder, and he'd have to literally taste it. He snarled and reveled in the man's terrified whimpers but the sound of a bolt action rifle halted him. *One of them has a gun!*

Suddenly Kersen leaped out of the brush, toppling the surveying equipment, which hit the floor with a *crack*. Donovan blinked in surprise. *Destroy their equipment. That's smarter.* Not just the little equipment like that, but the bigger, more expensive stuff, like the bulldozer.

Donovan, behind you! Kersen sent, his tail lashing.

As Donovan raised his head to look, he saw that a second man near the dump truck had drawn a revolver, and the weapon was trained on Kersen. *No! Not him.*

Time slowed—this was all going sideways. Kersen froze, gaze fixed on the gun. The supervisor under Donovan bucked. *I should kill him now. Make this worth it.*

I can't risk losing Kersen.

Donovan gave a massive roar, and the man with the gun fumbled it, almost dropping it in his panic.

Backing away, Donovan let the supervisor scramble away toward the flatbed truck, and then he dove at Kersen to put himself between the gun and his lover. *Get back under the brush, Kersen.*

Kersen snarled at him, and Donovan could feel his fury. *I'm not leaving until you do. You get back in the brush!*

The men were yelling at them now, throwing things to try to scare them away. The one with the pistol waved his weapon. One slip of the finger and that could be the end of them. Donovan lashed his tail in irritation; his ears were laid flat against his head, and his hackles were raised. The men seemed so small, so fragile. He looked once more at the trucks, the heavy equipment. Save his lover, or save the forest?

I can't risk him. Kersen needs to live. Cautiously, Donovan turned his back on the men to return to the brush. Since nobody had fired at them yet, the workers must either be reluctant to shoot a protected animal, or terrified. *It's all right, Kersen. We can leave.*

He took two steps, watching Kersen turn as well, when another explosion of orange and black burst out of the forest to the right of everyone. The new tiger, almost as big as Donovan, charged at the man holding the rifle.

Anwar, no! Kersen cried out inside Donovan's head, but it was too late.

Several things happened at once.

Kersen dashed toward his clan member. Donovan ran alongside him, to stay between him and the man with the revolver. The rifle went off with a terrifying boom, and there was a puff of dirt behind Kersen. Then Anwar pounced on the rifleman and chomped down on the weapon, tearing it from the man's grasp. Even as Donovan tried to process that, the second man fired his revolver and a searing pain tore through Donovan's shoulder. His foreleg gave out from under him, and he found himself sprawled in the middle of the road, far from protective cover.

The revolver fired again, and then one more time. Donovan waited for the pain or the end of his life, but the shots must have gone wide. Anwar ran past in a streak of movement, carrying the rifle in his mouth, past open-mouthed humans. Donovan fought against the burning in his shoulder to turn and see. The shooter was running from another tiger, clutching his hand. A fifth tiger was chasing the surveyor.

Gemi, get back here! That was Kersen. Donovan rolled and found Kersen standing over him protectively, glaring at the men who had fled to the trucks. The supervisor climbed into the cab of the flatbed truck, clutching a cell phone. The rifleman, wide-eyed and pale, stumbled his way over to the dump truck where another man pulled him inside, speaking rapidly.

Five tigers in a coordinated attack on armed men, and no one killed, miraculously. While one of the tigers must have bitten the fellow with the revolver, without the transfer of weretiger blood, there would be little danger of passing their infection. Donovan winced at the fire spreading into his chest from the bullet wound in his shoulder. Ironic that he was the best qualified to take the damned thing out and he couldn't do that. Worse, it was his right arm. Roark was going to tear him a new one if he couldn't perform surgery on animals any longer.

The rumble of a pickup truck approaching forced Donovan to rise up on his good legs. He needed to get away from the trucks and the men in case more of them had guns. *Kersen, Gemi, get back into cover. Call Anwar back. We need to leave before they bring reinforcements.*

As the pickup screeched to a halt, however, Donovan realized it was Roark. Bitari was with him, shouting and pointing at Anwar and Gemi. *Uh-oh. She's going to gut me for this, isn't she?* He sent Kersen the question. After all, he'd endangered both of her younger siblings.

The glare she sent him confirmed his fears.

Umm . . . Kersen sent, apparently unwilling to say more.

Roark honked his horn, and Donovan forced himself to limp forward. Should he make for the bushes, or for Roark? No place seemed safe, though the man who'd had the revolver was still fleeing. Gemi trotted back over to rejoin them. Anwar was running in a wide circle, leaving the chase to return to the group.

The supervisor rolled down the window of the flatbed truck and yelled at Roark in English. "Go away! The crazy tigers are attacking us! They grabbed the rifle—they're not normal!"

Roark stepped out of the truck brazenly, his stance and his size making him look like some Scottish high lord before battle. "That's right! You're trespassing on cursed land, you buggers!"

Donovan wanted to laugh. Of course as a tiger, he couldn't. Cursed land? What nonsense was Roark saying? He tried to take another step but could only limp, painfully. Kersen stayed glued to his side while Gemi moved to flank him on the other. This wasn't good. If someone shot at them, Donovan wouldn't be able to protect anyone. *I'm such a blasted sod.* He shouldn't have gone off halfcocked like that.

"Cursed?" The supervisor appeared doubtful, but then he looked over at Donovan. That made up Donovan's mind. Carefully, he began limping toward Roark. *He's brilliant.* If there was any chance of getting out of this and not earning the dangerous label of man-eaters, all of the tigers would have to behave so incredibly strangely that no one would believe the story.

Roark hardly glanced at Donovan, like it was no big thing to have three Sumatran tigers closing in on him. "That's right. You've bought yourself a bit of land here that belongs to the ancient gods. Even the locals don't venture near. They say that evil spirits enter the animals in this area. Spirits that like nothing better than the taste of human blood."

I'm liking your friend more and more. For a second or two, Donovan didn't recognize the gruff female voice in his head. Then he saw Bitari wink at him. So apparently the weretigers could communicate mentally when they weren't tigers. Or was that a clan thing?

If so, what did that mean for him?

The supervisor glanced nervously at Donovan, Kersen, and Gemi. "This is ridiculous. I don't believe in curses. You have trained these tigers somehow."

Roark laughed. "Yeah, I'm some fellow that works at an animal conservation center, and we've developed such a brilliant program that we can train wild tigers in the middle of the jungle." Despite his bravado, Roark was sweating. Three tigers could be trainable.

Donovan glanced at Kersen. *How many others from your clan are nearby?*

Kersen brushed up against Donovan's good side, nuzzling him. *Several. Anwar, lead them out! Have them form a line with us, and raise your hackles to my mate's friend here as well.*

From the forest, tigers began to emerge, a few crawling with stealth, others running full speed for the trucks and Kersen. Anwar rounded the truck and leaped in front of Roark, growling at him. Roark went pale but didn't move, much to his credit. He shot Donovan a worried look, though.

Bitari patted his hand and faced the supervisor, speaking English. "We go now! The forest very, very angry. More and more animals come, the longer we stay!" She pointed at the tigers, in case any of the men hadn't noticed them. "This is *Hutan Duri dan Cakar*, the Forest of Thorns and Claws. This is sacred land to my people." Her voice was almost as loud as Roark's, and Donovan wanted to pounce on her and lick her face . . . or at least the tiger in him wanted to. She was brilliant.

Kersen spoke in Donovan's head. *Growl at your friend too. We must all make a show of this.*

Donovan did, baring his fangs at Roark, trying his best to act like a killer even though his shoulder was throbbing, the blood flowing in a steady trickle down his front leg.

The supervisor ducked his head back inside the cab of the flatbed truck and rolled up the window. He started the engine, a welcome rumble to Donovan's ears.

We're doing it. I think we're actually doing it! This came from Gemi, and she sounded elated; her tail lashed back and forth with excitement. The truck's tires began to move, as the supervisor tried to back it up to get to the access road.

Kersen crept forward, still growling at Roark. Other tigers had joined, lining up beside Gemi and Kersen, a formation that had to appear remarkable and sinister to the corporate men. Kersen's tail brushed against Donovan. *Tell Roark I'm going to pounce on him, but I'll be careful not to hurt him.*

Donovan almost replied that he had no way to communicate with Roark at the moment, thanks very much, but then he saw determination on Bitari's face and he realized the message hadn't been for him.

"Mr. Roark, Kersen's going to pounce on you. Act like you're dying," she said in a deadpan voice.

Kersen leaped on Roark with a roar, snapping at Roark's throat.

Roark's scream was probably not just for show. The men in the truck shouted as well.

Donovan could have danced for joy. It wasn't likely that trained tigers would be going after their trainer like this. Even if they were all somehow trained, it would appear like they were wild now, and too countless to be under control. Who would believe them? He glanced at the bulldozer, driverless and abandoned, then sent his thoughts to Kersen. *Once they're gone, we could sabotage their equipment. But we must make sure to show that tigers were responsible—otherwise they'll blame Roark.*

Elation poured into Donovan from Kersen, and then Kersen was relating the message to others in the clan, as the trucks rumbled away. The tigers watched silently except for Kersen, who remained crouched on top of Roark, his mouth on the man's throat but carefully, gently licking the spot. Roark made an odd keening noise.

"Can you get off me now? Please? I'm really not comfortable with this." He sounded scared out of his wits.

Kersen eased off of Roark as the trucks disappeared into the distance. Bitari strode over to Roark and offered him a hand. She was grinning ear to ear. "You could be a movie star, Mr. Roark."

He gave a nervous chuckle, allowing her to help him up. The other tigers, the members of Kersen's clan, approached the bulldozer, some leaping onto the hood to claw at hydraulic hoses, lights, or anything else that could be torn off. Others tested their teeth on the continuous tracks, and then one managed to open the door and climb inside. As Donovan watched, the tiger slashed the seat, then gnawed at the controller joystick until it broke off.

A lance of pain through Donovan's shoulder brought his attention back to himself. He looked at Kersen longingly. *Can someone please fix me now? I'll just say one more time that I'm very sorry for causing this mess.*

Kersen walked over and licked his wound. *Yes. The clan has heard you. I will find a way to make all of this right.*

CHAPTER NINETEEN

Somewhere along the border of Gunung Leuser, Aceh Province, Sumatra
May 18, 2013

Kersen walked over to Roark, noting that Bitari hadn't let go of the man's hand yet. Had his sister finally met someone she found attractive? He wondered if Roark realized how rare it was for her to display emotions like this. Well, good emotions, anyway. *Bitari, warn Roark that some of us will be shifting back. We need to get the bullet out of Donovan's flesh.*

Bitari finally let go of Roark's hand. When she spoke, her tone was softer than usual. "Kersen says he's going to shift back, and so will others. Donovan was shot. You know how to remove a bullet?"

Nodding, Roark paled and stared at Donovan with his bloody shoulder, red streaks on his striped fur. "Donovan? Is that you?"

Donovan yowled, lying down on his uninjured side. His eyes widening, Roark ran over and knelt beside him. He started to reach out to inspect the wound, then stopped himself. "Wait. You're contagious, right? I need gloves. Don't worry—I have a small first-aid kit in the truck." He stood up and hurried over to the cab, his belly shaking as he yanked open the door.

Kersen considered shifting while Roark's back was turned, but then if Roark was going to perform surgery on Donovan, he needed to stay in this form. Only as a tiger would he be able to keep Donovan from instinctively lashing out at Roark. While Bitari might be eyeing Roark as a potential mate, that should come with the man's full consent to become one of them. *The way things should have gone with Donovan and me.*

He settled down next to Donovan and pinned the massive paws, leaning his head against Donovan's jaw so that any biting would be aimed at him, not Roark.

When Roark returned, he regarded Kersen with curiosity. "Uh, is that going to work? I remember what happened with the tigress— your sister. I'm not that eager to go trading in my skin for fur." He sat down and opened up the first-aid box, which was a lot bigger than Kersen had expected. Donovan panted, holding still. *Is he going to talk all day, or are we getting this thing out of me? I can't even bite on a belt! He realizes this fucking hurts. Right?*

Turning his head a bit, Kersen gave Bitari a look. *Tell Roark he needs to hurry. I think Donovan will revert more to his tiger-self the longer the pain goes on.*

Bitari did so, and Roark nodded, waving his hands. "I'm not the bloody surgeon—Donovan is. Hell, I'm mostly in charge of logistics." After donning gloves, he pulled out a small packaged scalpel, alcohol wipes, and an unopened bottle of water. "This is the worst possible place to do this—we should take him to a hospital as a human. But I know, I know—they'd start an investigation. For now, I'd rather try it with him as an animal. I'd probably faint dead away otherwise."

With that, he cracked open the water bottle and poured a third of it over Donovan's wound, flushing away the blood. "Damned fur. I suppose you're going to want me to stitch this up too." He opened one of the alcohol pads, grimacing. "This is going to hurt. Don't bite me, please."

If I faint, help him get me back to the village. I'm not even sure if he should try to remove the bullet. He could hit a major artery. Donovan's mind-voice sounded tired and in pain.

He must remove it. When you shift, there's no telling where the bullet will end up. Try not to bite or scratch. Try not to move. I'm here. Kersen ached for him, wished he could do something to help. The best he could manage was to lick Donovan's throat and face to soothe him.

Bitari studied the kit, her mouth pursed in worry. "Shouldn't you sedate him first?"

Without halting his work on cleaning the area, Roark shook his head. "Nope. Bad enough that we had to tranquilize your sister to work on her injuries. Big cats are notoriously unpredictable when it comes to sedation. I don't know if that holds true for your kind, but I'd rather not test it."

Kneeling beside Roark, Bitari held the items for him. "I see. Then we will have to protect you if need be. Kersen says he's ready. Do what you need to do, Mr. Roark."

Roark blushed, shrugging. "Sterling's actually my last name. Just 'Roark' is fine. Hand me the scalpel, and then the tweezers. Stand by with the gauze to stop bleeding if it gets worse." He exhaled a breath, and sliced into the wound carefully. Donovan yowled, clawing at the ground.

I'm here. I'm right here. You're going to be fine. Kersen couldn't help the undercurrent of fear in his mind-voice. What if he lost Donovan? He'd been alone, but he'd never felt how alone he was before. Meeting Donovan had shown him just how much he needed a companion. Someone who could love him and support him.

One of Donovan's paws gripped Kersen's shoulder, the claws digging in. Kersen grimaced but didn't move. Donovan's mental voice sounded stronger as Roark took the tweezers from Bitari. *I'm not going anywhere. I'll be damned if I find someone as amazing as you and then die from a stupid mistake. I want to be with you, Kersen. I want to be your mate.*

At that point, Donovan could have torn his arm off and Kersen wouldn't have cared. His heart soared, making him light-headed. *I want to be your mate as well. It might be too soon, but I think I'm in love with you.*

Kersen paused as Roark began to explore the wound with the tweezers and Donovan roared in pain, struggling frantically. Only with Gemi's help was Kersen able to hold him down. The next thing he knew, Sabtu and his brother from the village, both in human form, were kneeling nearby to help pin Donovan and keep him still.

"Sorry, mate," Roark said under his breath. He looked waxen, as if he were in pain rather than Donovan. "Think I can feel the bullet—didn't quite make it to the shoulder blade, thank God." Grimacing, he pulled, twisting his hand, most likely to avoid making any further damage as he extracted the bullet. It was covered in blood. Such a small bullet to cause so much trouble.

Roark dropped it into a piece of gauze and reached for the bottle of water. "I'm going to flush the wound again, and then I'm going to stitch it up. We'll put you on the best antibiotic we've got. Just hang in there. You're almost done."

That wasn't entirely true, Kersen learned. Roark poured the rest of the bottle into and around the wound while Kersen and the others continued to hold Donovan. Human screams rang out in Kersen's head—Donovan's screams, but the noises he actually made were all animal, a tiger in agony. Roark winced, tears glistening at the corners of his eyes as he resolutely cleaned the wound. Kersen doubted that much of Donovan was left conscious; this procedure had probably put him right back into his tiger-self for the rest of the day.

"Keep holding him," Roark said through gritted teeth. "Going to dab the skin with antiseptic—that'll hurt like a fucker. Then I'll use the topical pain killer and begin stitching."

True to his word, the antiseptic was the worst part; Kersen just concentrated on Donovan's head, his eyes shut as Donovan bit him on the shoulder, while Gemi and the others controlled the rest of his limbs. Roark worked quickly, and though Bitari was paler than usual, she stoically handed him clean gauze and then the needle and whatever they were using for the stitches. After the first stitch, Donovan calmed down, though panting heavily. His mind-voice was silent, but Kersen felt a reaching out, calling mate to mate, for comfort.

I'm here, Donovan. Keep hanging in there. Kersen tried to send what he was feeling, though he wasn't certain what to call it. He wanted Donovan to be all right. He wanted to see him laughing and smiling.

He wanted to be naked in Donovan's bed, holding him.

"Just a few more stitches," Roark muttered. Sweat dripped down his temples, and he blinked a few times, before Bitari reached over and dabbed at his eyes. He smiled at her gratefully. "You ever consider becoming a vet? You've got great focus."

She said nothing, but Kersen detected the hint of a smile. He couldn't help teasing her. *You like him. Don't even pretend that you don't.*

She snorted, flicking at his sensitive nose and whiskers. "You pay attention to your mate there." Roark looked at her in confusion, and she shrugged. "My brother. I heard you and he did not get along so well at first." She grinned. "He is a stubborn one sometimes."

As if she was one to talk! But Donovan was whimpering, and Kersen returned to licking at his ear, trying to calm him. Roark tied off the last stitch and let out a long breath. He smiled at Bitari. "Yeah, I gathered that when he kept trying to break into my facility. Hand me the gauze wrap there. We'll get Donovan bandaged up." He glanced up for a moment, frowning. "We need to clear out before they bring the authorities. I don't know how we're going to move him."

Bitari eyed Kersen. *Do you think he can shift back? I heard him earlier. He's been conscious the whole time?*

Since she wasn't speaking aloud, Roark stared at her blankly. "You went quiet all of a sudden. You have an idea?"

She held up a finger to him. "Shh. We shall see."

Kersen nuzzled Donovan again. *Are you still there? Donovan, can you send your thoughts to me? We need to get you somewhere safe.*

Pain! Hurts! It wasn't much, but there were words along with the sensations, which meant that Donovan's human mind was at least partially present.

Kersen gently tugged on his ear with his teeth. *I need you to shift back, Donovan. Can you do that? They can't transport you like this. You have to become human again.* It was like talking to a child—he wasn't even sure if Donovan could comprehend what he was saying. Roark continued to bandage the limb, quickly and quietly.

Hurts. Want to go home. Want to be with you. Still half animal, still very childlike, but it was encouraging. Kersen debated his options. He peered at his surroundings, noting that his other clan members had finished their sabotage. They'd leave plenty of evidence to show it had been tigers, in this bizarre aggression toward the machinery. Roark checked his watch nervously.

Once the bandage was on, Bitari taped it and tested it, pulling to make sure it would stay put. Kersen nudged Donovan firmly, with both nose and paws. *Get up. You need to either shift back to human or we need to walk you out of here. They may return soon. You don't want to be here for that, do you? Let's go home. You'll come home with me, yes?*

Donovan huffed. He tried to stand up, but rolled onto his back as soon as his injured shoulder started to bear weight. That wasn't going to work. *Home! Yes. With you. Want to be with you.*

For a moment, Kersen despaired that he wouldn't be able to reason with Donovan. But then a tentative question came into his head. *I'm . . . Donovan. Yes?* Donovan's mind-voice still seemed a bit childlike, but he was starting to sound more like himself.

Kersen gave him a toothy grin, panting. *Yes! You're Donovan. You're* siluman harimau, *like me. We're tigers and men. You need to become your man-self. It's important.*

Tiger. I'm a tiger. And I hurt.

Kersen nudged him again. *You're a man in a tiger's body. You need to be a man in a man's body. Do you want to kiss me? Do you want to have sex with me?* He kept pushing at Donovan, and with a growl, Donovan rolled over onto his feet, although he kept the weight off his injured shoulder, crouching in the dirt. Kersen sensed others from his clan gathering around, but he couldn't spare them a look. All his focus was on Donovan.

Mm, yes. Yes—want to kiss you. Wait. Donovan raised his head, and Kersen swore he saw the light switch on. Donovan blinked at him, his amber eyes alert. *I need to change back. How do I do that?*

Joy surged through Kersen. Donovan was back! And he was getting it. Kersen stood, making sure to keep his head near Donovan's to maintain eye contact. *Think of your human body. Remember what it feels like. Think of kissing me—you need human lips to do that, right? You can do it. I have faith in you.*

Okay. I'll try. Donovan closed his eyes, and Kersen took a couple of steps to give him room in case he succeeded. Shifting was about focus, and not being afraid to let the body transform despite the discomfort and pain it caused. Now that Donovan had human consciousness, he'd be able to do it as long as he didn't get in his own way. Kersen kept his thoughts carefully shielded, to himself. Fear was the enemy here. His biggest worry was that their time might be running out.

CHAPTER TWENTY

*Somewhere along the border of Gunung Leuser, Aceh Province, Sumatra
May 18, 2013*

I'm a man. I'm a man. Cripes, I'm a doctor and a man.

Donovan fought against the pain in his shoulder and the black hole that wanted to suck him back down and offer him oblivion. It wasn't death or anything as dramatic as that. It was more like another part of himself; perhaps what Kersen called his "tiger-self." All it wanted was to find a nice den and curl up and sleep for the next twenty hours or so.

With his mate. His feelings on that were so strong he couldn't deny it, though the logical side of him wanted to scream and argue that such a thing wasn't possible. He'd only met Kersen a few days ago! Relationships weren't supposed to happen like this. But he couldn't fight the incredible urge to hold Kersen tight and never let go.

And that was another problem. His mate was going to shift back, and if Donovan wanted to curl up with him, that meant he needed to be human too.

He wanted to be with Kersen for the rest of his life, if possible. Even if half of him quailed at the thought.

Donovan's toes were tingling like they were falling asleep. Was that the shift beginning? He dimly remembered what it had been like going from man to beast. Enraged, he'd wanted to kill the humans who were taking the forest. But the enemy was gone now. It was time to rest and heal.

Kersen, help me. I'm trying, but it's not working.

You're doing great. Keep concentrating. Kersen sounded confident.

Donovan imagined a hand, his hand, entwined with Kersen's, and just like that, his paws began to itch all over. Itching—it had started that way as a human, hadn't it? Before he'd turned into a tiger.

Keep remembering what it feels like to be human. As soon as you start to shift, I'm going to shift with you. Kersen's tone was not only encouraging; he was sending feelings of concern and care as well. And not simply concern. Love.

And I feel the same way for him. Donovan's heart beat faster. It was bonkers, falling for somebody so quickly. Yet it felt right.

Human hands, human arms, holding Kersen. That was what he wanted most right now.

The itching and tingling spread farther, from Donovan's toes to his elbows and up to his shoulders. His legs seemed to be being pricked by thousands of tiny needles. Heartened by the sensations, he concentrated harder on the physicality of being with Kersen. This morning they'd been lying together in bed, limbs tangled. The feel of Kersen's naked body beneath his had been amazing. Wonderful.

Pain flared up his spine, like someone had hacked off his tail.

You're doing it! Just relax and let it happen. I'll see you on the other side. Kersen's voice faded inside Donovan's head, as something powerful gripped his entire body. It was like being caught with a bad muscle cramp, except this one affected all his muscles at once. He screamed and then began to pant, trying hard to relax, but how did one relax when one was being turned inside out?

He was half-aware of falling onto his uninjured side. Voices came from far away, but he couldn't distinguish any words over the roaring in his ears. His jaw ached, and his teeth ached, and he was burning up from the inside.

Just let me not die. Let me be with Kersen again.

He blacked out.

When Donovan came to, he was wrapped in a blanket and strapped into the backseat of the extended cab in Roark's truck as it bounced along a dirt road. Kersen was sitting beside him, his arm holding Donovan, his shoulder supporting Donovan's head. Donovan blinked, looking up at the front seat where Roark and Bitari were sitting. Roark was talking as he drove, but over the rumble of the truck's engine, Donovan couldn't hear what he was saying.

His shoulder burned like someone had stuck a red hot poker into it. *Damned bullet.* What the hell had possessed him to go attacking the surveyors, knowing full well they'd have scouts and guards near the jungle? Had he been cracked?

Kersen nudged him. "How are you feeling?"

For a moment, Donovan could only stare into those soulful, amber eyes. It was almost weird to hear Kersen's voice out loud instead of inside his head, to see human eyes rather than feline. There was a bruise on Kersen's cheek. *Did I put that there?* He vaguely remembered struggling while they'd been trying to take the bullet out.

His voice felt rusty as he answered. "I'm fine. How is everyone else? You?" He took Kersen's hand, needing the contact, needing to feel Kersen's skin against his. As tigers, they'd been connected. Did they lose that when they became human?

A little smile crossed Kersen's face. "Everyone else is doing fine. Roark has been talking to your animal center, telling them not to speak of your absence or his, and to cover if the Chinese paper company we tangled with contacts the authorities and starts any kind of investigation. My people made sure to leave tiger tracks returning to the jungle, and then erased their trails back to the village. That should keep the corporation guessing. Meanwhile, we're taking you to your center to get antibiotics."

What would be happening right now if I'd killed that man? The guilt churned in Donovan's gut, knowing that he'd put Kersen at risk, Kersen's entire clan at risk. He clenched his free hand into a fist, ignoring the lance of pain that it caused. "I feel terrible. I shouldn't have lost my temper. I shouldn't have dragged you and your people to fight with the corporation like that." He shook his head. "Killing people and terrorizing the surveyors and contractors isn't the answer to saving the forest. But I was desperate."

"It's okay," Kersen assured him, patting his hand.

Their words must have carried to the front, for Roark commented next. "I've seen things today I never would have imagined, not in a million years. Men turning into tigers, communicating telepathically, and teaming up against a major corporation. I imagine they'll be furious when they return and see that bulldozer. Hard to get American parts here, so that should hinder them for a while. Long enough for us to try something else, anyway." He glanced at Donovan in the rearview mirror. "You doing all right? That was my first field dressing without your direction. I hope those stitches hold. Your beau there wouldn't even let me get close to check them after you'd switched back to yourself."

This time Kersen smiled. "I am sorry. It frightened me that he would not wake up." The smile crumbled, and moisture shone in his eyes. "I didn't want him to die when I'd only just met him." He didn't look at Donovan, until Donovan squeezed his hand. Then there was no mistaking the love in Kersen's eyes.

"I'm glad you came to stop me. I was an idiot. I'm sorry," Donovan told him. Without Kersen and his clan's intervention, it was likely that the scouts and guards would have killed him. *No more losing my temper and attacking humans. At least not as a tiger.*

Kersen's expression was a mixture of concern and regret. "I am sorry I was not able to stop you sooner. But it may all be for the best. Because of your actions, we have chased off the intruders for the time being. Now that the village is safe, however, the clan's next focus will be on you. Your partner says we must stop by your animal center for your medical care, but then we have to return to my village. My people will decide today if you will become a member of our clan." He bit his lip, lowering his head, and a vague wave of foreboding went through Donovan.

"What happens if they don't let me in?"

His eyes glistening, Kersen raised his head again. "Then you would be an outcast. And so would I. We are mated. There is no turning back now."

Donovan blinked at him, trying to process that. The way Kersen said it made it sound like they were married or something. They'd had sex. Kersen had never mentioned a lifetime commitment; hell, Donovan hadn't even been certain where he would be staying from day to day. "What do you mean, we're mated? Why would you be an outcast?"

Kersen's face gave away nothing. His voice was also carefully neutral. "While natural tigers do not develop strong ties to one partner, as *siluman harimau* we are different. It is uncommon yet possible for us to form a strong mental and emotional bond with our lovers. When that happens, we can communicate with them on every level mind to mind—as man, as tiger with human awareness, and even as our pure tiger selves. This happened when you were wounded. You should not be able to hear my clan mates until you are clan, but because of your tie to me and mine to them, now you can. This means you are my mate, and I will go wherever you go." Kersen swallowed guiltily. "I should have told you sooner, but I never believed this could happen so fast."

If anyone had said something similar to Donovan a day, two days ago, he would have been running for the hills.

So why did he want to dance for joy right now?

Donovan opened his mouth, but he didn't know what to say. His heart felt too large for his chest, like it was expanding rapidly. He'd been alone for so long, but here was Kersen, offering to go with him no matter how matters turned out.

It couldn't be that easy. It just couldn't. *My parents supposedly loved me, yet now I rarely hear from them. How can I trust that this will last?* Donovan pushed past the knot in his throat that wanted to choke him. "Kersen . . . your other clan members want to fight me. Now that I'm this tiger-thing, I've become vicious, overbearing." He forced himself to say the word. "Dominant. My anger—my *rage* almost led to your death. Are you sure you want to be with someone like me?"

Two worry lines formed in Kersen's brows, and his doubt came across through their connection, though he was obviously trying to hide it. Donovan's heart sank. *See? He doesn't truly want this bond with me. It's being forced upon him.*

Kersen rubbed his eyes. "Anwar is vicious. You are not. But I can understand you not wanting to fight for position in the clan. I'm sorry—this must all be such a bother to you." The vulnerability and doubt on his face twisted like a knife in Donovan's chest.

He was about to respond when Roark cleared his throat. "We're almost at Ketambe. I'll get you in and out as fast as possible."

Reluctantly, Donovan nodded. "We'll talk later about this, Kersen. I promise." *I've hurt him—perhaps I simply need to submit to*

all this and stop agonizing over these changes and the clan dynamics.
Being bitten wasn't his fault, and neither was our bonding. "None of
this is a 'bother.' Especially you."

When they pulled into the animal conservation center, Donovan
felt more like himself. He hurt like hell, but as Helena appeared with
better bandages and two bottles of medication, he forced a smile and
acted as if it were nothing.

"Roark did a decent job." She didn't ask questions—Roark had
apparently told everyone that they'd had a run-in with poachers.

It was as good a story as any.

With antibiotics in his system and a strong dose of oxycodone,
Donovan climbed back into Roark's truck, this time with his overnight
bag and some clothing that would actually fit.

His staff whispered to each other, glancing between Donovan
and Kersen, then falling silent when they noticed him looking. They
were probably uncertain about what Donovan was doing with Kersen,
but hopefully their acceptance would come with time.

Roark sighed as he started the engine. "Can't say I feel comfortable
about heading back to that village. I really thought they were going to
kill me earlier."

Bitari sniffed, adjusting her hijab. "That is because we did not
know who you were. This time we do. No worries. You have helped
our clan. We do not forget such things." She glanced at her brother
meaningfully, and Donovan hoped that was a positive sign.

Kersen had spoken barely a word while the staff had worked on
Donovan. Though he nodded at Bitari's words, he looked tired and
scared. "True. We do not forget things. But the clan also is slow to
change as well." He studied his hands, avoiding Donovan's gaze.

To that, Bitari didn't have an answer.

By the time they reached Kersen and Bitari's village, Donovan's
painkillers had kicked in, making the world seem faded. Donovan still
wanted to touch Kersen as much as possible; he hadn't let go of the
poor man's hand the entire ride. Kersen didn't seem to mind, though.
He'd settled into quietly watching the landscape, while Roark and
Bitari kept up a continuous stream of chatter from the front seats.

At the outskirt of the village, two men stood in the middle of
the road wearing full ceremonial dress with lavish red headscarves

and traditional Batak-style scarves, over their red and black robes. Donovan squeezed Kersen's hand nervously. Apparently the village was ready to make a statement, for good or ill.

Roark pulled up to them and stopped the truck. Bitari called to them in an Indonesian dialect, then opened the truck door as they shouted back something. "We get out here. They will escort you to the village center."

Kersen took a deep breath, letting go of Donovan's hand to exit the vehicle. Donovan followed, and noted that the two men immediately placed themselves on either side of him. It looked like he was the honored guest—or the despised criminal, if things went that way. They said something to Bitari and Kersen, who both nodded.

"We have to get dressed. I'll meet you there soon," Kersen said, giving Donovan a look that said he'd rather be at his side.

Donovan smiled with confidence he didn't feel. "I'll see you there." His throat hurt with want. *What if Kersen's wrong? What if his clan doesn't let us see each other again?*

He still had no idea what being a clan member would entail, either. Surely it came with rules, customs, obligations. His stomach did another nervous flutter. *And what do I say if they ask me to give up something I can't? What do I do then?*

With a slight nod, Kersen headed off toward the village with his sister, leaving Roark and Donovan with the village guards.

"Come with us," one of the men said in heavily accented English.

CHAPTER TWENTY-ONE

Unnamed Village, Aceh Province, Sumatra
May 18, 2013

Kersen's hands shook as he donned his clan clothes—loose black trousers and a red shirt and his *ulos* scarf over his shoulders with the tasseled ends hanging past his waist. Gemi ran a comb through his hair, trying to make him presentable. Drums sounded from that direction, which meant that they'd brought Donovan to the spot where the ceremony would be held, and they were probably washing and dressing him. Kersen grimaced. Donovan would no doubt hate all the fuss, but it was part of the ritual. Kersen needed to get there quickly, so that he could explain it to him.

They're washing away your old life, and your old ties to family and community. They're redressing you as a potential member of our family, our clan. Kersen sent the thought just in case Donovan could hear him, but didn't hear a response. Maybe they had to be near each other. Or maybe it was only a residual thing after they shifted back from their tiger forms—something that faded with time. *I have a lot to learn about how bondings work. If only I'd listened more to my parents when they talked about it.*

He pulled on his sandals and tied his headscarf. "Can I go now? I don't have to wait for Bitari, do I?" He should wait—she was eldest born. But he couldn't stand being away from Donovan for another second. *What if he's feeling forced into this? It isn't right. I never should have let myself get that close to him.* Sex didn't necessarily cause a mating bond, but the risk had been there, and he'd ignored it. He'd wanted Donovan too much.

Gemi almost dropped her scarf. "You'd better ask her. You know how she can be."

When Kersen peeked into his sisters' room, he found Roark standing by Bitari's mirror combing his beard. The clan didn't have clothing for Roark, but he'd taken a moment to groom himself after their fight with the corporate task force. He blinked in surprise at Kersen. "You clean up well. You look a lot better than when I first saw you."

Kersen winced, recalling how Roark must have regarded him then. "Yes, about that. I was trying to save my sister. I apologize for my actions. You probably thought I was a poacher."

Roark nodded sheepishly. "Aye. Thought I'd have to call the police."

Kersen closed his eyes. "That would have been humiliating. I'm glad you didn't."

When Roark laughed, Kersen opened his eyes in surprise. The big man clapped him on the back. "Me too. I told Donovan it was probably just some local teen trying to make mischief. Can't blame you for trying, though, given the situation."

In return, Kersen smiled at him and nodded. "Thanks." Roark might think better of him now, but how did the villagers see Donovan? Despite their dwindling numbers, too many of the clan members had become leery of strangers and of sharing their gift. Donovan could show them that there were good people who could be trusted, even people who weren't Indonesian. If only they'd accept him.

I miss you. I want you here. I feel silly in these clothes. That was Donovan's mind-voice, soft but there.

"I can still hear him!" Kersen said to Bitari, knowing that she would understand what he meant, who he meant. "He's my mate. I need to be with him right now."

She made a shooing gesture at him. "Well then, let us hurry and go!" She picked up her bag and led the way, leaving Kersen, Gemi, and Roark behind. Kersen ran to catch up, ducking through the low front door and climbing down the ladder of the longhouse, careful to keep his clothing in order.

It didn't take them long to reach the village center. By the time they arrived, the sky had grown overcast above them, threatening rain, but not just yet. A warm breeze was blowing in from the south, smelling of green things, of the forest. The whole village had gathered, the men in their black shirts and red scarves, the women in red skirts and white blouses, some with their hair falling loose with red bands around their heads, others wearing the hijab like Bitari.

Donovan was standing in the center of the gathering, near the village well. The ground was dusty here—there were no paved roads—but members of the clan had laid down woven grass mats, making a staging area for what Kersen hoped would be an initiation ceremony. Donovan's skin was damp; they had obviously bathed him with a wet cloth, wiping the dust of the jungle from him. Shirtless, he wore only a pair of black trousers and sandals.

He looked positively lickable.

When he spotted Kersen, Donovan tried to go to him, but Anwar and Sabtu held him back. When Donovan started to growl at them, Mentauri tapped him with her fan. "Easy, foreigner. Respect our ways. We have already cleansed you. To walk on the dirt now would be to undo all the preparations we have made." She turned and nodded to Kersen.

He stopped at the edge of the grass mats, longing to go to Donovan but aware that he couldn't yet. "Auntie. Can you tell me what the clan decided?"

She shook her head at him, gently. "Wait. Everything will happen in good time."

Once Bitari and Gemi joined him at the front of the gathering, one of the clan children offered them all *tuak*, or palm wine. Kersen took his gratefully, sipping it as Mentauri waited for the last of the villagers to arrive. There had to be over a hundred of them now, of all ages, from babes to the ancient ones with lined faces and silver hair. The old and the young didn't shift, which still left about half of the population, who were the ones who decided on matters pertaining to shifters, including voting on new members. Thirty years ago, Kersen's grandparents had come to the village after fleeing Bali, when the last tigers there died out. They'd made their case and been accepted.

Now it was Donovan's turn.

As the last stragglers joined the circle of villagers, Mentauri stepped forward. She was dressed all in red, from her skirt and blouse to the hijab covering her hair; the only other colors were her black *ulos* and a necklace of gold disks. She held up her cup of *tuak*, and said in a loud voice, "Clan members of the *suka siluman harimau*, as clan leader, I called you all to gather! I will speak in the tongue of this man, Donovan McGinnis, who seeks to join our clan. He has already taken in the blood of the *harimau rah*, the tiger spirit. He has taken the tiger form. And he has already bonded with another of our clan, Kersen anak Ingat. Therefore our decision today is an important one, as it will affect both of them."

Kersen's heart swelled at the mention of their bond, and he couldn't help looking into Donovan's eyes, seeking a connection. Donovan met his gaze, and then everything around them seemed to fade out. *I am going to be with you, no matter what.* Even as Kersen thought the words, he was sending them. He couldn't help it; the feeling was that strong. It didn't matter that they'd only met four days ago. What he felt was real. *I love you.* Even the fear of losing his clan couldn't surpass that certainty.

I love you too. Donovan's response came back clear and strong and suffused with emotion. Kersen blinked away the sudden moisture in his eyes. Mentauri was speaking again, but he couldn't focus on her words. All he saw was Donovan. All he wanted was to be on the mat with him, standing next to him, touching him.

You do? His heart swelled almost painfully.

Donovan smiled, almost sheepishly. *Yes, I do. I'm sorry for what I said earlier. Everything happened so fast it scared me at first, but I'm not at all sorry that we met, or that this happened to me. I think you're an amazing person, and even though fate threw us together, I think we're a good match. I want to know you much better.*

Me too. But I don't ever want to hold you back or be a burden. It was somehow freeing, being able to admit his fears mind to mind like this. He could sense Donovan's acceptance.

And I'm worried about having to fight others, and this whole dominance and hierarchy thing. Even Donovan's mind-voice sounded scared.

Kersen smiled as he sent out love and support to his mate. *I realize this must be difficult for you to admit. Don't worry. We'll figure it out together.*

Mentauri's words brought Kersen out of their silent communication. "Kersen? Will you come to your mate?"

Kersen's heart was pounding as he hurried over to Donovan and grasped both his hands.

Though Donovan looked like he wanted to speak, he kept his mouth shut, giving Kersen's hands a squeeze instead. His eyes held Kersen's and once again Kersen lost track of what Mentauri was saying.

It was with difficulty that he brought his attention back to the gathering around them.

"Kersen anak Ingat, you are taking this man, Dr. Donovan McGinnis, as your mate, correct?" Mentauri placed her hand on his shoulder, which helped to keep him present, when all he wanted to do at the moment was bury himself in Donovan's arms. He'd come much too close to losing him today when he'd only just found him.

"Yes. It is already done," he said before he even thought about it. As far as Kersen was concerned, a wedding ceremony would be simply a formality. He was already bonded with Donovan.

She chuckled. "I can see that. Dr. Donovan McGinnis? What say you? I know this is very new to you."

Donovan stared at her, wide-eyed and unprepared. "I . . . This has been the craziest week in my entire life," he began, shifting his feet. He turned to Kersen. "I never thought in a million years that I'd find someone who really understood me, who would be comfortable with my work to protect animals and forests. But Kersen does. We barely know each other, yet I say yes. I want to be with him for as long as he'll have me."

It was with difficulty that Kersen fought the urge to throw his arms around Donovan and kiss him. Instead, he grinned ear to ear.

Mentauri smiled and wagged a finger at them. "I saw it, you remember. I saw the spark when you first introduced him to me." To the clan, she said, "These two are mated and shall not be separated by anyone, man or beast." There was some light applause; Kersen doubted anyone was surprised at this first announcement, given the day's events.

Once the crowd settled, Mentauri continued. "As a village, we have discussed whether or not to let this Donovan McGinnis, this man who is not of Indonesian blood, to come into our tribe and be counted as family." Her tone had turned serious, and Kersen caught her gaze moving to Anwar, who stood at the back of the crowd. He wore a white bandage on one arm, where a bullet had grazed him, and he appeared grim-faced and silent.

A tremor of doubt crept into Kersen's heart. Anwar was the highest dominant male. What if he had voted against Donovan?

Silence hung over the gathering. Mentauri took a deep breath. "It was not an easy decision. It is obvious that Donovan is a dominant male, and I foresee several contests to decide if there might be a new alpha in the clan if he is allowed to join. Worse, he showed today that he can be reckless and violent. He endangered us with his attack on humans." She frowned at Donovan like a scolding school teacher.

Donovan grimaced, but he squared his shoulders and maintained steady eye contact. "I'm deeply sorry to you and to the clan, Mentauri. I made a poor decision. It won't happen again."

She grunted and nodded. To the gathering, she continued. "What's done is done. At least it prompted us all to protect our village. Clan members, know that Donovan broke a rule. That cannot be allowed to happen again, even if we did succeed in driving them off, thanks in part to Bitari and Roark."

Bitari looked more proud than Kersen had ever seen her. But Mentauri wasn't done yet. "Despite what happened today, I see value in the skills and connections that Dr. Donovan can bring to the *siluman harimau*. I researched his center, and I like what I learned. His tiger patrols catch poachers and remove snares that can harm us as tigers, and his website brings support from all over the world to protect our forest. As a clan member, he may be able to teach us what more we can do to assist such efforts."

This was good—very good. Kersen had been prepared to argue why the clan should let Donovan join, but it seemed that Mentauri had already done the work for him.

Anwar growled. "Get on with it, Mentauri. Some of us still have fields to work today."

She waved a hand at him. "Right. As I said, after discussing all these things, the elders have decided that we will let Donovan McGinnis join our clan and live here in the village, if he chooses to do so. We will of course expect both Kersen and Donovan to add to our breeding pool, in whatever way works for them." She looked Donovan up and down. "Do you accept?"

Kersen held his breath. But Donovan's hand only tightened on his briefly before he nodded. "Yes. I accept."

"Good." Chuckling to herself, Mentauri gestured to two other men. "Wash Dr. Donovan's feet. He is today new among us again, now a man of the *suka siluman harimau*."

As Donovan calmly raised one foot and then the other to allow their ministrations, elation soared through Kersen. This was it. The cleansing was a sign that they were welcoming him in. As soon as the two men were done with Donovan, Kersen grinned, squeezing Donovan's hand back. "So . . . that's it, then? He's one of us?"

Mentauri laughed, stepping forward to give them both hugs. "Yes, that is it—for the most part. Now you may dress him in the Batak fashion, and we will anoint both of you as a mated pair in the clan." Members of the clan around him started clapping, but he barely noticed them. All he wanted was to go back to Donovan's place with him and continue what they'd been doing last night.

Kersen wasted no time. He helped Donovan button up the red shirt, wondering where they had found one to fit the tall man, then helped him with the black *ulos* and the headband. They resumed holding hands, as Mentauri sprinkled them both with cinnamon and kaffir lime leaves, which were supposed to bring a good future for the two of them. One of the village elders, a wrinkled old man known only as Azur, spoke a prayer. Then it was done.

Clan members slapped Kersen and Donovan on the back, wishing them well. There would be a feast later, but Kersen wasn't particularly interested in that. Besides, Donovan seemed to be fading. Probably a combination of his adrenaline wearing off, or the pain pills and the gunshot wound. In any case, they could celebrate with the clan another time.

"My sisters will be out feasting for most of the night. I know my little room isn't much. But it's close," Kersen told Donovan.

"Lead on," Donovan said, without any hesitation. "I'd sleep on a bed of leaves right now, if it means we get to be alone."

Kersen grinned. "I think we can do better than that. To my room, then." At the very least, they'd get the chance to cuddle and have a real conversation after all the crazy events of the day.

I can't wait to put my arms around him. My mate.

CHAPTER TWENTY-TWO

Unnamed Village, Aceh Province, Sumatra
May 18, 2013

Kersen's room might be small, but it was nearby, and Donovan was happy to follow him there, as Gemi and Bitari left for Mentauri's house to work on the food preparation for the feast. Donovan's stomach growled at the reminder that he hadn't eaten all day, but truthfully he was more tired than anything else. And he wanted to spend some time alone with Kersen.

Inside Kersen's room, they stripped and curled up on his mattress, with Donovan spooning Kersen, lying on his good side. His shoulder burned, but it was too soon for another dose of pain medication.

"I feel like we should be celebrating with sex." Donovan yawned. "But I may have to wait till later on that. Would it be all right to return to my place tonight? Nothing against your room, but this mattress isn't doing my back any favors."

That prompted a laugh and a nod from Kersen. "I like your place better too. You have no idea how nice it is to have privacy like that." Kersen rubbed Donovan's hands, which had been scratched up during the craziness earlier. He sighed. "I'm probably going to fall asleep as well. Do you truly think we've protected that piece of forest?"

Donovan shrugged. "We've given them a few obstacles. They may need to find different staff willing to go to that particular location, and they'll have to repair their bulldozer. Maybe that'll cause a few weeks' delay." He nuzzled the back of Kersen's neck. "But there will be others. I wish that stupid bill hadn't passed."

Kersen brought Donovan's hand up and kissed it. "We'll think of something. All the villagers can come up with ideas, and we can all work together. If tigers keep 'attacking' their equipment and costing them money, they may decide this area's not worth it."

A twinge of fear passed through Donovan. "Be careful. They'll likely hire more guards and shoot tigers on sight after today."

"Pfft. We will outsmart them. It's not like in the forest where we don't know where the traps will be. They will have to bring their equipment on roads or cleared lands. And unless they're willing to hire an army, we shifters far outnumber them. We'd be able to slip past whatever they come up with." Kersen's confidence helped, and eventually Donovan smiled.

It was a good feeling, knowing that he had allies as of today, and more friends. Family, even. "I can't believe everything that's happened. I can't believe I'm one of you now." He raised his head to look at Kersen, who hadn't stopped grinning from the moment that Mentauri told him to dress Donovan. "I'm really home, aren't I?"

Kersen gazed at him. Donovan wanted to drown in those amber depths, but he had to lie back after a bit when his shoulder protested. Then Kersen spoke, and it sent a delicious shiver through him. "You didn't think you were home before? Yes. You are home."

Mulling over all the places he'd lived, all the sterile, temporary housing his parents had occupied in their various quests to save the planet, Donovan realized he had never felt this content. He snuggled closer, relishing the scent of his mate and the warmth of his skin.

They slept.

Later, they went back for part of the festivities—after a long nap, hunger had woken both of them, and the village was filled with the scents of cooking. Donovan ate two bowls of a spicy chicken dish with jasmine rice and stewed vegetables, while Kersen went right for the lamb dishes. Members of the clan greeted them, clapping them on the backs and offering congratulations. They had both put their ceremonial clothes back on, as apparently this was still part of both the mating and the initiation traditions.

Donovan was trying to figure out if "*siluman harimau*" was the actual name of the clan or what they were as weretigers. He knew it meant "invisible tiger" and that it had to do with the sorcerers who had first learned the art of shape-shifting. That part remained unbelievable to him. But the clan seemed content to merely call themselves that, and so he went with it.

As soon as Donovan and Kersen finished their plates, they made their good-byes. Donovan knew he had a lot of learning to do—he needed to know more Indonesian, maybe some Batak, and he needed to learn all the names of the villagers. In addition, he needed to learn how clan hierarchy worked. According to Mentauri, Anwar and the other dominant tigers would want to fight and measure his strength against their own. That idea still made his stomach twist with dread. Lastly, he needed to find out what their other customs were, so that he didn't go and make an arse of himself.

Fitting others into his life was a new thing for Donovan; he'd never had a family, not really. Having Kersen and all of his family and clan felt like the beginning of something big.

Sometime during the afternoon, Roark and Anwar had retrieved his Jeep from the animal conservation center. Anwar joked that he'd be paid back when Donovan was able to fight with him, which wouldn't be until both of their wounds were healed.

As dusk settled into night, Donovan drove his vehicle home with Kersen beside him, relieved to have time for just the two of them. He parked the Jeep in front of his house and wasted no time in getting Kersen to the door, opening it for him. "I feel so . . . I can't even describe it." His world had gone bonkers, and yet he felt happier than he had in a long time. A very long time.

Kersen rubbed against him, and Donovan suddenly flashed back to how that had felt when they were tigers, when he'd been shot, and Kersen had comforted him. A sweet hurt filled his chest.

"It feels like you're finally who you are meant to be?" Kersen asked. "That was how it felt like for me. When I started shifting."

They walked into the foyer, then to the bedroom. Donovan stripped off his *ulos* and his sandals. His clothes were in his backpack, but they stank of sweat and grime.

Kersen removed his sandals, shirt, and *ulos* next, then he was working the buttons free on Donovan's shirt, easing the fabric off of him carefully. The wound in Donovan's shoulder still burned, but the painkillers had muted it to a low buzz. Donovan grabbed Kersen's hips, pulling him in for a fierce kiss, ignoring the spike of sensation his movement caused.

"At last," Kersen sighed, kissing him back, his hands sliding around to fondle Donovan's arse. His lips were firm and demanding; apparently he'd learned a bit about kissing in the past couple of days.

"Mmph," Donovan agreed. He tried to squeeze Kersen in tighter, but then his shoulder complained. He wasn't sure if it was lust or the drugs making him lightheaded. "I need to move over to the bed," he said by way of apology. It had felt so good, yesterday, lying on top of Kersen, feeling their different textures. He loved how smooth and youthful Kersen's skin was, the contrast in tone. Nobody else enticed him so much.

"Yes." Kersen's hands worked at Donovan's trousers, easing them off. "On the bed naked," he emphasized, not stopping until all that was left on Donovan was the bandage over his shoulder.

Donovan frowned. "Maybe I'd better be on bottom this time." The last thing he needed to do was open up the wound by putting strain on it. "What do you think?"

Donovan thought he detected the trace of a blush in Kersen's cheeks. "I've never, um, topped before." Kersen's eyes roamed over his body, sending a peculiar heat through Donovan. "That might be interesting to try."

How exciting, to be a person's first, in any way. Donovan swallowed in a throat suddenly gone dry, his nerves racing. "I've bottomed once. It was at university, and we didn't really know what we were doing. It wasn't my favorite." He smiled. "But I'd love to try it with you."

For a second, Kersen looked panicked. "You mean you didn't like it? We don't have to. I bet I could—you know—sit on top? I saw it once in a sex show." He rubbed at his cheeks. "I'm sorry I don't know more. There wasn't . . ." He shrugged. "There wasn't much chance to try things, growing up. I'm afraid I'll botch it all up and hurt you."

Touched by his concern, Donovan reached out, placing his hands on Kersen's chest, wanting to steady him, relax him. "Hey. I haven't tried a whole lot myself. I was always focused on my work, on my studies. It's okay. With you this would be something special." He let his gaze slip down to the trousers hugging Kersen's slim hips. On an impulse, Donovan dropped to his knees, working the trousers open, letting them fall to the floor. "I've been wanting to do this all day."

He pushed Kersen's briefs down, exposing his cock, and then took Kersen into his mouth without delay, wanting, needing to let the man know that it was all right. They were together now. He wanted to *be* together. In every way possible.

Kersen gave a soft cry, his hands raking through Donovan's short hair. "Yes! Please." His hips canted forward, and Donovan hummed in the back of his throat, loving the feel of the swollen cock in his mouth, the taste of pre-come and Kersen's unique flavor.

He wouldn't be able to stay on his knees; the pain from his wound would force him to take it easy soon. But Donovan wasn't about to let an opportunity like this go. He took Kersen as far down as possible, wanting to be overwhelmed. When he couldn't breathe, he backed off, licking his way around the foreskin and the head, lavishing attention on the organ. Kersen moaned, low and needy.

"I can't . . . I can't do this for long," Kersen pleaded, one hand stroking Donovan's cheek. Yet he wasn't moving.

Donovan let him go. "I can't either. But cripes, you taste fantastic. I wanted to do at least that." Shakily, he got to his feet. "I'll be good and lie on my back now. You can take over."

Kersen laughed. "This is so different. Here—tell me where the lube is." He offered a hand, and Donovan sat down on the bed with him, scooting back in order to get comfortable.

With a sigh, Donovan laid back. "First drawer, night table. Condoms are there too." This was nice, being able to just lie here and watch someone else do the work. He couldn't remember the last— no, he couldn't remember *any* time—that he'd been able to do this. "You're so sexy. Did you know that?"

"No fair trying to distract me." Kersen was really blushing now. He reached for the lube. "And we don't need condoms. You're going to find that you'll never have another cold or virus again. Something to do with the differences between the immune systems of humans and tigers."

Donovan stared up at Kersen, the implications sinking in. "So you can't get STDs?"

Kersen nodded, smiling. He tipped the bottle over Donovan's cock. Donovan's stomach contracted at the sexy look on his mate's face, as lube spilled over his cock. "That's right."

"Enough clinical talk." Donovan sighed as Kersen began to stroke his cock, slow smooth strokes, which only heightened his pleasure. "Remember that I'm not eighteen. Take your time. I want this to last." His breath hitched when Kersen's other hand played with his balls. "Oh. That feels so good."

Kersen's smile turned diabolical. "I thought so." He continued to stroke as he rolled Donovan's balls between thumb and forefinger in his other hand. "I'm doing what I like done to me, when . . . you know. When I play alone."

That was an enticing image. Donovan smiled, half tempted to close his eyes. But he wanted to watch Kersen, to see the expressions on his face as he topped for the first time. "You've giving me ideas." He bit his lip as Kersen's thumb flicked a particularly sensitive spot under the hood. "Mercy?" As much as he was enjoying the foreplay, he really wanted what was coming next.

"Mercy." Chuckling, Kersen let go of Donovan's cock only to trail his hand down the perineum to Donovan's arsehole, rubbing in circles over the sensitive flesh. Donovan almost forgot to breathe. "You ready?" Kersen asked. "I don't want to hurt you."

He's so sweet. How did I get this lucky? "You won't. I'm so bloody ready right now." Donovan took a deep breath, letting it out slowly. "If something hurts, I'll let you know." But at this point he barely even felt his shoulder.

Kersen nodded with satisfaction, and then pushed in a bit with his finger, before withdrawing it. Donovan groaned. He wasn't sure if Kersen meant to tease him like this or if he was just nervous, but God, it was driving him crazy. "Please," he begged. "I need more."

"I'm sorry." Kersen's smile faltered. "I just—I haven't done this. So I am figuring it out." He added lube to his finger and pushed it in deeper.

Donovan groaned again. "It's okay. You're not hurting me at all. Take whatever time you need to explore." *Want him to take me now, but patience is a virtue, right?* He shifted his weight, spreading his legs farther. "Add another finger."

When Kersen did so, the ache was delicious. It also helped keep Donovan's mind off his wound. He motioned to Kersen. "Come here. I want to kiss you while you do that."

Kersen leaned in closer. "You like this? I think you're almost ready. You feel tight—but not too tight."

Instead of answering, Donovan put a hand on the back of his head, pulling Kersen into a hard kiss. Kersen's fingers curled inside him, sending sparks of pleasure through him. Donovan growled, nibbling at Kersen's lower lip. In response, Kersen began fucking him with his fingers, until the two of them were grinding against each other, writhing on the bed.

"Now, please," Donovan gasped, as Kersen withdrew his fingers. "Now would be good."

"Yes." Kersen's voice sounded rough with need, which only made Donovan want him more. He kneeled up, and Donovan was able to watch as Kersen slicked up his cock.

They needed to do this again, preferably when he wasn't wounded, maybe on a Sunday morning when they could take their time, and he could enjoy watching Kersen like this. It was really fucking nice to watch another man getting ready to stick his cock in Donovan's arse. "I'm such a git. I can't believe I haven't tried this side more."

A half smile on his face, Kersen glanced at him. "Me too." He lined himself up, rubbing against Donovan's entrance as he began to push forward.

Donovan concentrated on pushing out. Steadily, he felt himself being entered, the ring of muscle protesting a bit, but not too bad. He wanted it too much to care. "Come on," he urged, placing a hand on Kersen's hip. "I need you."

"I need you too." Kersen's eyes were intent on Donovan. He thrust forward, deeper, and ecstasy filled his face. "Oh! You're tight. That feels . . ." He bit his lip, pushing in even deeper, until Donovan felt balls brushing his arse. It burned, but in a good way.

Donovan's hand tightened on Kersen's hip, holding him in position for a few seconds, until his body started to adjust. He brought his other hand down to his cock, to either slow himself down or speed himself up; whichever was necessary. Looking into Kersen's face, he smiled. "Don't go easy on me. I want you to really fuck me."

Kersen nodded. He pulled halfway out, then drove home. Donovan cried out, not expecting the rush of sensation, but he squeezed Kersen's arse for him to continue. His other time bottoming hadn't been anything like this. Was it because he'd been inexperienced? Or was being with Kersen just different altogether? He suspected it was a combination of the two.

It was very different, knowing that somebody needed you, that they wanted to be with you. Forever.

At the second thrust, Kersen whimpered. Donovan was right there with him. He loved seeing the pleasure in Kersen's face, to know that they were both experiencing something new, something wonderful.

Bracing himself on his hands, Kersen began a steady rhythm, leaning in to rub his cheek against Donovan's, nuzzling him. Donovan let his hands roam and explore, greedily taking in Kersen's luscious body. Oh, there were benefits to bottoming, all right. He even dared to play with Kersen's sac, squeezing and gently kneading.

Kersen moaned, thrusting harder. They kissed, fighting for control of each other's mouth, and Donovan began to lose track of who was doing what; it all felt so glorious. His hand was partially trapped between them, but that was fine. He was drunk on sensation, drunk on Kersen.

With his next few thrusts Kersen began hitting something incredible. Donovan had no idea if it was his prostate, or just a really good spot, but he knew that he wasn't going to last much longer. "Close, Kersen. Just like that. Oh my God . . ." Ignoring the twitches in pain from his shoulder, Donovan began stroking his cock faster, and Kersen sped up as well, the slapping sounds of his thighs against Donovan's arse making a lewd music between them.

All of a sudden Kersen bit him on the side of the neck, a hard bite that would surely leave a bruise.

Donovan cried out as the first shot of semen spurted out of his cock. Kersen held on, and Donovan submitted, the climax rocking through him as Kersen fucked him hard. *Never let anyone into my life before. Until you. Only you.* The words, the thoughts came from deep within Donovan, and somehow he knew that Kersen heard them, now that they were joined this profoundly.

Kersen let go of his hold on Donovan's throat to whisper in his ear. "I love you."

Then he reared up and thrust in hard, coming.

A thrill went through Donovan; rarely had he gotten the chance to see someone in the throes of ecstasy like this. His arse would no doubt be sore tomorrow, but it was worth it. When Kersen shuddered with aftershocks, Donovan drew him in close, holding him to his chest, letting him rest.

Kissing the side of Kersen's face, he whispered back, "I love you too." So strange, the connection between the two of them, and yet so wonderful.

They lay there together for several moments, not speaking. Not needing to speak. Eventually Donovan heard an echo of Kersen's voice inside his head.

Can I move in now?

Donovan laughed. The words had come with such love, such happiness.

He answered out loud, as Kersen raised his head to look at him. "Yes. Definitely."

Kersen smiled. "My mate."

Tigers didn't usually mate for life. But this bond, Donovan had a feeling, would last forever. He nodded. "My mate."

Outside, the sounds of the rainforest sang on, undisturbed by men.

EPILOGUE

Gunung Leuser National Forest, Sumatra
November 18, 2013

"Gemi's five kilometers to the west of me, and she's found more evidence of illegal burning. Didn't you want to take pictures of that?" Kersen's voice rang clear over the handheld radio, and Donovan smiled at Amin and Anwar, who were helping him to search for snares.

Six months since Donovan had joined the weretiger clan. Kersen, Gemi, and Anwar had all joined the Tiger Patrols under Donovan's supervision, and their insights into the forest ecosystem were extremely valuable. While Anwar had beaten Donovan in the fight for alpha dominant in the clan thanks to his greater experience, they'd managed to become friends shortly afterward, and now Donovan was training Anwar in how to search for signs of poacher activity.

Meanwhile, Kersen had advanced to the level of leading his own patrols. Twice the patrols meant twice the illegal activities they could find and stop.

"We'll head straight there. Any signs of poachers in the area that I should be aware of?" Donovan signaled for his patrol to follow and began walking faster, ducking under vines and low tree branches. He didn't need Kersen to tell him where he was; he could feel his mate, better than any radar detector.

"Haven't found anything today, thankfully. I'll notify Gemi that you're coming." While Kersen didn't say the words, Donovan knew that meant Gemi would be shifting back from tiger to human.

Kersen ran a very specialized patrol team—smaller in number, but utilizing members of his village in their animal form as an extra way to detect anomalies in the forest. Yes, it came with the risk of encountering a snare, as Gemi had before. Yet even she said she'd been careless that day.

They'd learned a lot in six months.

Breaking into a light jog, Donovan considered how he'd present the new evidence. While the clan's stunt and sabotage of a bulldozer had delayed the corporation long enough for the animal conservation center to file the first lawsuit, other companies had swiftly begun taking other chunks of land released from protected status by the Aceh Council. Those lands were farther away, so they didn't directly impact the village, but they were still a loss. Roark was tirelessly working with other conservation groups to file more lawsuits, in the hopes that at least one of them would make its way to the national court. After all, this was supposed to be federal land, not provincial.

Members of the clan had conducted further sabotage to any company venturing too near the land by the village, to the point where stories were starting to circulate that the place really was cursed. So far, they'd managed to keep everyone away. The good news was that there was one lawsuit that was gaining traction, heavily supported by conservationists. This one focused on the burning of forested areas, particularly a peat moss zone of the forest that was one of three remaining habitats for the Sumatran orangutan. In Indonesia, it was illegal to burn rainforest for clearing, even if it was okay to use the land. And some of the loudest conservationists were those trying to protect orangutans.

If Gemi had found additional evidence that might strengthen the case, it could mean palm oil companies would have to pay millions, perhaps billions of dollars in fines.

That might be enough to keep them away permanently.

Donovan began running faster, checking once in a while to make sure that Amin and the porters were able to keep up. He sent his thought out to Kersen, still amazed that they could communicate over such large distances mind to mind. The radios were more for Roark and the other staff's benefit. *Did Gemi say how bad it is? I'm coming toward you.*

It's pretty bad. I'm heading there, and I'll probably reach it before you reach me. There was sorrow in Kersen's mind-voice, and Donovan couldn't help but send something of a mental hug. Kersen returned with a wave of gratitude. *Hey, tonight, we should soak in that large tub of yours. All this running is making me sore!*

Donovan snorted out loud, skirting around a boggy area. *You're sore? You're over ten years younger than me. Still, soaking in a bath sounds wonderful.*

There was a silent laugh from Kersen, and then Donovan was forced to slow down as he noticed Amin and the porters falling behind. Groaning, Anwar slowed as well. Donovan was about to ask Amin how he was doing when his radio went off.

He stopped to answer it. "Donovan with Alpha Patrol, over."

Roark's bright, cheery voice came out so loud that Donovan had to adjust the volume. "Hey, mate! I have some good news for you."

"Yeah? Is it one of your court filings? Gemi may have found further evidence for you." While Roark should have been listening to the radio chatter, it was possible he'd been busy at that particular moment.

"No, although I understand this particular case has a trial date set for January. But this is still good. The Leuser ecosystem was just named by the World Conservation Union as one of the most irreplaceable protected areas in the world. Imagine what that title's going to do for our cases!" Roark sounded like he was almost dancing, and Donovan couldn't help but smile.

Bitari's acrid voice came on the line. "Apparently it's in this month's *Science* magazine. Roark's been on the phone all morning with other agencies."

It wasn't precisely a victory, but it was another solid step toward one. "That's brilliant. Thanks for letting me know." World organizations putting pressure on the Aceh government would force the province to crack down on the reckless destruction of the rainforest. The *siluman harimau* would finally be able to relax.

"No problem, mate. Bitari told me what Gemi found, by the way. Shame to have to send them more pictures, but perhaps with this extra bit of news it'll have a greater impact. I told you we'd stick it to them!"

As Roark spoke, the others caught up to Donovan and looked at him questioningly, no doubt wondering what he was smiling about.

"That you did. I'll radio once my patrol reaches Kersen's."

"Good luck. I'll talk to you later. Over." Roark cut off the transmission, and Donovan related his message to his patrol. Then he mentally shared it with Kersen.

Sounds like tonight we'll be celebrating as well as relaxing. There was a definite sexual undertone to Kersen's thoughts this time. Donovan hoped his blush didn't show. Roark was always moaning about how affectionate Donovan and Kersen were, even on the job. Then again, Roark didn't have ground to stand on, since he and Bitari were always blowing kisses at each other.

Can't wait. Let's hurry up and get this work finished.

As he resumed jogging, Donovan imagined all the animals, all the precious living things trying to survive in the forest. Roark's news really was a blessing. The more the world cared, the less corporations would dare infringe upon the protected lands.

And the safer Kersen, Donovan, and their home would be, for generations to come.

GLOSSARY
OF INDONESIAN WORDS
(MOSTLY BAHASA, THE NATIONAL DIALECT)

anak	son (of)
boleh	able to, can
dengannya	(with) him
gulai	an Indonesian curry with spicy peppers
gunung	mountain
harimau	tiger
hutan Duri dan Cakar	literally "forest of thorns and claws"
ingat	remember (Balinese Indonesian)
jadian	false, fake
kawin	marry
keluarga	family
kau	you
maka	then
manusia	man
rah	spirit
siluman harimau	invisible tiger (weretiger)
suami	husband
suka	clan
tuak	palm wine
ulos	scarf from the Batak culture

AUTHOR'S NOTE

The inspiration for this book came from an image I had seen online designed by Erin Lark that featured a bearded man, clearly Caucasian, with a younger, tattooed man who was obviously indigenous to the Pacific Rim. Looking at the two men, I immediately envisioned a story between a conservationist and a native who was also a weretiger. From there, I delved into research. The native's appearance and tattoos steered me away from most places that have tigers—I considered India, but Indonesia seemed the more interesting choice. While a lot of Indonesia is Muslim, the people of Bali are primarily Hindu, and embrace tattoos, while Muslims do not. This also made sense, because there once was such a thing as the Balinese tiger. The last recorded Balinese tiger was killed in 1937, although it was estimated that some Balinese tigers survived into the 1940s and 1950s.

So I chose Sumatra as the setting. From there, I learned about the plight of the Sumatran tiger. The numbers are horrifying: in 2005, there were estimated to be only about five hundred Sumatran tigers left.

There are now believed to only be about four hundred Sumatran tigers remaining in the wild. These are confined to a few national forests on the island of Sumatra, including Bukit Barisan Selatan National Park, Kerinci Seblat National Park, and Gunung Leuser National Park. Of these three, Gunung Leuser is under the greatest threat, since most of it lies in Aceh, a province that was in civil war for years and is still struggling to determine what is best for the land and people of the region. As of 2016, it was estimated that there are one hundred Sumatran tigers living in the Gunung Leuser National Forest.

I selected the dates for this book with a reason: on May 19, 2013, the *Jakarta Post* (Indonesia's largest online newspaper) ran a story about how a Change.org petition directed to the president of Indonesia had become a worldwide phenomenon, with over a million people signing the petition. The petition called for the president to stop the local governments, in particular the Aceh Province, from allowing private companies to utilize large swaths of supposedly protected rainforest land for commercial purposes. This petition seemed to have some effect; there were later articles about the Aceh government starting to crack down on illegal poaching, logging, and farming. However, it is still an ongoing problem.

The events mentioned in the epilogue came from this article from January 2014, which in addition to mentioning the *Science* magazine announcement, also highlighted a landmark decision where Indonesia fined one palm oil company about nine million US dollars for their illegal burning of areas in the Tripa Peat Swamps, located within the Gunung Leuser National Forest.

There's a more recent Change.org petition (as of March 2016) that is again calling attention to the Indonesian government the importance of preserving the rainforests. I encourage readers to check this one out, or see if there are any others that are current. Readers can also learn more about current efforts by organizations like Worldwildlife.org and United Nations Educational, Scientific, and Cultural Organization (UNESCO).

Another thing to check out is Sumatra's Tiger Protection Units, the inspiration for Donovan and Roark's organization, which is funded out of Canada. (There really is an animal research and conservation center in Ketambe, but it seems to be currently abandoned.) And specifically to protect Gunung Leuser National Forest, there is the Leonardo Dicaprio Foundation that highlights news that impacts the rainforest there.

My call to readers is this: go out there and see what is happening in the world, including the threats to magnificent creatures like the Sumatran tiger. Support efforts to preserve habitats and protect wildlife. I'm a cat person; I've always been a cat person. It breaks my heart to think that in my lifetime, another great cat species may go extinct.

We cannot let that happen.

Spread the word.

Dear Reader,

Thank you for reading J.T. Hall's *Forest of Thorns and Claws*!

We know your time is precious and you have many, many entertainment options, so it means a lot that you've chosen to spend your time reading. We really hope you enjoyed it.

We'd be honored if you'd consider posting a review—good or bad—on sites like **Amazon, Barnes & Noble, Kobo, Goodreads, Twitter, Facebook, Tumblr,** and your blog or website. We'd also be honored if you told your friends and family about this book. Word of mouth is a book's lifeblood!

For more information on upcoming releases, author interviews, blog tours, contests, giveaways, and more, please sign up for our weekly, spam-free newsletter and visit us around the web:

Newsletter: tinyurl.com/RiptideSignup
Twitter: twitter.com/RiptideBooks
Facebook: facebook.com/RiptidePublishing
Goodreads: tinyurl.com/RiptideOnGoodreads
Tumblr: riptidepublishing.tumblr.com

Thank you so much for Reading the Rainbow!

RiptidePublishing.com

ACKNOWLEDGMENTS

I want to give a huge thank-you to the individual who conducted the cultural review and gave me extremely valuable notes about the Indonesian cultures and languages. Included in the notes were reminders that not every situation is black-and-white, and this is also true of the struggles between the locals living near protected wilderness in Sumatra and the plants and animals being protected. While it is vital to protect the forests that are left, there also need to be viable options for the nearby communities to sustain themselves as well. I acknowledge that this is a complex issue.

And, as always, I want to commend and acknowledge my editor, Carole-ann Galloway, who worked tirelessly with me on this for months while my personal life was in complete chaos. Thanks for putting up with me and keeping me going!

Last, I want to acknowledge my partner of eleven years, TK, who had to endure my nights upon nights of being "absent," sitting beside her with a laptop in my lap and my head in another world. She also helped me immensely with the climactic scene and ideas on how to beat a corporation. I love you always.

ALSO BY J.T. HALL

The Oddities series
Murder Once Seen
Fraud Twice Felt

Friday at the 7-Eleven
Vice and Exploitation

Hard Hat series
The Foreman
The New Hire

About the Author

J.T. Hall has been writing for many years under this name and others, and has appeared in magazines, anthologies, and online and print books. She earned her BA in creative writing from the University of Arizona, her Master's in education from Argosy University, and works as an independent technical writer for state and federal programs.

In what little free time she can find, she volunteers for the LGBT community and is active in the leather scene. As an open bisexual, J.T. is passionate about the LGBTQIA spectrum and speaking up for minority rights. She has a teenaged daughter and a partner of over ten years of Japanese American descent. Every spring they have two "must visit" events: the Matsuri Festival and the Renaissance Faire. They live in sunny Arizona with three adorably cute dogs, three black cats, and a hamster who loves peanuts.

Social Media:
Visit J.T. Hall's blog at: jthallwriting.wordpress.com
Facebook: facebook.com/profile.php?id=100005608068142
Twitter: twitter.com/JTHall7
Goodreads: goodreads.com/author/show/7035533.J_T_Hall
Newsletter, with announcements of new releases, sales, and special sneak peeks: eepurl.com/4TQCn

Enjoy more stories like
Forest of Thorns and Claws
at RiptidePublishing.com!

Wet Heat
ISBN: 978-1-62649-407-7

Wolf's Clothing
ISBN: 978-1-62649-411-4

Earn Bonus Bucks!

Earn 1 Bonus Buck for each dollar you spend. Find out how at
RiptidePublishing.com/news/bonus-bucks.

Win Free Ebooks for a Year!

Pre-order coming soon titles directly through our site and you'll
receive one entry into a drawing for a chance to win free books for
a year! Get the details at RiptidePublishing.com/contests.